DIGGING THE WOLF

A WEREWOLF PARANORMAL ROMANCE

STEFFANIE HOLMES

BACCHANALIA HOUSE

Want free books, exclusive giveaways and exclusive sneak peeks at upcoming Steffanie Holmes paranormal romance books? Sign up for the mailing list to get the scoop - http://www.steffmetal.com/subscribe

❀ Created with Vellum

1

ANNA

"*A*nna, can you hand me my other trowel, please? I just dropped mine down that crevice."

Beside Professor Frances Doyle, Ruth – the senior graduate assistant – sniggered as she shot in a deer skull with the theodolite, the surveying instrument we used to create a three-dimensional plotted map of all artefacts and features. Two years ago it would've been Ruth doing all the fetching on site, but now she was senior to me, and I was the one scampering around after our scatterbrained professor like a faithful dog.

Sighing loudly – for my sigh would never be heard over the driving rain outside the cave – I picked myself out from underneath the rock shelf I was using as shelter and splashed over to the mouth. This was the third trowel Frances had lost down that bloody crack in as many days, and every time I'd braved the elements to replace it, the weather was worse.

We kept all the site tools in a lockable chest just outside the cave mouth, which meant I had to lie on my stomach and slither through a tiny hole while muddy water trickled down my bra, and then stand up in the howling wind and driving rain, all so my dopey lecturer could lose her tools again.

This was not what I had imagined archaeology would be like.

When I'd started my degree at Loamshire University, I had visions of swanning around exotic locations in a white tank top and Bermuda shorts, getting a glorious tan while I uncovered glittering jewels and treasures of long-lost civilisations. I've wanted so badly to get away from Crookshollow my entire life. As a teen, I'd worked my arse off for top marks and had got accepted to Cambridge University, but after my father died, I had to give up my place to stay close to look after my mother. Giving up my spot at one of the best universities in the world to live at home had been one of the hardest things I'd ever done, but I'd consoled myself by remembering that at least I'd get to travel to far-flung locales as part of my degree to dig up the remains of the past. My dreams absolutely *did not* include spending four of the coldest weeks of my life stuck in the middle of Crookshollow Forest with Frances Doyle, the mad professor of neolithic cave art.

And the worst thing was, I only had myself to blame. All the third-year archaeology students were required to undertake a four-week field trip on a site of their choice throughout the world. The university had relationships with several ongoing excavations, so we had our choice of locales ... Greece, Italy, Egypt, Ecuador, Australia ... It was the highlight of my entire degree.

I put in my application for a classical villa site in Sicily, and was informed I'd got the spot. But that was before Becky Masters – the stupidest girl in our entire class, the girl with the perfect blonde hair and perfect nose and perfect tinkling laugh whose passing grades came solely from the fact she was shagging the classical pottery professor – got hit by a bus.

She didn't die, but her perfect little nose had to be recon-structed, and her arm had been broken in three places. Poor

Becky, everyone said. Stuck in hospital with a broken arm and a mushed-up nose. Poor Becky, who missed the cut-off date for applications and was stuck at a dig in Crookshollow Forest. Poor Becky who really, *really* wanted more than anything in the world to go to Sicily with Professor Hicks to study classical pottery *in situ* ... wasn't there a student who would consider swapping her place with Becky so she could continue the work that inspired her?

That was the spiel Professor Hicks gave me when he called me into his office and suggested I be the one to swap places with Becky. "You're such a good student, Anna," he said. "I'm sure you will excel wherever you are placed. You would be doing a great kindness to a fellow student, and I would definitely look upon this kindly when it comes to making your recommendation for postgraduate study."

Because I was such a pushover, and I liked Professor Hicks and wanted to please him, and I didn't want to be the cruel person who said "fuck off" to a girl who'd just been hit by a bus, I agreed. So Becky took my spot on the Sicily dig, and instead of relaxing in the sun beside a Minoan palace with my friend Katie, or excavating pharaonic treasures in the Valley of the Kings with Sinead, I got stuck in a soggy English cave twenty miles from home during the coldest month of the year.

Fuming silently at my miserable situation, I lifted the lid on our toolbox. My hand closed around one of the many trowels we had on hand. One of the first lessons I learned on the site was that an archaeologist would never get far without a spare trowel, or ten. I stuffed a second one in my back pocket, knowing Professor Doyle would inevitably need it before the day was out. The biting wind whipped across my face, the cold stinging my filthy skin.

I knelt down at the cave entrance and slid inside, feet first, pulling my body through the gap. Rain pounded against my face, dripping down the collar of my jacket, wet droplets crawling over my skin.

"Thanks," Frances said, barely even glancing at me as she grabbed the trowel and continued to scrape away at the dirt layers in her quadrant. In the quadrant opposite hers, Ruth and Max – the other graduate student – were laughing as they used the theodolite to map the edges of an area of blackened dirt that signified the position of a hearth. I seethed inwardly as I noticed Ruth's clothes were mostly dry and free of mud.

We were working in a raised area near the rear of the main cave complex, above the natural water level – so even through the entrance was like climbing through a waterfall, the actual site itself was mostly dry. The site was clearly a living floor for the neolithic inhabitants of the cave – functioning as a kitchen, judging by the cutting tools and piles of animal bones we'd uncovered. Foxes and birds and even bones of wolves from when wolves were still common in England had all been dragged back to the cave and eaten. The dietary habits of the neolithic cave dwellers were of particular interest to Max, who was completing his thesis on the subject. And Ruth was pleased with the charcoal samples and dried seeds we'd found inside the hearth, which she would be analysing for her doctoral thesis once we returned to the university. But so far, we hadn't uncovered any treasure. Glittering jewels, Greek vases and gold funerary masks were not abundant in neolithic caves, and that meant I couldn't find much to interest myself on the site.

I bent down to help Frances scrape off the remaining layer of soil on her quadrant. As I rolled the edge of my trowel over the surface, the corner of a small bone became visible. It was probably the rib bone from a fox, judging by the size and shape of it, but animal bones weren't exactly my area of expertise. I placed it in a small bag, wrote a number on it, and left it in place to be shot in with the theodolite, once the other two had finished with it in their quadrant.

While I worked, I watched Frances, her messy brown hair falling out of her ponytail and spilling over her shoulders, her face streaked with smudges of dirt where she had itched her nose or pushed her glasses back up over her eyes. She didn't even wear gloves when she dug, and her hands seemed to be permanently stained from the dark soil of the cave floor.

"What's the time?" she asked absentmindedly as she scraped down the edges of the quadrant, her wrinkled hands making expert work of the corners of the square.

"Three-thirty," I answered, pulling my phone out of my pocket and squinting at the screen. There wasn't any reception in this remote corner of the forest, so my expensive smartphone had become nothing but a heavy portable timepiece. Smears of mud ran across the screen from where I'd been checking it frantically throughout the day, looking forward to knock-off time so I could get back to the camp and out of my mud-soaked clothes.

"Oh! So late already! That new ranger was supposed to be here around three. He might already be outside."

"What happened to Daniel?" The county required a forest ranger to accompany us throughout the excavation, ostensibly to ensure our safety but really to make sure we didn't damage any fragile forest ecosystems. Ranger Daniel Davies had been living at camp with us for the last two weeks, although he didn't hang out much on site, preferring to spend his days inspecting the hiking trails and bridges in this area of the forest. He was a cheerful guy, and a lot of fun to have around. He was also the ranger who'd found Ben's body, so I felt a connection to him, even though he was scrawny and kind of ugly.

"He got a call the other day saying his flat had been broken into, so he's had to go back to Liverpool," Frances replied. "Can you go and meet the new ranger? He's probably wandering around, wondering where the cave entrance is."

"Either that or giving us red crosses for health-and-safety violations," Ruth piped up. I stiffened at the words. Most archaeologists had a blasé attitude towards health and safety on site, believing their "common sense" would prevent an accident. I was the opposite. I was the only one on the team wearing my hard hat in the caves. I wanted more safety procedures, more lectures, more equipment. But I had my reasons.

A flicker of panic crossed Frances's face. If a ranger deemed a site unsafe, they could shut it down. Daniel had been pretty chilled out, but who knew what this new ranger was like? "Find him and take him back to camp and show him the run of the place. Don't let him come down here until we've had a chance to … to clean things up. Tell him I'll be back around six to brief him. I want to finish shooting in these features."

Why couldn't she have told me all that before I'd crawled back down the hole again, saving me a trip? I sighed again. She wouldn't be Mad Frances if she had.

I crawled out of the cave again, just as a large four-wheel-drive truck pulled up along the narrow dirt road near the site. The truck parked up, and I jogged towards it, my feet slipping against the muddy ground. I knew I must look like a golem rising out of the mud, but forest rangers tended to be pretty grubby themselves, and it wasn't as if I were showing up for a date. I had my hard hat on, which was the only important thing.

"Hello," I began, as the door swung open. "I'm—"

My words died in my throat as the new ranger stepped out of the car. His tall, muscular body towered over mine, biceps bulging from the rolled up sleeves of his work shirt. He wore dark jeans and workboots with the laces loose, and looked like he'd just stepped off the set of a "Hottest Rangers" calendar shoot. On the edge of his sleeve, I caught the outline of a black and grey tattoo encircling his upper arm.

But most of all, it was his eyes that had me frozen. Deep, pools of dancing green flicked over my body, appraising me. He gave a curt nod, a stray dark brown curl falling over his eye. Another curled around his ears, the rest pulled back in a tight ponytail, like a Viking warrior preparing for battle. A line of stubble ran along his broad jaw, giving him a wild, untamed look.

He was beautiful, and here I was, wearing baggy dungarees, a shirt that had belonged to my father, and mud caked over every inch of my body.

"H-h-hello," I plastered a smile on my face and extended my hand to him. A strange electrical energy sizzled along my veins. The air around us suddenly became thick and heavy. My stomach flipped, and not from anything I ate. What was happening to me? The ranger was hot, but he wasn't Tom Hiddleston or anything. Why did I feel as nervous as a PhD candidate about to defend their thesis? "Welcome to the Crook-shollow Caves. I'm Anna Sinclair, from the University of Loamshire. I'd be happy to show you around—"

He stared at my hand extended in front of him, an expression of cruel disdain crossing his handsome features. "No thanks," he said, looking me up and down, his scowl deepening. "I don't deal with students."

My face flushed with heat. I stared down at my boots, hoping he wouldn't notice. *It figures someone this hot is a complete prick.* "Dr. Doyle is down in the cave." I pointed to the cave entrance. "She won't leave until this evening, and it's pretty cramped quarters down there anyway. If you want to talk to her, you'll have to wait until—"

"I have a job to do, and that job includes spot inspections of the work area." The ranger shot me a defiant look, then stalked over to the cave entrance. I longed to just walk away and leave him to sort himself out, but I was curious to see how his meeting with Frances would go. He was definitely going to make her put on a hard hat.

So I followed him back to the cave entrance, rubbing my arms through my shirt in an attempt to drive out the strange heat tingling through them. The ranger knelt down in front of the tiny hole, sticking one leg in first, than the other. I was hoping he'd get his enormous, sculpted, arrogant shoulders stuck, but he managed to slide through easily, the rain hardly touching him. Sighing, I crouched down and slid in after him.

By the time I'd wriggled through the entrance, he was already stomping through the water towards the site, his face set in a firm line. Frances stood up, and dusted off her hands. "You must be the new ranger. You don't have to come down here, you know. I understand it's a tight fit."

She didn't say it, but her resentment at his presence was written all over her face, unobscured by the brim of her nonexistent hard hat. Frances hated the county intrusion on her work. They were required by law to oversee the excavation, but Frances saw Crookshollow Caves as *her* site. She'd literally written the textbook on neolithic caves in England. She didn't want some ranger who didn't know a flint tool from an arrowhead telling her what to do, especially if he was as prickly as this character appeared to be.

He didn't shake her offered hand, either. "I'm Luke Lowe. I'm replacing Daniel. Can you tell me what procedures you have in place for preserving the ecosystem within the cave? I notice a stalagmite broken off by the entrance."

I cringed. I'd done that accidentally on the first day. A stalagmite formed over tens of thousands of years, through water dripping through cracks in the rocks. One misplaced swing of the theodolite tripod, and I'd knocked it off. And judging by Luke's expression, I could be glad he didn't know it was me.

"I have a full environmental report waiting for you back at camp, Mr. Lowe. Anna will show it to you. I have a lot of delicate work to do here, and I'm sure you'd rather get out of the rain."

"The rain doesn't bother me. What bothers me is your lack of personal protective equipment—"

"Nonsense." Frances practically pushed him towards the cave entrance. "I wouldn't want you to catch a cold. I'll give you a full tour of the site in the morning, I promise. The weather is supposed to clear a little by then. Anna, take our guest back to the camp and get a pot of tea boiling. You might as well finish up for the day, and we'll be along presently."

"I'll take Mr. Lowe, if Anna would rather stay behind. It doesn't look as though she's finished her quadrant yet," Ruth piped up. I snapped my head around, watching her smile broadly at Luke and tuck her chin-length blonde hair behind her ears. For some reason, this turned my stomach more than it should have.

"That's fine," I snapped. "I can do it." I didn't want to be alone with the new ranger, but I wasn't giving Ruth the satisfaction of flirting with him for the rest of the afternoon. "Finish my quadrant for me, would you? You must be *dying* to pick up a trowel again after a whole day carrying around that heavy tripod."

Ruth gave me a filthy look. I couldn't be certain, but I thought I saw a flicker of amusement pass over Luke's face. But when I glanced at him again, it was gone, replaced by his now-familiar sour expression.

"This way." I gestured for him to follow me back through the cave entrance and out into the rain. I jogged down the path, glancing back to make sure Luke was following me. He took long, graceful strides, having no trouble keeping up despite the fact he looked as though he were only taking a leisurely stroll. More of his hair had fallen out of his ponytail, and the rain plastered the curls to his face, making him appear even more attractive. An image of him naked under a shower flicked across my vision, and I was so shocked at the thought, I whirled around and ploughed straight into a tree.

"Argh!" I flopped backward, landing on my arse in a puddle. Mud splashed across my shirt and soaked through my already sodden dungarees.

"Careful," Luke called over the downpour as he strode past me. He didn't help me up. What a plonker. I cursed myself for fantasizing about him.

I trudged after Luke towards the camp, trying in vain to wipe some of the mud from the seat of my dungarees. The five of us were camping in a clearing around four hundred metres from the cave network. We had Dr. Doyle's rickety old caravan as a kitchen and field office, a small tin gardening shed that functioned as artefact storage, and a collection of leaking pup tents that we slept in. I led Luke up the stairs of the caravan, and shoved open the door.

"Take your shoes off," I ordered him, as I hung up my hard hat, kicked my boots off and stomped into the kitchen, not caring that I was smearing mud everywhere as I located the tea and filled the kettle. We had a half-packet of biscuits left, and I knew Frances was saving them for when the new ranger arrived, but I didn't get them out. Luke didn't deserve the last chocolate finger.

"Why? It's not exactly the Ritz in here. And with you shuffling around, it looks like the set of *Attacked by the Mud Creature From the Deep*." He kicked off his boots, though, which was more than I expected, and left them in front of the door. Without waiting for an invitation, he pulled out one of the stools at the counter and sat down, picking up one of Frances's field note-books from the stack on the counter and flicking through it.

I bit back a million retorts that threatened to spill out of my mouth. I had to be nice to this guy, no matter how rude he was to me. One word from him and Frances could be shut down. And as much as I resented having to be here, I liked her, and I didn't want to be the reason she had to stop work in the caves. That, and I needed to pass this course if I had any hope of getting into a master's programme.

So I took a deep breath, and tried to calm my racing heart and that weird, thrumming heat in my veins. What was it about this guy that made my whole body feel like I'd placed my finger in an electrical socket?

"Do you take milk and sugar?" I slammed a couple of cups down on the counter, harder than I'd intended.

"Just a splash of milk," Luke said, not looking up from his reading. "Tell me about what you've discovered about the site so far."

"Wouldn't you want to quiz Professor Doyle on that?" I demanded. "After all, I'm *just a student.*"

As soon as the words were out of my mouth, I wanted to take them back. What was wrong with me? I never spoke like that to anyone. I was the biggest pushover in the world. The very fact I was in this hellhole instead of Sicily was testament to that. But this guy had me completely on edge.

"Feeling feisty, aren't we?" Luke must have sensed my discomfort, for he gave me a smile that was slightly friendlier. He set down the notebook and looked up at me, those wicked green eyes sizing me up. A wet lock of hair flopped down over his eye, and he reached up and tucked it behind his ear. I gulped. If only he thought of me as anything other than an annoying student not worth his time ... he was just the kind of guy I'd go for, my deepest, sexist fantasies come to life. "I can see that you don't like me."

"I ... it's not ... I just ..." I backed away from him. Everything was going wrong. I was not used to being confronted like this, not when my veins were thrumming with tension. "I don't know you. You just seem as though you don't really want to be here."

"Then you misunderstand me. I want to be here very much." His eyes bore into mine. "And not just because of the caves."

My heart pounded against my chest. Did I read that right? Was this incredibly arrogant, incredibly handsome man *flirting* with me? I don't think anyone had ever flirted with me before. "I ... er ..."

I must be wrong. He couldn't possibly be—

"Let me get that tea." Luke stood up, his body inches from mine in the tiny kitchen. The air around me crackled with electricity. More than anything in the world I wanted to lean forward, press my body against his, and feel his lips brush against mine.

No.

I had to resist those thoughts. I wasn't ready for men again, not after what had happened to Ben. And I certainly wasn't ready for a man like this, who was cocky and confident and looked as though he sat firmly in the shagging-his-way-across-the-English-countryside camp. This guy would tear my heart out and dip it in his tea.

Luke reached around me and went to pick up the milk. My skin crawled with heat, the urge to touch him screamed inside me. My eyes locked on his lips, wondering what it would be like to kiss them, to feel his tongue slide against mine—

"I can do it myself," I said, my words coming out cold and harsh as I tried to rein in my desire. I snatched the milk from his hands and stepped back, splashing some into his mug. "Don't think that just because you're the ranger here, that you can intimidate me with your mere presence. I'm not impressed by guys like you."

"What makes you think I'm trying to impress you?" Luke said. A wicked grin spread across his face. "That's probably enough."

"Enough ..." I glanced down. While I'd been talking, I'd still been pouring out the milk. A little white waterfall flowed over the edges of his cup and down the side of the cupboard. "Oh, shit!"

"Don't worry." Luke grabbed some paper towels from the dispenser and started mopping it up. "I'll take care of it."

"Wait," I hated the way my voice whined. I held out my hand for the towels. "I'm sorry. That was uncalled for. It's been a long day, and I am very damp and cold and grumpy. Let me do it."

I reached out to take the towels from his hand, but he yanked them away. "I said I'll take care of it," he said, shortly. "You just sit over there and try not to touch anything else."

I moved across to the other side of the counter, a safe distance away from those rippling shoulders and piercing eyes. *I must've been mistaken. He wasn't flirting. He's just made it clear he's not interested.* I should have felt relieved, but all I felt was the flush of embarrassment, mixed with bitter disappointment.

Luke finished mopping up the spill and threw the towels into the rubbish. He threw his mug in the stack of dirty dishes on the bench, grabbed another one from the shelf, fixed his own tea, then set it down on the table across from me, as far from me as he could get in the tiny space. He pushed my own mug in front of me. "The caves," he said. "Tell me about them."

"Frances can—"

"I didn't ask Professor Doyle," he said. "I asked you."

Not looking up from my cup, I stammered my way through a basic description of the site, how an extended family had probably lived in the caves for several generations, using them seasonally to store food and take shelter when the weather turned.

"And you haven't found any cave paintings, anything like that?"

I shook my head. "Cave paintings are extremely rare, especially in this period. Conditions have to be just right, or they'll be destroyed. I don't think we'll find anything as interesting as that here."

"What's that on your wrist?" Luke asked, pointing to the silver bracelet I'd been playing with subconsciously.

Hastily, I covered my hand over the cool metal band. My father had given me the bracelet when I'd got my GCSEs. "I'm so proud of you, Anna," he'd said as he slid the cool metal onto my wrist. "I know you're going to do amazing things." He'd died two weeks later, and I hadn't taken it off since. Just touching it reassured me when I was nervous, and being in the same space as Luke Lowe made me incredibly nervous.

"The environmental regulations clearly prohibit the wearing of jewellery in the caves." Luke frowned. "It could get snagged on the rocks and cause damage to the caves, not to mention the fact that jewellery on any site is a health and safety concern. Your party has already broken off that stalactite. If I see any other damage in the caves, I'm going to ask you all to leave."

"It ... it's just a bracelet." I said, a lump rising in my throat. "I'm being so careful. You have no idea. I'm the only one wearing my hard hat. Surely that's more important—"

"It's all important. That bracelet is not allowed. You need to take it off."

"Okay. Fine." I could barely get the words out. Tears battled against my eyelids. I tried to blink them back, but they spilled over, crashing down my cheeks. I couldn't stay there with him, not while I was crying. My whole body flushed with the shame of it. I turned my head away, pushed my stool back, and shoved my feet into my boots.

"Anna, wait!" Luke called out, but I was already out the door and fleeing to my tent.

Once inside the privacy of my canvas walls, I collapsed on my sleeping back, the tears flowing thick now. What was wrong with me? I'd been feeling okay for a month now. I hadn't cried about Ben in a few weeks, and we'd buried Dad years ago ... so why was I so upset now? Luke was right, the bracelet was against the rules. And I knew better than anyone how important obeying the rules was.

It was that guy, Luke. His arrogance had got inside my head. Maybe I wasn't as over Ben as I thought, because just the thought of Luke flirting with me made me feel sick.

Why did Luke have to come here at all? Why couldn't they have sent a non-attractive ranger? And most of all, why was my own body betraying me? Why did I want him so badly, even though I also hated his guts?

2

LUKE

*W*oah.

Anna Sinclair.

Woah.

The moment I stepped out of the car, her scent hit me like a brick wall. Light and floral and utterly delicious, she was like a rare flower blooming in a barren field. I knew from the moment her aroma wafted across my nostrils, she was meant to be mine.

And that knowledge was terrifying.

As she stalked through the forest towards me, panic rose in my chest. This was not supposed to happen. I'd come back to Crookshollow for the caves. I was here for one reason only, to prevent any of my family's dark secrets from being drawn to the surface once again, to ensure my father could rest in peace without the past being dragged up again. And now that the site's discovery had been made public, there was also the possibility that some other wolf might show up here, eager to lay claim to my family's old territories. I had to be on my guard. I couldn't have any distractions.

As I watched her bite her lower lip with nerves, and my cock stirred to life, I knew Anna Sinclair was going to be one hell of a distraction.

This can't be happening. I had it all planned out. I'd fabricated a story about a robbery to trick the last ranger into resigning. I'd managed to flirt my way through the job interview with Bev, the fifty-something head ranger with hair like burnt straw, and I'd landed the job as the new park ranger in Crookshollow Forest, overseeing the archaeological excavation. All I had to do was sneak into the cave at night, find the paintings, destroy them, and check that no other wolves were in the area. Then I could retreat back into the wilderness and continue my mourning in peace.

I never could have anticipated that my mate would also be here. But here she was – the woman I was destined to be with, the women who my body already ached for – offering me a mud-caked hand to shake.

I didn't dare take it. The air between us already sizzled with electricity – with the unknowable and unavoidable force that drew me to her. My veins surged with heat, and the wolf within pressed against my skin, threatening at any moment to burst forth and claim his mate. If our skin touched, I couldn't guarantee I'd be able to control myself, and jumping the young archaeologist and doing her up against a tree before I'd even said, "Hello, terrible weather we've having," might be considered a little rude. So I stared at her hand, and she retracted it.

My rudeness rankled her, and her beautiful face set in a firm expression, her cute nostrils flaring slightly with anger. God, that was hot. Note to self, make her angry again. She was trying to lead me to the camp, but I knew I needed to see the cave first, to leave my scent there, lest any other wolf showed up trying to claim it as their own. Plus, I wanted to see if it still matched my father's description.

Anna pointed out the entrance. It was small, barely wide

enough for me to wiggle my shoulders through. This made perfect sense, as it meant only one wolf could enter or exit at a time. This made it easier to guard against warring packs. Unfortunately, it hadn't saved my father's family from a grisly death.

I was hoping Anna would shimmy through the gap first, so I could watch her gorgeous arse slide down into that dark hole. But she hung back, waiting for me. I shoved my legs through the hole and slid down.

Inside, the cave was surprisingly bright. Floodlights illuminated the raised floor of the work area, their cords extending out through a smaller hole in the roof and hooking up to the solar panels I'd noticed resting against the rocky ledge outside. The light reflected off the shallow pool of water at my feet, a small river that ran across the entrance and deeper into the cave.

I glanced around, taking it all in. The cave floor, the vaulted room, the little river by the door. It was just as my father had said it was—

I raised my nose into the air and sniffed. A hundred snatches of scent wafted through my nostrils – mostly the smell of rats and foxes and other small animals that had taken shelter here. The distinct odour of another wolf was absent. Good, I was the first one here. Hopefully, there wouldn't be any others.

As I waded through the shallow river, I raised my arm, rubbing my underarm as casually as I could across the rocks. I noticed one of the stalactites in the cluster by the entrance had been broken off. A shudder of rage tore through my body. Archaeologists pissed me off so much. All they were interested in was evidence of human achievement, human beauty, human triumph. Meanwhile, they stomped around in beautiful natural landscapes, destroying things that took thousands of years to form, and didn't even bat an eyelash.

I spoke briefly to Frances Doyle, the head archaeologist. She was annoyed at my presence. She wasn't wearing her hard hat, which I made a mental note to write up later. In fact, of all the team, only Anna was wearing the correct safety gear. Her hard hat looked adorable perched on top of her head.

Even though I was standing in the home of my ancestors, a place we'd long since thought buried and hidden forever, I struggled to concentrate as I became aware of Anna Sinclair behind me, her soft breathing, her teeth biting down on the edge of her lip, the shape of her breasts through the wet fabric of her shirt—

My blood ran hot, my whole body desperate to claim her. How was I going to survive sharing a campsite with her? I'd been here five minutes and I was already imagining what she'd look like rolling naked in the mud while I took her—

No. Focus, Luke. You're not here for a mate. You're here for your father.

My father. The pain of his loss temporarily cooled my blood. It had only been a month since he'd died, and I still couldn't believe he was really gone. All my life, it had just been the two of us. I longed to talk to him, to have his opinion on what I should do about Anna, but he'd never give me his wisdom again.

Through the haze of my thoughts, I heard Frances order Anna to take me back to the camp and put the kettle on. Good. Maybe I'd be able to collect my thoughts away from this place. This time, Anna led the way out of the cave. I clambered out behind her with as much dignity as I could muster, deliberately running my palm along the cave wall, smearing a scent path that should deter any other wolf.

Anna stalked in front of me, that sensuous arse of hers swaying seductively, even in her mud-covered dungarees. She must be feeling the effects of the attraction, too. I noticed with a not inconsiderable amount of joy that she was staring over her shoulder at me. She was staring so hard, in fact, that she ran right into a tree and fell down into the mud.

She looked miserable sitting in that puddle in the pelting rain, her dungarees bunched up around her boots. I wanted desperately to help her up and wipe all the mud off her arse with my hand, but I knew if I touched her, I would be claiming her as mine. And as tempting as she was, I couldn't do that. She was perfect, and I was a broken, damaged man, carrying secrets that would chill her soul.

If only I could get my body to see sense. It was going to be very, *very* hard to keep my mind on the task at hand.

AN HOUR LATER, I lay on my inflatable mattress, my stomach rumbling and a stack of field notes on my chest that I should have been studying. But instead, I was staring at the ceiling and thinking about Anna.

I'd been rude to her in the caravan, when she offered me tea. I'd been even more rude trying to get information from her about the site. I'd even flirted with her a little, just to see how she'd react. Surely, she must feel the same energy between us, the same deadly attraction?

Well, Anna may have been my mate, but she certainly didn't know it. She was a shy little thing, always biting her lip instead of saying what was on her mind. Normally, I would never be interested in a girl like that, so eager to please, so desperate to be liked that she never disagreed. I could tell she'd wanted to tell me to fuck off with my attitude, or to fuck her with my cock. But instead, she apologised.

And *then,* when I cornered her about her bracelet, she'd burst into tears and run away. The pain in her eyes when she put her hand on that silver band tore at me. Something had hurt her badly, and it had to do with that bracelet. And like an idiot, I had chewed her out about it.

This is never going to work, I told my brain. *I don't want to be with anyone, least of all a shy archaeologist. I've been alone my entire life, and that's just the way it's supposed to be. I have my own pain to deal with. I don't need to take on anyone else's.*

You're *an idiot.* My brain whispered back. *Maybe she's exactly what you need.*

PROFESSOR DOYLE COOKED a dinner of stew and potatoes. The stew burnt to the bottom of the pan, and tasted mostly of charcoal. The potatoes were so lumpy they could've spelled DON'T EAT ME in Braille. The team ate in silence, although it was clear from their faces that this was the calibre of meal I could expect to get used to.

After dinner, Frances handed around drinks from the fridge and each person settled into their own activities. I hoped this might be my chance to speak to Anna and apologise for upsetting her, but just as I was about to move in, Ruth plopped down next to me and shoved a beer under my nose. "I'm so passionate about sustainability," she gushed, as she tipped her cider into a disposable coffee cup that would release enough methane into the atmosphere during its inevitable trip to the bottom of a landfill to turn the ozone layer around her ditzy head into a doily.

I choked back my gathering scorn and spoke to Ruth politely, listening with half an ear as she prattled on about the Save the Whales project she'd been involved in back at the university. My eyes remained fixed on Anna, who sat at the far end of the caravan, under the window, drinking her beer in short gulps as she buried her face in a science fiction novel. She wore a pair of reading glasses that made her doe-brown eyes appear even larger.

"—and I raised enough money to pay the petrol for one whale protestor's boat—"

"Excuse me." I broke Ruth off mid-sentence as I stood up, and walked over to where Anna was sitting. Max looked up from the rummy game he was playing with Frances and shot me a horrified look that clearly implied what he thought of my decision.

"May I?" I gestured to the space beside her.

"It's a free country," she replied. Her cheeks flared red as I plopped down beside her, close enough to breathe in her intoxicating scent, but not close enough that we actually touched. She pushed her glasses up her nose, and continued to stare down at the page.

"You're reading Heinlein?" I glanced at the title of her book. *Stranger in a Strange Land.* A lump rose in my throat at the title. That had been one of Dad's favourite books.

Anna nodded. "Re-reading, actually. I love all of Heinlein's stories." She blushed deeper, as though she'd somehow revealed some deep personal secret.

"Me, too," I said. The electricity between us sizzled, pulling me towards her like two opposing charges. "I love the way Heinlen uses the character of Smith to force the reader to view their own preconceptions."

She nodded, her fingers tracing the edge of the page. "Exactly. I read this book for the first time when I was fourteen. Every few years, I reread it. And I always get something different out of it. That's what I love about Heinlen – people think *Stranger* is all about Heinlen presenting his ideal world in the form of Smith's 'religion.' But that's not it at all. He's inviting you to think, not to believe."

"Yeah, that's it exactly." That was seriously insightful. "What other authors do you like?"

"Oh, all sorts." She looked up at me then. Her eyes lit up as she spoke. "I've read all the classic science fiction authors, of course. Asimov, H. G. Wells, Frank Herbert. I especially love science fiction when it crosses with horror."

"So a big Lovecraft fan, then?"

"Oh, definitely. Give me Cthulhu over sparkly vampires any day." She grinned. "I do like some fantasy books. Writers like Laurell K. Hamilton and Patricia Briggs who take old legends like vampires and werewolves and bring them into the contemporary world. There's this amazing author named S. C. Green who wrote these dark steampunk books set in a Georgian London infested with dinosaurs. My friend Derek got me onto those – he is always giving me new books to read. He's studying mythology so he digs that kind of stuff."

"What's your favourite creature?"

"Werewolves," she said instantly. "I love how primal and protective they are. Werewolves are all about family. I totally dig that."

If only you knew, I thought ruefully, marvelling at where this conversation had gone. I pointed to the crinkled book cover. "So you've had that book since you were fourteen?"

Anna shook her head. "I got this copy from a second-hand bookshop in Crookshollow. My dad gave me a beautiful hardcover copy for my fourteenth birthday. But I wouldn't take that to a site. My books are precious, especially ones from my dad."

"A woman after my own heart."

She smiled then, a genuine smile that made my heart pound against my stomach. "Oh yes?"

"I have a small cabin in Sherwood Forest," I explained. "I go there when I'm not working. It's pretty tiny and very basic – there's no mobile reception and you have to bathe in a little stream outside. But I keep all my books there." In my head, I imagined her sitting beside me before the fire, her feet over my knees as she leaned back against the sofa, a book open on her lap, those adorable glasses perched on her nose.

I hadn't been back to the cabin since Dad died – everything there bore his scent, his unmistakable presence. I couldn't face being there alone. But the idea of Anna being there with me made a return trip seem instantly palatable. *The things we could get up to in that stream ...*

"It sounds heavenly," she said, her voice slightly wistful. "I live with my mum in a flat in Crooks Crossing. There's not a lot of room, so I have to keep my favourite books in boxes under my bed. Even then, there are several boxes stashed in the loft."

"You live with your mum? So your parents are divorced."

Anna shook her head. My stomach sank as I realised what that probably meant. Anna looked away, her whole body stiffening. Her hand flew to her wrist, which the silver bracelet still defiantly encircled.

"I have to go," she whispered, the book falling from her hand and clattering on the floor.

"Why?" Disappointment surged through me. I was actually enjoying talking to her. I wanted to find out more about what books she liked, about her family, about her studies and what had made her want to be an archaeologist. But for some reason, her father's death – for that had to be what it was – kept her closed off from me. But it didn't have to. I reached out to her, willing to say anything to get her to stay and talk to me. "Anna, I know how you feel. My father—"

"I just ... I can't ..." She grabbed her coat and swung herself up, racing for the caravan door and sprinting into the wet evening as fast as her legs could carry her.

∾

I STAYED in the caravan for another hour in case Anna came back, but she didn't. I got stuck talking to Ruth and Max about reality TV shows – a sickness I had yet to succumb to. As a ranger, I didn't have the chance to watch much TV, and when I did, my taste lent itself to western films and Star Trek reruns, not the inner monologues of ten stick-thin models posing as seductive lampposts in an avant-garde advertisement for a lighting company. While I tuned out their inane discussion, I mentally ran through my conversation with Anna, trying to figure out where I had gone wrong.

Her father. I'd assumed he was dead, but what if I was wrong? What if I just assumed that because that was my situation? What if Anna's father was in jail? What if he was in jail for something he'd done to her?

If that was true, that was pretty heavy. I got why she wouldn't want to talk about that with a stranger, especially not in the caravan with Frances and Ruth and Max listening. Fuck, I was an insensitive idiot.

Try again tomorrow. I hadn't completely fucked up. Yet. Even though I didn't want a mate, I was becoming more intrigued by Anna Sinclair. Maybe it was that pain I'd seen flicker across her face – a pain that felt like a mirror of my own.

That decision made, I stood up and loped off towards my tent without wishing the others goodnight. As I strode across the campsite, the moon rose higher through the trees, taunting me with its pale light. In two days' time, she would be completely full. The itch pulsed through my veins, making me feel nervous, jumpy. I scratched my cheek furiously, out of habit, but nothing could sate the itch of the moon heating my wolven blood.

I was staying in Daniel's tent, which he'd left set up for me after leaving in a hurry to deal with the emergency I'd invented for him. I was lucky I had a dodgy friend in Liverpool (are there any other kind of friends from Liverpool?) who was willing to break into his flat for me. He hadn't stolen anything, just messed the place up enough that Daniel would need to spend time cleaning it as well as filing reports with the police. He'd taken two weeks' leave, which should be more than enough time for me to do what I'd come to do.

Luckily, Daniel had set up his tent a good fifty metres from the others, between the camp and the caves. I'd at least have some privacy. Most of Daniel's things were still inside. I unzipped my rucksack and took out my bottle of *Lycan* pills. They weren't the usual ones I took, but I'd heard good things about Clara – the local witch in Crookshollow village – and she'd assured me these were even more potent. Hopefully, the pills would keep my wolfish persona in check while the moon was high. Otherwise, I might do something I'd later regret, especially with the delectable Anna around.

I downed a couple of pills, and waited. The itch did seem to abate a bit. Good. I had something important to do that night.

The moon rose higher, and the itch throbbed through my whole body. I gritted my teeth and held my hands at my sides, resisting the urge to scratch my skin raw, the way I had done as a child.

Instead, I counted the minutes on my watch. *Eleven thirty ... eleven forty-three ... eleven fifty-seven ...* When I was sure everyone else was asleep, I grabbed my torch, a crowbar, and a notebook from my pack, and made my way swiftly and silently from the camp towards the caves.

It was better to get the job over and done with. Then I could focus my attention on Anna.

The seam of basaltic rock ran through the forest for miles, and I knew that a huge network of caves ran through it, carved out by the movement of the earth and the paths dug by water rushing ever downward. People had inhabited the caves since the neolithic period, but not many people knew how recently they had been occupied.

I had to keep it that way.

It took me a few minutes to find the cave entrance in the dark. I sniffed the air again, but it was hard to distinguish the smells. Everything out here was tainted by the intoxicating scent of Anna. I could smell her footsteps as clearly as if she'd wandered through a tub of butter.

I shimmied through the tiny hole, my boots splashing in the water. Now that the rain had finally stopped, the pool around my feet wasn't nearly as deep as it had been earlier, although it was still slippery. I flicked my touch on, and made my way carefully over the rocks and across the site.

The archaeologists had used string lines to create a grid of twelve squares (or quadrants, as Anna called them) across the living floor, and they were systematically clearing away the stratigraphic layers of each square, recording all the artefacts and features, and mapping notable finds into the theodolite to create a three-dimensional spatial map. So far, it didn't look as though they'd ventured any further back into the cave. That was a good sign.

Even when the cancer had eaten away at his mind and body, my father remembered the layout of the cave as though he'd been there just yesterday. I knew from his description the cave paintings were located in a tunnel leading down from a secondary cavern located through a small fissure at the end of the living floor – the flattened area where prehistoric people had made their home in the cave. I needed to find them before Frances and her team did, and destroy them, if there was even anything left. Nearly a hundred years had passed since they'd last been seen. Nature might have already taken care of things for me.

I picked my way carefully along the wooden planks placed between the quadrants, and scanned the rear wall with my torch. It only took a few moments to find what I was looking for, a small opening in the back wall of the cave, at about waist height. I pushed my torch through first, resting it on a protruding rock so it pointed back towards me. I squeezed my shoulders forward, and wriggled my body into the tiny hole, using the wall behind me to kick off with my feet.

It was a tight fit, but after a few moments of sweating and shifting and grunting, I managed to slip my arms through. I used the rock in front of me to pull my torso into the darkness. I stood up, dusting myself off, and shone the torch around me. I was standing in a long fissure between the rocks, the roof of the cave at least three metres above my head. I manoeuvred my way between the two sloping faces. At the end of the fissure, the room opened out into a large cavern. In the far corner, a pool of water reflected the light of my torch back at me. Dark openings led off to the left and the right.

Dad said it was the left tunnel. I jumped down onto the next stone and headed towards the opening, the crowbar on my back clanging against the rock as I swung myself around.

Back here, the rocks were dry, the ground beneath me crumbling stone. At the entrance, I shone my torch down the tunnel, bouncing the light along the walls, searching for the coloured designs that marked the paintings. I couldn't see anything.

"You've got to be here," I muttered under my breath, bending up to check the ceiling of the tunnel. This was exactly where he'd said they'd be. So why couldn't I see—

"What the hell are you doing?" a sultry voice demanded from behind me.

Shit. I was caught.

3

ANNA

*L*uke whirled around, the light of his torch temporarily blinding me. "Anna, you startled me."

"I might say the same thing," I said, suddenly nervous. Not twenty minutes ago, I'd been tucked up warm in my sleeping bag, trying to forget about the way Luke had smiled at me when I said how much I love Heinlein's books. I had been drifting off to sleep, imagining what it would be like to kiss Luke's soft lips ... but then I'd realised I didn't have my book with me. Had I left it in the caravan when I'd run away from Luke, or had I dropped it somewhere outside on the way to my tent?

Dammit. That was the only book I'd brought along to read. Without it, I'd have to resort to talking to people. And between Ruth's sickening suckup-itude, Frances's scatterbrained inattentiveness, and Max's overall leery strangeness, I wasn't that keen on the idea.

So I'd sighed, and sat up to pull on my socks and boots. I had realized that I was wide awake now, and the thought of the book sitting in a puddle outside hast just been more than I could bear. It was like I'd told Luke: my books were precious, even the battered second-hand copies. I'd pulled on my jacket and stepped out into the frigid night. I'd retraced my steps across the camp to the caravan, but hadn't been able to see it on the ground anywhere. Peering in at the window, I'd noticed the book sitting on the edge of the chair. I went inside and grabbed it, relief seeping through my body as I clutched it under my arm. I had been heading back to my tent when I'd seen Luke creeping off towards the caves.

It had been curiosity that compelled me to follow him. But now that I was here, confronting him wearing only my pyjamas, thermal underwear, boots, and jacket, I realised just how dangerous this situation could be. I barely knew Luke. Just because he was gorgeous didn't mean he didn't have some nefarious purpose. As far as I knew, the guy could be unstable. And I was alone with him, without my hard hat, in the dark, in an unexplored section of the cave. No one else knew I was here. If he killed me now, they wouldn't ever find my body.

I'd just made all the mistakes I'd promised myself I'd never make.

"I asked a question," I said, trying to stop my voice from wavering. Luke stared at me with wide eyes. His mouth moved, but no sound came out. Fancy that. I'd actually rendered him speechless.

"Luke?" I prodded, careful to keep my voice stern. No sense in letting him sense my fear.

"I'm just ... checking up on some of the details of your excavation." Luke nodded firmly. "Frances's notes weren't very expansive. I thought I'd come here and try to get a sense of things *in situ*."

"This area of the cave hasn't been explored," I said, my voice shrinking in the cavernous space. "That fact was in the notes you were reading. It's dangerous to come here by yourself, especially at night, especially if no one knows where you are."

"You know where I am," he growled, those fierce green eyes flickering over my body. With a flush, I remembered that I was wearing my hideous pink thermal leggings underneath my Snoopy pyjama pants. Could this day get any worse?

"We shouldn't be in the caves at night," I repeated nervously. "I believe a certain ranger told me it's against the rules."

"Do you ever do anything that's against the rules?" he asked, closing the gap between us in a heartbeat. He still hadn't touched me, but my body flooded with warm, pulsing energy. How was it he could make me feel this way? Especially when I'd just caught him red handed doing something he shouldn't.

"I ... er ..."

"I thought so." Luke stepped closer. "Anna, I can explain. I—"

"Argh!" I screamed as something swooped down from the darkness and flapped beside my face. I dropped my torch as I flung my hands up to protect my eyes from the screeching bat. My stomach turned as the bat's furry body slipped through my fingers and scrambled into my hair, its wings twitching as it tangled itself deeper.

The torch clattered on the rocks below, bouncing down the steps and plunging into the pool. The light went out.

"Fuck," Luke swore. "Stand still!"

"I can't stand still. There's a bat in my hair!" I wailed, flailing my hands around my head. I turned to run back down the fissure, but instead I crashed into Luke, sending his torch flying from his hands. It hit the rocks with a crash, and the light flickered out, plunging us both into complete darkness.

Tears welled in my eyes. The bat's feet scrabbled against my head, yanking my hair so hard the entire side of my scalp felt as though it were being pulled off. Luke's hands battled in my hair. He swore again as the squabbling intensified. Finally, the bat released me, and I heard its wings flapping away into the darkness.

"Ow." I touched the side of my head. My scalp felt tender. But at least it was still there. Luckily, I'd already had a tetanus shot.

"Anna, are you okay?"

I nodded, biting my lip. After a moment of silence, I realised how stupid that was. "I'm fine," I said, my voice cracking.

"I can tell. Here, hold on to me," Luke ordered. I reached out, grabbing for his elbow, but instead, my fingers brushed the fabric of his jeans. I felt the button on his fly. Shit. I'd grabbed him right—

"If you wanted an excuse to grope me, you just had to ask," he said, laughing.

"Shut up," I shot back, heat flaring in my cheeks. I was lucky it was so dark, he wouldn't be able to see how beet-red I must be. I reached up, clamping my hand around his forearm. The warm sensation raced through my fingers, down my whole arm, lighting all my senses on fire.

Woah. The heat was intense. It wasn't just my hormones on overdrive. The heat penetrated every layer of my body, spreading through my limbs and circling through my head. My chest swelled with intense emotion. I gulped back the urge to ... I'm not sure whether I wanted to cry or laugh or kiss Luke or push him away or beg him to marry me. The intense sensation swirled around my head, and in the darkness, it was even more disorienting. I squeezed Luke's arm tighter, reassuring myself that he was there, and that I was standing upright still.

"Luke," I asked, tugging at my hand. "I feel—"

"I know." His deep voice came through the dark. Confident, reassuring. "Don't think about it right now, Anna. We need to focus on getting out of here. Can you follow behind me?"

"I ... I think so."

Luke's fingers closed around mine. The warmth in my body surged. Slowly, Luke felt his way back up the fissure, squeezing his way between the gap. I kept close at his heels, my other hand feeling my way along the rocks, re-establishing my bearings. Every few moments he squeezed my hand. I squeezed back, assuring him I was fine.

"You're good at this," I remarked as we emerged onto the site and Luke picked his way carefully around the quadrants without disturbing any of our cuttings.

"I can see well in the dark," he said, then sucked in his breath, as though he'd said something he shouldn't.

"That's interesting."

"Is it?" He slid down a rocky ledge, then turned to grip my waist with his strong hands. Before I could say anything, he'd lifted me down, and crushed my body against his powerful chest. My face was millimetres from his. His hot breath warmed my lips. The energy between us sizzled. "I can think of much more interesting things right now."

Kiss me, my body screamed. In the dark, my senses worked in overdrive, assailing me with Luke's intoxicating masculine scent, the sensation of his fingers gripping me, the press of his bulge against my thigh.

"Luke—" I murmured, not sure whether I was protesting or begging.

"Anna." His husky voice grated against my ears. His breath caressed my cheek. And then, he pressed his lips to mine.

I pressed back. My whole body shot with fire. It was as though the kiss connected us by more than just our lips.

Luke teased apart my lips, his tongue running against mine, dragging me deeper into his embrace. His hand cupped my cheek, holding my head against his as though he couldn't bear to break the seal. His other hand burned the small of my back.

In the darkness, every touch, every sensation spiralled out of control. He burned all around me, a star going supernova, trailing a line of fire across my universe.

I tangled my fingers through his hair, pulling it out of its tie and enjoying the way the silky threads fell through my fingers. I'd never been with a guy who had long hair before. Ben's hair had been your standard number-two cut ... *No,* I didn't want to think about Ben. Not now—

Too late. Ben's face was dancing on my vision. That carefree smile he'd worn as he'd kissed me goodbye for the last time ... his battered face staring up at me at the morgue, stiff and lifeless. My body stiffened.

Luke pulled away. "We ... shouldn't do this," he breathed.

"It's a bad idea," I agreed, leaning forward to kiss him again, wanting to drive out the vision of Ben. Luke moaned as my lips touched his, and I melted back against him, losing myself in his wonderful touch.

He tore himself away again. "Anna. We have to stop."

"You don't want this?"

He laughed hollowly. "That's not it at all. You were the one who just stiffened up."

"I don't want to talk about that right now. I just ..."

"Look, it's fine." Luke shrugged away from me. My heart beat against my chest. How had this gone so wrong? Why had I thought about Ben at all ... thinking about him wouldn't bring him back. "We can just go back to the camp and forget it ever happened."

"But ... you kissed me?" Panic rose in my chest.

"Yes." He sighed. "And I want to push you up against that rock face and fuck you senseless."

My whole body flushed.

Luke continued. "But aside from the fact we risk getting stalactites in some very unfortunate places, I'm not sure it's such a good idea. We're supposed to be working together."

Now my face flushed with embarrassment. Luke was right. If we did ... anything, it was going to be awkward as hell for the rest of the dig. I was supposed to be doing my best job to impress Professor Doyle so I could get a recommendation for my master's course. Luke was supposed to keep all us archaeologists in line, and prevent the kind of accidents that had killed my dad and Ben. It wouldn't look good if anyone found out that we were shagging.

Disappointment surged through me, followed by an intense wave of sadness. For a minute there, I'd been completely ready to expose myself to Luke, both figuratively and very, very literally. I'd finally let down that wall that had been closed off ever since Ben had died, and the only thing on the other side was a guy who couldn't even begin to comprehend the enormity of that. *You have to remember that Luke doesn't have all this baggage. To him, you are just a shag. Probably one of hundreds of women. That's why it's so easy for him to just pull back. He can just get it somewhere else. Don't read more into this than it is.*

"Yeah, I guess you're right," I said, keeping my voice steady. At least in the dark, he couldn't see the tears threatening to spill down my cheeks. *This is what happens when you let yourself be vulnerable,* the voice inside my head warned me. *You get hurt.*

We scrambled out of the cave without touching and walked back to the camp, keeping a wide distance between us. The silent night stretched between us, filling the void with hanging, unanswered questions. The waxing moon beat down on my back, illuminating the forest with long shadows. I watched Luke out of the corner of my eye. He walked tall, his shoulders back, his head high, almost as though he were a dog sniffing out a scent. He showed no hint of disappointment or sadness at all.

You made the right decision, I told myself, even though the disappointment still bit into me.

Luke walked me to my tent. As I stooped to open the flap of the tent, he cleared his throat. "Anna, I—"

"It's fine," I said. "You were right. Goodnight, Luke."

I glanced up at him then, and caught his gaze. His eyes locked with mine, the stare so intense, so primal, it gave me a start. How could he be so blasé about things back in the cave, and then look at me like *that*?

Luke turned away, his mouth curling up at the edges ever so slightly. "Goodnight, Anna. Sweet dreams."

I pulled up the flap of my tent and crawled inside. I scrambled around in the dark and found my phone, which I clicked on to the torch app to give me light while I took off my jacket and socks. My sleeping bag had never looked so inviting.

Weariness washed over me as I crawled down into the bag, pulling the flap right up around my chin. I trembled, but not from the cold. The heat still pulsed through my body, and I could still feel the traces of Luke's fingers against my skin. What a bizarre, frustrating, sad night.

As I closed my eyes and tried to force my mind away from Luke and the kiss, my hand closed around my wrist, seeking out the familiar bracelet that always helped to calm me. Panic seized me when all I felt was skin.

I bolted upright, wide awake once more. I flicked on my phone torch and looked at my wrist under the light. It was bare. I turned out my sleeping bag, flipped over the air mattress, and scrambled through my stack of clothing. Nothing.

My bracelet was gone. I'd lost it somewhere in the cave. It was the one item I had left that reminded me of Dad, that gave me strength when I needed it, and I'd lost it.

Tears pricked at my cheeks. I buried my face in my hands. *You're an idiot, Anna. This is what happens when you let your emotions take over. You have to stay away from that ranger, for your own good.*

4

LUKE

*A*fter my encounter with Anna, I couldn't sleep. I tossed and turned, my body surging with desire for her. The connection between us called me to her, and it was all I could do to prevent myself throwing open the flap of my tent and running naked across the camp to find her.

Probably not the best look, if Frances or Ruth caught me.

I'd hoped the kiss would dissipate some of the sexual tension between us, but instead, it had turned up the heat. But as soon as she'd stiffened up, I'd realised we had to stop. I knew it was a bad idea. It was bad for her because she had to suck up to Professor Doyle for her grades, and because there was clearly something in her past that made her cautious around me. And it was especially bad for me because I needed to stay on high alert for other wolves, and I had to find and destroy the paintings, something that was going to be hard as long as Anna was keeping her eye on me.

But maybe now she would pull back. It had taken everything within me to pull away from her, and I could see the disappointment and embarrassment written all over her face as we'd walked back to the camp. I hated the idea she thought I didn't want her, but I was used to being thought of as a bastard, so it made sense, even if it was messing with my hormones, big time.

Your hormones … or your heart. The thought made the itch flare against my skin. I growled and scratched furiously at my legs, but the itch didn't subside. I didn't want to think about Dad, or how much I missed him, or how much I wished I could talk to him about Anna.

The full moon was two days away. I rolled over, punching the sleeping bag cover stuffed with clothes that served as my pillow in an attempt to form the lumps into a comfortable shape. Even though my head burned with barely concealed pain, my veins still pulsed with desire. Several long, grey hairs pricked through my skin, sticking up out of my arms and back like porcupine quills. *Get control of yourself, Lowe,* I scolded myself, rubbing in vain at the itch on my neck. *This will only get worse.*

AT SOME POINT I must've fallen into an agitated sleep, for the next morning I woke with a start, my mind reeling from a dream in which I was chasing my father through a forest, only to burst into a clearing to find him and Anna kissing.

You're going nuts, I told myself, trying to shake off the images. My dreams always got vivid and disturbing close to the full moon. Usually I paid them no heed, but my father's death was still too raw in my consciousness for his appearance not to affect me.

The pain of his absence gripped me like a vice. I wrapped my arms around my shoulders, trying to will it away, but it pulsed just below my skin, a nagging, hopeless desire to see him again. I wished he could be here with me, telling me the stories about his childhood here in the forest. I wished he could give me some advice about what to do about this intense physical longing now I'd found my mate. I longed to introduce him to Anna, and listen to them talk about books all night long ...

But none of that would ever happen. I had to face that fact, and move on.

I threw off the covers, pulled on my work trousers and shrugged on my coat. I wasn't going to sit here and think about it.

The rain had returned during the night, and it pelted me in huge drops as I emerged, bleary eyed, from my tent. The rest of the team were already in the caravan. I could see them moving around through the windows. I pulled the hood over my face and jogged through the trees towards them.

He's dead. He's dead.

A flash of memory. The first time my dad ever took me hunting. We were living in the Black Forest in Southern Germany, and I had just turned eight. When the full moon claimed us, instead of hiding me in our cabin while he went out alone, Dad took me deep into the woods, further than I'd ever gone before. Strange scents overwhelmed me, but he showed me how to discern different trails and map the forest with my nose. We sat together on top of a hill and watched the stars move across the sky.

"Your grandparents are up there somewhere," he told me, pointing with his snout to the Milky Way smudged across the deep sky. "They're shining down on us, along with the rest of the Lowe pack. We're the last ones left, Luke."

"We don't need anyone else." I hated how wistful he sounded, how lonely. I wasn't lonely. I had him.

He'd ferreted out a rabbit from amongst the brambles, and I'd chased it along a ridge before cornering it by the river and killing it with a single bite to the throat. I remembered the way the adrenaline coursed through me, my heart pounding in my ears as I closed in for the kill.

As we enjoyed our feast that night, Dad offered me the choicest haunch. "I am proud of you, Luke. You will be a fine wolf. One day, perhaps you will be the one to make the Lowe pack great again. If anyone could, it would be you."

It would be you.

I spun around, and slammed my fist into the nearest tree trunk. Pain cracked across my knuckles, but the sting tore me back to reality, away from the memories. I glanced up at the sky, just visible through the bare branches. A few lonesome stars twinkled against the early morning haze.

I'm here now, Dad. I promise you I will succeed. I won't let our family legacy be one of dishonour.

I sucked in a breath. *Time to get over feeling sorry for yourself, Luke.* I needed to have all my wits about me if I was going to get back to destroy the paintings without arousing suspicion. And I needed to keep my cool around Anna. It was better for both of us if we didn't get involved.

I pushed open the caravan door. Ruth and Frances looked up from the table, one giving me a gleaming smile, the other, a disdainful look. Anna's eyes flicked briefly to mine, and then she glanced away, suddenly engrossed in her porridge. Not wanting to make her more uncomfortable, I took a seat at the opposite end of the table, and intentionally provoked Ruth into a conversation about fossil fuels. If Anna was going to play at ignoring me, then I could follow her lead.

5

ANNA

*a*ll through breakfast, I kept sneaking looks over at Luke. He sat down at the opposite end of the table, and was hanging off Ruth's every sycophantic word. *He's forgotten about the kiss awfully quick,* I thought angrily. *He's obviously going to have no trouble bouncing back.*

If only things were so easy for me. After last night's kiss, I realised how ready I was to move on, to attempt to date again, to maybe make myself vulnerable. Ben wasn't coming back. The grief had dulled from the roar in my ears, the relentless voice screaming over every interaction, *He's dead, he'll never hold you, or kiss you, or make you laugh ever again.* I no longer stood in the supermarket queue and failed to comprehend how everyone around me was just going on as normal. Didn't they understand what had happened? Didn't they know I had lost the one guy who loved me? Didn't they know my whole world had stopped?

But now I was ready to hit play again. I wanted to thaw the numbness in my veins, to unclench my body and *feel* again. But I had to be careful who I trusted with that. I wanted so badly for it to be Luke, but watching him flop his hair out of his eyes while he laughed at Ruth's inane jokes, I realised it couldn't be him. He was probably the world's greatest shag, but didn't know how to be that person for me.

"I'm finished." I pushed back my chair. The words sounded hard, final.

"Alright." Frances grabbed my bowl and frowned at the pile of porridge I'd left behind. "Don't go into the caves until I'm ready to join you. We're not allowed there by ourselves—"

"I know." I shoved the door open, cringing as it banged against the side of the caravan. I hadn't meant to push it that hard.

"Anna, wait," Luke called out to me, but I raced across the camp without looking back.

I took my toothbrush and a cup of water and brushed my teeth behind my tent. Then, I went over to the artefact storage and started work on cataloguing some of the artefacts from the previous week. We were always behind on cataloguing – it was supposed to be done in the evenings, but after a hard day on my knees in the cave and then chewing my way through one of Frances's "meals" (and I use the term in its loosest possible sense), it's much more appealing to curl up with a beer and a book.

I pulled up the chair behind the small desk and started transferring notations from our notebooks into the database we'd been creating. The mundane work started to calm me, to ease away the tension in my nerves. But then, just as I thought I was ready to face the day again ...

"Anna."

His voice sent a shiver through me. I could feel the weight of his body in front of me, the way the air around me seemed to shift to accommodate him. Goosebumps appeared along my arms that had nothing to do with the cold.

I didn't look up from the laptop. "Go away, Luke. I have to concentrate on this work."

"You're angry with me."

"I'm not." I tried to keep my voice even. "I'm just busy."

"You just feel the sudden urge to catalogue artefacts at six thirty-three in the morning?"

"Yes. I've had two cups of coffee. I need to burn off the energy."

"If you're feeling wired, I can think of a much more enjoyable way to burn it off." That familiar smirk had crept back into his voice.

I looked up at him then, setting my face into an angry line. "You were the one who broke things off last night. So you don't now get to come over here and flirt with me like nothing ever happened."

"I was just teasing." He grinned. "It's nice to see you reacting. I knew there was a lioness beneath that geeky exterior. Besides, we both decided it was better to leave things be last night."

"If you say so." I rubbed a fleck of dirt off the edge of a fox bone.

"You're not wearing your bracelet."

I glared at Luke, my hand falling over my empty wrist. Old habits die hard. "I was informed it was a health and safety risk. So now it's not a problem."

"If this site is going down for violations, it won't be because of that bracelet. Go put it on, seriously. I won't tell."

"I can't." The words choked in my mouth. "I lost it in the cave last night."

"What? Why didn't you say anything?"

"It doesn't matter." I kept my eyes glued on the fox bone. I didn't want him to see the tears brimming in the corners of my eyes. Having Luke see me cry once was embarrassing enough.

"Looking at your face right now, I can tell that isn't true." Luke leaned over the table. His scent overwhelmed me, that rich, earthy smell that spoke of wildness and untamed lust.

I opened my mouth to speak, but I couldn't get any words out without bursting into tears. So I said nothing. The space between us felt non-existent, inconsequential. Heat from his body leapt at me, like flames dancing under the moonlight.

"Anna?" Luke prompted, his face wearing an expression of recognition. The sight of it shocked me. I was so used to people looking at me with pity. *Poor Anna ... her daddy was crushed in a factory accident ... poor Anna, her boyfriend fell into a ravine and cracked his head open ... poor Anna, everyone she loves seems to die on her ... poor Anna ...*

But Luke's face didn't say *poor Anna*. It said, *I get it.* I wondered if he'd put two and two together from the way I'd reacted when he'd asked about my parents. But that look ... it told me he'd been there. He understood. He'd lost someone close to him, too. The pain sat close to the surface, just under his skin. He still saw their face in his dreams, and still remembered things to tell them, as though they'd just popped out to get the milk.

"I—" I wanted so badly to confide in him. The words were on the tip of my tongue. I pushed out a breath, trying to push the words out as well.

"Oh, Luke!" Ruth called out. The spell between us broke. I jerked my head back, seeing Ruth waving her arms madly in an attempt to get Luke's attention. "Come with me and I show you that really interesting fungus I was telling you about."

Luke cast a look back at me. He sighed. "I have to go." The fact he looked so annoyed about it made my heart soar.

"Yeah."

"But we'll talk later, okay?"

"Sure." My stomach clenched. I wasn't sure he was ready for what I had to tell him, but maybe if I scared him away with all my heavy shit, it would solve my Luke problem once and for all.

I wasn't quite ready to brave Ruth's over-the-top flirting, so I stayed in the shed, listening to the rain hammer against the roof while I scrawled notes in our field book and typed frantically into the database. Tin sheds are extremely useful objects with many potential applications, but creating cosy workspaces was not one of them. After forty-five minutes of blistering cold wind howling across the desk and trying to thaw the pen nib against the tips of my fingers so I could continue writing, I'd had enough. The others would all be in the cave by now, which was at least sheltered from the wind. If I had to be miserable, I might as well be miserable in the cave, with a trowel in my hand.

You never know. You could find a buried treasure. Wouldn't that make Ruth's face red?

With that image cheering me up somewhat, I bundled up in my jacket, gloves and scarf, found my trowel, and headed over to the caves. The rain came down in thick sheets, slamming against the exposed skin of my cheeks as I struggled to run in all my layers. For the first time, I felt relieved as I got down on my knees and slid through the muddy tunnel entrance into the cave.

"Nice of you to join us, Anna." Ruth gave me a smug look as she punched buttons on the theodolite. Luke stood in front of her, holding up the measuring staff. He grinned when he saw me. I didn't return the smile. Instead, I went to my quadrant and started scraping down the next layer. My trowel made a reassuring slap against the damp earth – a sound I fantasized I would hear if I decided to slap Ruth's snotty mouth.

The day dragged on for an eternity. An icy wind shot through the tunnel, burrowing through my layers of wool and nylon and chilling my bones. I waited for a chance to escape to the back tunnel and look for my bracelet, but Frances was so intent on her work, she kept going right through lunch. Luke ignored me all day, the bastard. Instead, he helped Ruth operate the theodolite, even laughing at her inane jokes about whales and seamen.

" ... oh, you'll love this one. I learned this one at a Save the Whales rally in London. What's Moby Dick's father's name? Paper Boner." She threw back her head and let out a high-pitched giggle. Luke gave a short laugh.

"Gag me with spermaceti," I whispered under my breath. After what he'd said to me this morning, the way he'd looked at me, I thought Luke was trying to be my friend, or my ... something. But then he was over there with Ruth, not even looking in my direction. He could've offered to help me in my square.

As the day wore on, Luke and Ruth's obvious flirting grated me more and more. By 4pm, my whole body shook with rage. *How dare he make me feel like this? How dare he put on this ridiculous display in front of me? He was the one who was walking around the caves at night, he was the one who kissed me, he caused me to lose my bracelet ...*

At the thought of my bracelet, my stomach twisted with fear. That was the most precious thing I owned, more precious even than my first edition of *Stranger in a Strange Land*. If I'd lost it in the mud, I'd never forgive myself. I was going to have to sneak back there, completely on my own.

The thought sent me into a spasm of fear. I'd been to all the pre-excavations safety lectures. I knew how dangerous caves could be. And I knew, better than anyone, what could happen when someone ignored safety precautions and forged ahead on their own. But I *had* to find that bracelet. I just *had* to.

Frances started packing up for the day. Heart pounding, I helped her clean off and pack up the tools, trying not to look in Luke's direction. He gave me a short nod as he walked by, following Ruth back to camp with the theodolite slung over his shoulder like it was a school satchel. I didn't nod back. At least I didn't have to contend with him right now.

I helped Frances lug the last of our equipment out through the tiny entrance and lock the tools up in the safe. The rain had eased off a little, falling in a steady mist across the forest, but the wind still bit deep. My heart pounded. It was now or never.

"You did good work today, Anna," Frances said, pulling her mittens on over her stained fingers. "One more day on your quadrant and you'll be able to move to another area."

"I'm excited about that," I said, picking my words carefully. I pretended to pat down my pockets, searching for something. "My area isn't yielding much of interest."

"That's true for a lot of archaeology, unfortunately. It's not all dodging rolling boulders, dismantling booby traps and dragging up treasure." Frances smiled.

I held up my own stained hands. "Don't I know it? Listen, you go ahead. I'll be right back. I just realised, I left my trowel behind. I don't want it to get lost."

Frances shrugged her shoulders. "Leave it. You can get another one in the morning."

"It's just … I really liked that trowel. It's the last one left with the left-handed grooves." I glanced back at the caves. "Go on. Don't worry about me. I'll only be a moment. I know exactly where it is."

"I'll go back with you." Frances grabbed her torch from her belt.

"No!" Frances glanced at me in concern. I grinned, realising I'd yelled too loudly. *Way to play it smooth, Anna. You're no good at this subterfuge stuff.* "I mean, there's no sense both of us going back in there and getting all dirty again."

"I'm not supposed to let anyone on the site by themselves. Luke could shut us down."

"Luke is already back at camp with Ruth," I said, her name coming out more sarcastically than I'd intended. "He'll never know. I could have been back by now, and you could be sitting down to a nice hot cup of tea."

"You're right. Sure." Frances didn't look sure. But she peered over my shoulder again. Luke hadn't looked back. Frances tossed me her torch. "If you're not back at site in ten minutes, I'm going to be very angry."

"Thanks." I bolted back towards the cave. *Ten minutes.* Just enough time to go back to that cavern and look for my bracelet. I slid down the cave entrance, clicked on the torch to fight the deepening gloom, splashed across the small stream, and carefully picked my way through the site back to the crevice.

Squeezing through the tiny gap, I found myself again in that familiar cavern, the dark mouth of the adjoining cave gaping at me from my left. I shone the light of Frances's torch over all the rocks, but I couldn't see my bracelet. Panic rose in my throat. The clasp probably got broken when the bat was thrashing around in my hair. That meant it had to be around somewhere.

Or, it fell into the water with the torch. Tears sprang in the corners of my eyes. I shone my light into the pool, but couldn't see anything shining back through the murky water. *No, don't give up just yet. Keep looking.*

I scanned the rocks again, moving in a grid pattern, searching every inch. It definitely wasn't there in front of the pool. Perhaps it had fallen off closer to the mouth of that tunnel Luke was inspecting ...

I walked over to the tunnel entrance, shining my light across the ground, inspecting the edges of the tunnel for crevices or shelves it could have fallen onto. With every step the knot in my stomach tightened. *It's not here. Why isn't it here?*

A lump rose in my throat. To prevent myself from breaking down into tears, I tried to distract myself by wondering about Luke. Why had he come back here in the first place? I crept closer into the cave and peered inside. *He'd almost seemed as if he'd been looking for something. And he'd been carrying a crowbar ... it just didn't make sense.*

I stepped inside the cave, stooping to fit under the low ceiling. The floor sloped away from me. If I'd dropped the bracelet here, it might have slid deeper into the tunnel. It was worth checking while I was here. I might not get another chance.

That's probably how Dad justified lifting the guard on that machine, a voice inside my head railed. *And how Ben decided to climb along that ravine without the right equipment.*

My stomach turned at the thought, but I couldn't bear the idea of being without that bracelet. I just had to be careful. I moved forward, carefully testing where I placed my boots, using the wall to support my weight. One wrong move here, and I was in deep trouble.

You shouldn't be here, I scolded myself. *This is so dangerous. If you slipped and hit your head, they wouldn't know where to find you. Like father, like daughter ...*

My light caught something bright on the wall. *What was that?* I shone the torch up at eye level, and nearly dropped it in surprise.

I was staring at a cave painting. And not just any cave painting, one of the most elaborate examples I'd ever seen. The wall had been smoothed out – you could see the tool marks at the edges – and the surface cleaned and painted with a grey hue to serve as a background for the work.

And what work it was! I moved my torch across the wall and over the ceiling, taking in all the details. In the top corner, a family of wolves hunted in the forest. Towering trees rose up around them. They had a hare surrounded. A larger wolf advanced upon it while three smaller wolves – the cubs? – guarded its back, preventing escape.

Another scene showed the wolves sitting and lying on some rocks. In the middle of the rocks was a black circle. The cave entrance? Did the early cave dwellers observe wolves in the woods?

The next scene was the strangest of all. It looked to me like the wolves standing up on two legs, and one of them was not really a wolf any longer, but a man, with shaggy hair and human eyes. He wore dark shoes and walked like a man, but he still had a tail and paws and claws and a snout like a wolf.

In the next scene, humanoid figures hunted the wolves, holding sticks set alight. The wolves ran onward, away down the dark tunnel. In the corner was a woman with long, wild hair. She was weeping, her tears forming a river that cascaded off into the distance. I held my torch up and shone it downward. I could make out the gleam of more paintings further down the tunnel. The place was absolutely covered with ancient art.

My mind reeled. *This is incredible.* I was standing amongst some of the most elaborate, ancient, and well-preserved cave paintings in the world. This might be the most important neolithic discovery ever made in England. And I had discovered it. Me, Anna Sinclair, nerdy archaeology student and science-fiction nut.

Or did you? My mind shot back. *Why had Luke come back here the other night? Was this what he was looking for?*

The thought unnerved me. It was a big coincidence that Luke had been looking in this tunnel the day before I happened to discover these paintings. But that only presented me with more questions. How did Luke know the paintings were here? These tunnels were unexplored. There's no way paintings this elaborate had been discovered and documented without being known to Frances. And if Luke did somehow suspect the paintings were there, why was he carrying that crowbar? Was he planning to destroy them?

Two things were for certain. I'd just made a brilliant archaeological discovery, the kind of discovery that could define my entire career. And there was definitely something our new ranger wasn't telling me.

6

LUKE

I gritted my teeth against Ruth's onslaught of inane conversation, and kept my eyes on the caravan door. After a few moments, Frances stepped through and kicked off her muddy boots. But Anna didn't follow her.

"Where's Anna?" I demanded. Ruth shot me a filthy glance from behind the stack of vegetables she was chopping.

Frances stammered out a response. "She's ... just gone back ... to pick up a trowel she dropped."

"Back to the toolbox? Or into the caves?"

Frances shifted her weight from foot to foot. "In the cave. But she's perfectly safe—"

"You're not supposed to allow *anyone* in those caves alone, not even for a moment," I scolded her, as I shoved my chair back. My chest tightened. Anything could've happened to Anna. "This is ridiculous. I've already warned you about this. I could have you shut down for this."

"She was just going back to get a trowel," Max said, grabbing a beer from the fridge. "What's the big deal?"

"She's very forgetful and clumsy," Ruth said, relinquishing the dinner prep to Frances with a look of resigned disgust.

"I don't care if she's Saddam fucking Hussein." I grabbed a torch from the shelf by the door of the caravan and shoved my feet into my boots. "I'm not going to let her bleed to death after falling down a chasm while you all sit here badmouthing her." I jabbed the torch at Frances's chest. "When I get back, we're going to have a little chat."

She opened her mouth to protest, but shut it quickly when I fixed her with a glare. "I'll come with you," she said in a small voice, handing the knife back to Ruth.

"Fine." I stormed back towards the cave, my heart pounding against my chest. The idea of Anna down there, alone, filled me with dread. I shouldn't have tried to distance myself from her today. I'd just wanted to give her space to think, even though being away from her made my whole body ache with need, and my ears rang from being in close proximity to Ruth's incessant chatter. *I should never have let her out of my sight for a moment.*

What if she's hurt? What if she's disappeared? What if another wolf has turned up? The pain of losing my dad was still raw under my skin. I couldn't bear to lose my mate, too.

What if she discovered the paintings? At that moment, I wasn't even sure I cared any more. I just wanted to make sure she was okay. Visions of her body bent and broken against the rocks surged against my eyes. I jogged faster.

Footsteps crunched in the leaves behind me. "Luke, wait up." Frances sprinted up alongside me. I grunted at her, but didn't slow down. At least with Frances out here with me, Ruth would be inside cooking dinner and it might be in at least some way edible.

"There she is!" Frances pointed, her pinched features softening.

And sure enough, there was Anna, jogging across the forest towards us, her auburn ponytail bouncing along behind her, and her shapely thighs undulating even under her layers of thermal gear. Relief washed over me. My arms ached to crush her against my body, to hold her tight and never let her go.

Anna stopped running when she caught sight of us, and waved frantically for us to follow her back to the cave. "You won't believe this!" she cried out. "It's amazing."

Shit.

Anna was an archaeologist. The only time archaeologists ever got that excited was a) when the local pub did an Indiana Jones–themed quiz night, and b) when they discovered some incredible remnant of a lost civilisation. A remnant like a cave filled with intricate paintings.

Before I could stop her, Frances dashed towards Anna, her skinny arms swinging like chicken legs, her archaeological discovery radar going off the charts. "What is it?"

"It's in the caves. Quickly, you have to see. You won't believe it!"

Frances overtook Anna and squeezed through the tiny mouth of the cave. Anna made to follow her but I grabbed her, pulling her close to me. Her eyes were wild, dazed by what she had seen.

"What were you doing, going into the caves all by yourself?" I demanded.

"Oh, I don't know. That same thing you were doing," she shot back. *Fine.* I deserved that.

"So, did you find them?" I covered up my concern for her with a sneer.

"Did I find the mysterious cave paintings you knew about all along? Of course I did. What I want to know is, how did *you* know they were there?"

"I meant your trowel. That was why you went back into the cave in the first place, according to Frances." I glanced down at her hand. "You don't have it with you."

"No. I dropped it in the cave. I was quite surprised, you see."

"I'd believe you. Except that I saw it sitting at the back of Frances's toolbox. Yours has the red handle, doesn't it?"

"That's my spare," Anna said, her eyes darting nervously.

"You didn't drop your trowel. You were looking for your bracelet."

"So what if I was? It was your fault I lost it."

"How do you figure that? If you're going to blame anyone, I'd be pointing fingers at Ozzy Osbourne's friend who got tangled in your hair."

"If you hadn't been snooping where you didn't belong, I wouldn't have followed you, and none of this would've happened. Go on, Luke, tell me why you were hunting for the paintings with a crowbar in your hand?"

"You seemed so timid yesterday," I said grinning, trying to distract her. This wasn't the time to tell her about my family secrets. "Where did this lioness come from?"

"She was provoked," Anna growled, but the corners of her mouth turned up in a slight smile.

"Come on, Anna," Frances yelled from the cave entrance. "You've got to show me what you found!"

"I've got to go," she said.

"Going to get Frances to help you find that missing trowel?"

"Exactly."

"You're a really horrible liar." I sighed, releasing her.

"Takes one to know one. I ask you again, how did you know those paintings were there?" she demanded. "That section of the cave has been completely unexplored."

"I know they were there because I am descended from the person who drew them."

Her eyes regarded me. "But that doesn't make any sense. Those drawings are tens of thousands of years old. How can you—"

"Are you sure about that?"

"I'm the archaeologist here. Of course I'm sure." But she frowned slightly. "You're not making any sense, Luke."

She rubbed her forearms. She was still wearing the clothes she wore on the dig – a flannel work shirt with the sleeves rolled up. Now that the sun had set, the frigid air caused goose pimples to raise along her arms.

"You're cold." I shrugged off my jacket, and wrapped it around her shoulders. "Come on, back to camp with you."

"No way. I've got to show Professor Doyle these paintings, and you need to tell me what's going on."

I opened my mouth, the words on the tip of my tongue. Staring into those eyes, that had yesterday been so reserved but now sparkled with life and defiance, and feeling the heavy thrum of our connection pulsing through my veins, I hoped I was making the right decision in trusting her.

"Anna!" Frances yelled from the cave. Anna glared at me pointedly.

"Later," I whispered. "Tonight. Meet me by that rotting oak stump where the road meets the hiking trail. I have something to show you."

She nodded, and whirled around, sliding down into the cave and disappearing into the gloom. I followed her, my stomach in knots. What the fuck would I do now?

7

ANNA

I shifted from foot to foot, my teeth chattering even through my thick jacket. Where was Luke? Why did he want me to meet him here, nearly half a kilometre from the campsite?

It had been an eventful evening, and my body ached with weariness. I'd taken Frances down to show her the paintings and as predicted, she was suitably awed. "This discovery is going to make my name!" she screeched, hugging me so tight she cut off circulation to my arms. She'd insisted on getting Ruth and Max back to the site with the camera, tripod, and floodlights to take some preliminary shots, while I spent an hour on the satellite phone to Professor Carter – the department head at Loamshire University – describing the find for a press release to go out the next day.

"You'll need to send through some photos," he'd said, his voice tight with excitement. "As crisp and hi-res as possible. It's going on the website tomorrow."

"Professor Doyle is taking some now," I'd replied. "They'll be in your inbox first thing." I stifled a yawn as I jammed a power bar into my mouth. Frances was too busy on the site to bother cooking dinner, which was at least a small blessing.

After the phone call, I had to go back to the cave, where I spent another couple of hours helping Max reposition the lights to get the best possible shots. Frances finally called it quits at 11pm, giving me just enough time to eat another power bar, clean my teeth and pull on some clean-ish, dry-ish clothes to go and meet Luke.

And now here I was, my bones aching with cold, my mind reeling with fantastical theories, and he wasn't even here.

Disappointment surged through me. Here I was, getting my hopes up about this guy, thinking he understood what I was going through, but he was just playing me. He was probably watching me from his tent, laughing at how pathetic I was. My cheeks burned. Screw this. I was going to bed—

Footsteps crunched through the forest behind me. A few moments later, Luke emerged from the trees, his hands stuffed inside the pockets of his jacket, his breath coming out in hot steam. Under the moonlight, he looked even better – the gloomy night only seemed to highlight his strong features and wild eyes.

"Well," I said, struggling to speak through my chattering teeth. "I'm here, freezing my tits off. What's your explanation?"

"You will catch your death out here," he said, wrapping his arms around me and pulling me to his chest. Instantly, his body warmth radiated through my jacket. I wanted to tell him to let me go, but I was far too cold and he smelt so, so good.

"You were the clever one who chose this spot. The faster you talk, the sooner we can go back to your tent—" My face flushed with heat as I realised what I'd said. "I mean, our tents. *Our* tents."

Luke laughed, his husky voice reverberating through my whole body. Damn, he was gorgeous when he laughed.

"Fine. I'll get right down to it. Those paintings aren't neolithic."

"How do you know that?"

"Because my grandmother painted them."

"What?" That didn't make any sense. "But how did she manage that? This cave wasn't even discovered until five years ago."

"Wrong. It was inhabited by my family for at least two centuries before that." Luke's green eyes bore into mine. "Anna, I'm going to tell you something that's so profoundly unbelievable, you're going to think I'm crazy. But I assure you I'm not. And I need you to just wait for me to finish explaining, and I promise I'll show you all the proof you need. Okay?"

"Can't we do this back at the camp, where it's warm?" I balled my hands into fists and pulled them up into my sleeves. But it was no good. My fingers were quickly losing all their feeling.

"I can't risk anyone else overhearing. And you can't tell the others what I say, either." He pulled out my hands and sandwiched them between his own. The heat was so intense, the ends of my fingers tingled. "Do you promise?"

"Promise what?"

"Not to breathe a word of this to anyone?"

"Fine, fine." My face was going numb. "Just tell me."

Luke took a deep breath. "I'm a werewolf."

I snorted. *He can't be serious?* I yanked my hands away, showing my fingers back into my sleeves. "You brought me out here, in the middle of sub-zero temperatures, to make up some stupid campfire horror story."

"It is no story. I am a werewolf." Luke stepped back, bracing himself against the rotting oak. "Watch."

I glared at him, wanting to turn away and leave him there in the cold. But curiosity ate away at me. I wanted to know what his game was, why he was trying to grab me with this cock-and-bull story.

Luke locked eyes with me, his gaze intense. At first, nothing happened. But then I noticed his face was changing. The bones beneath his skin seemed to be moving, elongating his nose, rear-ranging his cheekbones, flattening his skull. His ears moved back on his head, the lobes growing up and outward. His eyes remained locked on mine as his chin and nose joined in a snout, his teeth curving down into two long, sharp canines.

What is going on? What is happening?

Luke dropped to the ground, standing on all fours. His clothing tore from his body as the muscles in his shoulders bulged, reaching up to fuse with his neck, throwing his head back at an impossible angle. His back arched, and his legs and arms bent and shifted, the knees snapping backward with a crack.

This cannot be happening. My whole body went rigid with fear, my heart hammering against my chest. I staggered back-ward, preparing to run. But I couldn't tear my eyes away from the incredible scene before me.

Luke threw back his head and howled, the sound echoing through the silent night. What stood before me was no longer the handsome ranger who'd held me against his warm skin. It was a grey wolf, its eyes regarding me with cool, calculating precision. It stuck out a pink tongue and licked along its lips, revealing a row of sharp, white teeth.

My heart leapt in my throat. I fought through my terror, turned on my heel, and ran back towards the camp. Behind me, the leaves crunched as the creature took chase. I poured on speed, my body screaming with protest. Those long, razor-sharp canines flashed across my vision. At any moment, it would be close enough to pounce—

"Anna, wait!"

Luke's voice. I dared a glance back over my shoulder, and saw him running through the trees towards me. Moonlight glinted off his body, his skin glistening with sweat. His hair had come free, and it trailed behind him in the breeze.

He was completely naked.

Shit. I slowed, still moving towards the camp. "Don't come any closer."

"Please, Anna. I'm sorry for scaring you." He stopped in his tracks, planting his bare feet in a wide, powerful stance. I stopped also, leaning forward on one foot, ready at any moment to dart away. My heart pounded against my chest. Had I really just seen him turn into a wolf? Maybe it was my imagination playing tricks on me. Some kind of mirage caused by the moonlight? Maybe Ruth had snuck hallucinogenic drugs into my tea?

"Luke?" I gasped out.

He didn't say anything, just fixed his beautiful green eyes on mine.

I looked down, not wanting to stare into his eyes any more. Big mistake. My gaze fell on his naked hips, covered with more tattoos of wolves howling and tigers stalking across his taut muscles. His cock stood out between his legs. He was huge. And rock hard.

My whole body pulsed with excited energy. Even though I was terrified, my body wasn't. It was flushed with heat, as though some primal aspect of me was aroused by seeing Luke hard for me.

Luke was hard for *me*.

I folded my arms across my chest. "Okay, fine." I took a few shaky breaths. "So you're a werewolf. How does it work?"

"Werewolves have existed alongside humans for tens of thousands of years, probably much longer," he said, his eyes locked on mine. "It's a genetic trait, passed on from parents to cubs. The dominant genes pass through the male line. There are very few female werewolves – most of us choose a human mate who carries the necessary genes to create wolven cubs."

"That's ... interesting." I gulped, wondering why he was looking at me so intensely as he spoke of mates.

"I can shift whenever I want, as you've just experienced. When I shift, I'm in complete control of myself. It's still my human mind, just in the body of a wolf. Werewolves live longer than humans – about a hundred and fifty years. I also have a lot of primal, animal instincts," he glanced down at his hardness, and when he looked up, he was grinning. "As you can clearly see. But I would never hurt you, or anyone else. I'm still me underneath all the fur."

"Then why did you chase after me?"

"Because you ran," he said simply. "And because I don't want to let you get away."

"That sounds an awful lot like a threat."

"It's not meant to be threatening." Luke wiggled his crotch suggestively. "It's meant to be sexy."

The corners of my mouth twitched up into a faint smile. "So the thing about wolves and the full moon isn't true? You don't just change as soon as the moon rises?"

"Oh, it's true." Luke's face darkened. "Everything I've just told you changes when the moon is full. Then, I have no choice about the shift. I become a wolf, and I have no control over my behaviour. I am a wild beast, unbeholden to anyone, not even my own conscience. That is why I work as a ranger. When the full moon approaches I can retreat into the forests for days, and live out the curse without hurting anyone until I become human again."

"Suppose I believe that you're a werewolf—"

"I am."

"Fine. You're a werewolf. I don't understand what this has to do with the caves."

"The caves were the home of my family, the Lowe pack," Luke said. "The pack controlled much of the Crookshollow territory. They would come here to these caves during the full moon to live out their wildness, where they wouldn't injure anyone in the village. Most werewolf packs have a safe place in the wilderness to go as a family during the full moon. Those places are fiercely guarded by the pack to prevent other wolves coming in and claiming them as their own territory."

"That makes sense."

"Fifty years ago, my father lived here with his pack – my grandparents, and his two brothers. Something awful happened. My father never spoke much of it, but from what little I gathered from him, there was an accident one night in the village. A baby was killed in its bed, mauled to death by a vicious animal that had got in through an open window above the cot. That same night, villagers had seen a wolf skulking around the town. The villagers put two and two together – they knew it had to have been someone in my family, as we were the only werewolf pack left in the area. And so they came to the caves with blades and torches, in search of the killer. They murdered my grandparents and uncles in revenge for the killing. Only my father survived."

"How?"

"My grandmother was not a wolf, but a human woman with an artistic talent and an incredible prophetic power. She saw the villagers coming in a vision. My grandfather and his two oldest sons were out hunting, and so she could not warn them. Instead, she painted the last images on the wall, hoping they would see it when they got back to the cave. She then ran into the woods with her youngest cub, my father."

The weeping woman in the picture. "So now I'm supposed to believe there are such things as psychics?" I said, but as I watched his expression, my protests died away. The way he spoke of his family, his voice trembling ever so slightly when he talked about his father ... as hard as it was for me to compre-hend, I knew Luke spoke the truth.

"Oh, it's all true. Psychics, witches, werewolves, vulpines, bran ..."

"Bran? Vulpines? Now you're just making words up."

"Bran are raven shapeshifters. Vulpines are fox shifters."

"You're kidding me." There was a whole smorgasbord of weirdness out there in the world.

"I am not. There are actually some pretty infamous vulpines and bran living in Crookshollow right now. This area attracts supernatural creatures and paranormal activity like you wouldn't believe."

I unfolded my arms, balling up my freezing hands and stuffing them into the cuffs of my jacket. "Okay. Fine. Let's say you've convinced me with your miraculous shapeshifting abili-ties, and I believe all this supernatural mumbo jumbo actually exists. Let's go back to this wild tale of yours. You said humans don't know werewolves exist. So how come they all came to the caves after your family?"

"Some humans do know. In fact, there were times on earth where most humans knew. Many of the Norse and Saxon gods of legend are actually famous shapeshifters. The Egyptian pantheon, too. Shifters were often considered to be powerful sorcerers and advisors and held positions of power. But since Europe became Christianized, shifters have realised it's better to remain hidden. Although there are still humans who know about us, especially in supernatural centres like Crookshollow. You've heard the stories about what used to go on there, the witch burnings and hauntings and such?"

I rolled my eyes. Of course I knew. The town had been playing up its supernatural past ever since I could remember, using it as a ploy to lure more tourists. My friend Derek loved this stuff; he was always dragging me to arcane bookstores or on some local ghost hunt.

"Well, many of those witches burned were actually werewolves. The witch trials were what drove the last of the wolven packs out of England, to the forests of the continent, or further abroad. But my family stayed. My great-grandfather and my grandfather loved this land and the people, and they wanted to hold it at any cost.

"There was a powerful family in the village – the Peytons. Robert Peyton was the local bishop, so he had a tremendous power over the county. He delivered infamous sermons calling down fire and brimstone upon all, that brought in people for miles around. Church attendance in Crookshollow skyrocketed, and so did a renewed intolerance for the supernatural. He hated my family for no reason other than what they were.

"Peyton's chance to rid Crookshollow of my pack came, when that child was killed in the village, torn apart by an animal mere days before its christening. Because of this horrible act, Peyton incited the village against my family. He called down from the pulpit that we were the children of Satan – shapeshifting demons who came into the village at night and took their children. The fact the child hadn't been christened cinched the story. Peyton assembled a mob. They came for my family with pitchforks and torches. There was no trial, no evidence. They murdered my grandfather, my grandmother, and their two sons. My father was the only one who escaped with his life."

"That's horrible."

"That's life as a werewolf," Luke spat, his body shaking with anger. "Always on the outskirts, always running, always hiding and hoping your true nature isn't discovered."

"You showed me your true nature," I said, touching his arm. "I haven't run away yet."

"You tried."

"Of course I did. You had big scary teeth. But I'm not running away now. So who did kill the child?"

"That's just the thing," Luke said. "We never knew. My father carried this horrid guilt with him his entire life, as though he secretly believed one of his brothers might have done it. That's why we hid in the forests – he preferred to be alone, to escape the Lowe legacy, rather than to fight for it."

"So why did you come here?"

"My father died last month," Luke said, his voice catching. His words brought forth a wave of empathy more powerful than I'd expected. I knew all too well the pain he was going through, the burning anger at the universe, the memories that flooded you when you least expected them, the way you felt isolated from the rest of the world, part of a secret society you never wanted to join.

"I'm sorry," I whispered, wanting to say more, but not knowing what to say. Even people like me who'd lived with death for so long grew tongue-tied about other people's grief. It was the British way.

"It's okay, not your fault. He'd been ill for some time, but ... I saw an article about the excavation in the paper. I showed it to him. I thought it might cheer him up to know that our old haunt might have some archaeological significance. But instead it drove him crazy. For days he rolled around in bed, halfway between sleep and waking, mumbling about the paintings and the curse of our family ..." He choked. "The stress of it broke him; it allowed the cancer to take over. It was all my fault."

"Luke, no. It wasn't."

"You weren't there." His voice grew hard again. "You can't know. Only I know. The last words he spoke to me were 'Don't end up like me, Luke. Don't live your life paying for the mistakes of the past.' So I came here to bury the past forever."

"That's why you were in the caves with that crowbar? You were going to destroy the paintings?"

Luke nodded. "I knew that if you guys found them they'd get a ton of attention. My grandmother was fascinated by neolithic art – she deliberately used the same styles and pigments used to create ancient cave paintings. It tickled her that one day they might be thought to be older than they were. But there's no reason to bring up the whole story again, not now that everyone in the village has more or less forgotten it. It's not as if the paintings would be missed. They aren't archaeologically significant, which your professor is going to discover as soon as she does some in-depth analysis."

"But they're part of your history, your heMargaretge. Doesn't that mean something?"

"Not everyone wants to hold on to the past," he said. "Only archaeologists."

"Not all archaeologists want to hold on to the past," I said, two faces flashing in front of my eyes – my father and Ben. "Some of us want desperately to forget."

"We have more in common than you'd like to admit," he said, a harsh sadness passing over his features briefly. In an instant, that grin was back on his face, the sadness he'd shown before erased in a moment, replaced by glimmering eyes and a cheeky smile. He stepped towards me, his muscles rippling as he moved.

"Can you point that thing somewhere else?" I asked, my cheeks flushing hot as my eyes fell once again on his rigid cock. I tried not to imagine how good it would feel to ride that.

"Why?" Luke said simply. "It's like that because of you."

"Er ... I ..."

Luke was on me in a moment, his powerful arms wrapping around my body, the heat of his hands pressing into my back.

His hardness rubbed against my thigh, and an ache rumbled deep inside me, yearning for us to be closer still.

"We were discussing something really serious before," I said, desperately trying to buy myself time to think. Luke's scent intoxicated me, driving out any rational thought. There was a reason this was a bad idea ... I just couldn't remember it right now.

"Just say the words," he whispered. "And I'll leave you alone. I've done it before, though it tore me up inside. But I want you, Anna. I want to feel you beneath me, writhing in ecstasy."

"Luke, I ... I'm not sure ..."

"Can I help you make up your mind?"

He pressed his lips to mine.

The touch sent a surge of heat through my body, an energy that reached from our lips right to my toes. My fingers tingled, my core throbbed with need.

God, he tasted so good. His soft lips mashed against mine, a hint of stubble above his lip scraping against my skin. His tongue slid against mine, wrapping around me with delicious warmth.

This is a very bad idea, my brain screamed. *You barely even know this guy, and what little you know about him suggests he's an arrogant ass with an interest in destroying priceless archaeological discoveries. Not to mention the fact he's a werewolf. A werewolf. He could claw you to pieces—*

Unfortunately, Luke's intoxicating scent and delicious mouth dissolved the voice before it finished its thought. I drifted away, the chill in my limbs expelled by the heat of our embrace.

Without breaking our kiss, Luke scooped me up in his arms. He lifted me easily and started walking back towards the camp, his torn clothes lying somewhere in the forest behind him.

"Whose tent?" he whispered against my lips.

"Yours," I whispered back. "It's further away."

Luke picked his way through the forest with ease, holding me as though I weighed nothing. Every few steps, he stopped to clasp me to him, kissing me passionately. His hair fell over my face, tickling my skin. Occasionally, the voice in my head surfaced, reminding me that this was a bad idea, that I wasn't ready, that I would regret this in the morning. But all my protests dissolved in Luke's kisses and the thrumming energy that enveloped us, drawing our bodies together like magnets. Maybe my head wasn't ready, but my body couldn't wait to be naked beside him.

Inside his tent, Luke lay me down on the bed – an air mattress covered with two furs and an arctic sleeping bag. It looked like the boudoir of some kind of modern Viking. Luke grabbed his phone and pulled up an app of a flickering candle, which he placed on the ground beside the bed.

"For atmosphere," he grinned.

"If only it was a roaring fire," I said, my teeth chattering from the cold air.

Luke tugged off my boots, kissing the tops of my socks, and slid alongside me on the furs.

"Let's see if I can't do something to warm you up," he said, as he tore off my shirt. Buttons pinged against the canvas as he tossed the useless fabric aside. My bra was next. He snapped the straps right off as though they were made of pasta. His eyes gleamed as he gazed down at me.

"Fuck, you're gorgeous," he whispered, his gaze dancing over my body. I flushed with heat, his words pulsing through me. Luke buried his face in my neck, trailing a line of kisses over my skin. My body lit up under his touch as he dragged his teeth over the sensitive skin behind my ear. I moaned, dragging my fingers across his back, enjoying the way his muscles responded to my touch.

Luke's kisses trailed across my collarbone, and over the rise of my breast. He cupped my breast in his hand, pointing the nipple up towards his mouth. He blew against the sensitive bud. All the hairs on my body stood on end.

His eyes glued to mine, Luke bent down and sucked my nipple into my mouth. I cried out as the sensation arced through my chest. He nibbled and sucked, pulling each nipple into his mouth. In seconds, I was moaning against him, my whole body lit with sparks.

Luke pulled back, a cheeky grin lighting up his whole face. "I know it's hard," he said, as his fingers crept across my stomach towards the fly of my jeans. "But you're going to have to be quiet. Unless you want to wake up the entire camp to tell them what I've been doing to you."

"You sound awfully confident."

"I have good reason." Luke bent his head and took one of my nipples in his mouth again. I gasped as his warm tongue slid over my sensitive skin once more. *Damn him ...*

I missed this. I missed the touch of a man, the warmth and intimacy of skin against skin. Locking eyes with a lover and feeling as though you were the only two people in the world. And when your lover was a werewolf ...

"You're being so gentle," I told him as he dug his thumbs in the waistband of my jeans. Just having his fingers so close to my core made me ache harder. I bucked up my hips, urging him to go faster, but he didn't relent.

"Because I *know*," Luke murmured back, as he reached over my head and pulled a condom from his wallet. "Both of us are still reeling from the trauma of grief. I don't want to frighten you with my wolf nature. I want this to be good for you, so I'm controlling myself."

"Is that so?"

"If it's any consolation, I'm finding it bloody difficult," he growled, as he tore open the packet with his teeth and rolled the condom onto his shaft. "All I want is to be inside you, to ride you like the wolf I am."

That deep rumble in his voice made me shiver all over, and not from the cold. "What if I want to meet this wolf?"

"Are you sure about that?" Luke's eyebrows knitted together. He curled one of his fingers over the edge of my underwear and I groaned. "You can't take it back."

"I'm sure."

Luke groaned. He planted his lips against mine, but this time, the kiss wasn't tender. It was *fierce.* His tongue forced my lips apart. One hand remained hooked in my waistband, the other cupped my face, pulling me towards him.

The hunger in his eyes pulled me deeper. His warmth enveloped me. I became lost in the wildness of him.

Luke tore off my jeans and underwear and plunged his face between my legs. His tongue found that special spot, and he attacked it with all the ferocity of his feral form. The ache in my body intensified as he drew me closer to climax. Every hair stood erect, every nerve ending focused on the work of his tongue.

"Oh, Luke!" I dug my fingers into his hair.

In the flickering glow of his phone, I could just make out Luke's dancing eyes and wild grin, as he battered me with waves of pleasure. Sparks leapt from my skin, my whole body aglow with dazzling fireworks, my skin like molten lava flowing from my bones.

I came with a shudder, my entire body convulsing as the lava overflowed and buried me in heat. Red welts appeared in my eyes, and for a few moments the world completely vanished, replaced only by the roaring in my ears and the fire licking my veins. As the pleasure ebbed, leaving me sleepy and sated, Luke crawled up beside me, wrapping me in his arms, that grin of his wider than ever.

"Well, I guess I did tell you to be quiet," Luke laughed, holding up the edge of his fur. I flushed with embarrassment – I had torn a hole right through it.

"Don't be embarrassed. They say it's the geeky girls who turn into demons in bed." He planted his lips on mine. "I can't wait to find out."

As his tongue slid over mine, the ache between my legs returned, more persistent than ever. I wanted Luke just as much as he wanted me. Luke rolled me over, so I was lying on my stomach against the furs. He grabbed my hips with his hands, his fingers digging into my skin. I cried out with pleasure as he plunged me back against his cock, penetrating me with one quick motion.

I threw my head back, moaning as his whole length entered me, and we became one. I'd expected it to hurt, because of the size of him, and how long it had been for me, but all I felt was an incredible sense of fullness, of power. The sense that something inside us that had been searching for the other had finally been united.

Luke started to rock against me, one hand supporting himself, the other running over my skin, fingers drawing lines of fire across my back, down my arms, over the edge of my breasts. As he moved inside me, the ache gnawed at me, the pressure building once more.

As my body lit up beneath Luke's touch, my heart soared. Maybe it was the way Luke murmured my name as he drove into me. Maybe it was the hunger in his eyes, a hunger reserved for me. For the first time since Ben's death, I felt powerful, invincible, capable of anything. I was wild.

Luke rode me like the animal he was, leaning forward and crushing me against his body, his hands snaking over my skin. His teeth dragged across my neck, sending shivers of delight through my whole body. He thrust faster, building towards his own release. His cock stiffened, and the sensation of his impending orgasm drove me closer. The ache turned into a roar, and my body slipped over the edge once again, the lava bubbling up from inside my skin.

I started to cry out and the pleasure swept over me. "Bite me," Luke growled, holding his hand in front of my mouth. I bit down on the flesh of his thumb as the lava scorched my veins.

"Anna," Luke growled my name, his voice hitching as his whole body stiffened. He came with a mighty thrust, his cock reaching deep inside of me, touching every part of me. His eyelids fluttered shut and a few moments later, he collapsed beside me, his breathing hard.

"Fuck ... " he gasped, wiping sweat from his forehead. "Anna, that was incredible."

I flopped back against Luke's pillow, my body still tingling. Luke draped an arm across my naked chest, the weight of it reassuring. I waited for the joy to fade, for a sense of guilt to erode the tiny piece of freedom I had claimed back. But it didn't come. Ben's voice, for now, was silent.

"So ..." I breathed. "This is what it's like to sleep with a werewolf."

Luke beamed. "Did it fulfill your wildest fantasies?"

"It was okay."

"Just okay?"

"Yeah." I grinned. "It needs practice."

"Oh, really?" Luke stroked the edge of my breast. "And are you offering to help me sharpen my skills?"

"I'm available any time you need, wolf." I settled back against his shoulder, listening to the rain pelt down on the roof of the tent. My eyes fluttered closed. For the first time since Ben had died, I felt ridiculously, gloriously happy.

8

LUKE

I rolled over in the morning, my arm falling over Anna's sleeping body. She lay on her side, facing me. Her delicate features appeared relaxed and serene. A lock of hair fell over her eye, and a thin trail of drool extended from her mouth to the pillow.

I grinned. She looked so adorable. Heat radiated off her body, and the pull of our bond tugged between us. I shuffled closer, pressing my body against hers as the heat sizzled across our skin. The itch beneath my skin burned into hers. The full moon would begin today, and I needed to be well away from the camp. I couldn't predict how I'd behave now that Anna was my mate.

My mate. The thought sent a fresh shiver through me. I noticed a dark smudge on Anna's shoulder from where I'd bitten her, marking her as mine.

She *was* mine. The thought sent a shiver of joy through my body. I reached out and grazed my fingers across her soft cheek. *I could stay like this all day ...*

... all day ...

For the first time, it occurred to me just how much light was streaming through the tent's canvas. I reached over her and grabbed her phone from on top of the torn remains of her jeans.

"Shit!" I grabbed Anna's shoulder and shook her. "Wake up. We overslept."

"Huh?" Anna opened one lazy eye. Upon seeing me beside her, she leapt out of bed, evidently forgetting she was wrapped up in a sleeping bag and managing to topple into the side of the tent.

"Luke, what are you ... " her voice trailed off as the night evidently came back to her. "Shit."

"Shit is right," I shoved the phone under her nose. "We overslept. It's quarter past eight."

"Fuck." The curse word sounded so hot coming out of her full red lips. She scrambled around the bed, searching for her clothes. "I have to get out there. Frances has all these plans for uncovering the paintings today. I wasn't at breakfast so they're probably looking for me and—"

Her face fell as she held up her torn shirt. "You ruined my clothes," she moaned, grabbing the buttons from the tent floor and throwing them at me. "I can't believe this!"

I scratched at the itch crawling under my skin, biting back the urge to grab her, to throw her down on the bed and make her call out my name again. "I told you the wolf in me was too close to the surface. You didn't seem to care at the time."

"But *all* my clothes?" Anna inspected the seams on her jeans with horror. "I have nothing to wear out there and all my clothes are in my tent and they will know—"

"So?" I squeezed her beautifully-shaped arse. "I don't care if they find out. Besides, I think you look much better without clothes."

"*I* care." Anna's lower lip quivered. She looked dangerously close to crying.

"Hey, babe. Don't worry." I shuffled towards her, arms open. I wanted to find some way to make it right for her. "We'll find a way out of this."

"How?" Anna sniffed, turning away from me and balling up her hands with frustration. "I have to somehow get to my tent, by walking past the rest of the camp completely naked!"

I reached for a pair of boxer shorts, pulling them over my hard-on. From the look of terror on her face, it didn't look as though I'd be getting a repeat of last night any time soon. I tried a different tack. "I don't see the problem. We're consenting adults. We're allowed to shag, you know."

"They can't know," she whispered. "It ... it will get back to the university. Everyone will talk about me. I can't deal with that."

Somehow I doubted that was really the reason, but I didn't call her out on it. This definitely wasn't the time.

"Just wait until the team has left for the site and sneak over." Then I remembered the way I'd yelled at Frances yesterday. She thought I was only one infraction away from shutting her site down. There's no way she'd risk leaving the camp until Anna and I presented ourselves.

"Can you run over to my tent and grab some clothes for me?" Her voice quivered.

"Oh, yeah." I grinned. "They're not going to suspect anything if they catch me rifling through your stuff. Here." I tossed her a shirt. "Put this on over your jeans, and tie your jacket on over the top. No one will see that it doesn't fit, and it's long enough to hide the tear in your jeans."

She stared at the shirt for a couple of moments, then grabbed it from my hands. "Great idea, thanks."

"See? I'm more than just a pretty face."

Anna pulled on all the clothes and shoved her feet into her boots. My body ached with disappointment to see her beautiful body covered up again, but she couldn't very well stay in my tent fucking all day. More's the pity.

"How do I look?" She smoothed my shirt down over her ruined jeans.

"Absolutely fucking gorgeous. Just a moment," I grabbed her just as she was lifting the flap of the tent and pulled her in for one last, lingering kiss. Her scent devoured me, the softness of her tongue against mine making me even harder. My veins burned with the itch of my inner wolf and the tug of the connection between us. I pulled back before I tore all her clothes off again. My cock jerked in protest. "Okay." I patted her arse. "Now run for it!"

Anna yanked the tent flap open and stepped outside. I grabbed the flap from her hand just as she let it fall, and watched her as she made her way towards her own tent ... just as Ruth came around the corner, carrying a clipboard.

"Anna!" she called out. "You weren't at breakfast. You've got to get going. There's so much to do. Frances has a film crew arriving any minute. Where have you—" Her words died on her lips as her eyes fell on my face, and then dropped down over my body. Only then did I realise I was standing in the entrance of my tent, wearing only my boxers and an enormous erection, staring after Anna, who had very clearly just come *from* my tent.

Fuck.

"Well," Ruth smirked, her eyes flashing as she tapped her pen against her clipboard. "This *is* interesting."

"I was ... er ... that was to say ..." Anna stuttered. She was turned away from me, but I could see the back of her neck turning crimson.

Shame overwhelmed me. This was all my fault. Anna was so worried about making a good impression on Professor Doyle and I'd ruined it for her. My mind reeled. *Think, Lowe. You need to come up with some reason for her being in your tent.*

"I've just been giving Miss Sinclair a private forest safety lecture," I explained, keeping my voice stern. "Of all the health and safety violations I've observed here on the site, hers has been the worst. Wandering into those caves at night unaccompanied?" I sneered at Anna. Her face crumpled. I wanted to run to her and wrap her in my arms, but I pressed on, desperate for Ruth to believe me. "It was irresponsible and could have ended very badly. So, I thought it best if Miss Sinclair underwent a practical experiment."

"I'm sure." That smirk hadn't left Ruth's face.

I glanced from Anna, to Ruth, and back again, then burst out laughing as though the awkwardness of the situation had just occurred to me. "Oh, I see what this looks like. You don't honestly think I'd be sleeping with *her,*" I said, my voice dripping with disdain. "Rest assured, if I had a woman in my bed last night, you'd have heard her crying my name the whole length of the valley."

"Oh, I am sure." Ruth's mouth tugged at the corner.

"I am teaching Miss Sinclair about survival tactics, in case one found oneself lost in the forest and had to use one's clothes to create a shelter or make a signal. Unfortunately, Miss Sinclair was using her jacket as a shelter last night, and she tore her clothes on a bush, so I lent her some others rather than let her freeze." I pointed down at my rapidly deflating erection. "She just happened to catch me at a somewhat embarrassing moment, as you can see."

I was proud of my ingenious lie for solving the problem. Ruth looked disappointed, but at least somewhat convinced. When Anna turned around to face me, I was surprised to see her face red with fury. Her hands were balled at her sides. I'd just saved her arse, and she was pissed off. *Really* pissed off.

"If you guys will excuse me," she said, her jaw clenched, her face flushing with anger.

I watched her stalk off towards her tent, desperate to go after her, but not able to with Ruth still watching. I ran over everything I'd said in my head, but couldn't come up with anything that might've triggered Anna's response. I remembered the way she'd shut down the other night, when I'd asked her about her father, and how worried she'd been when she woke up. I wondered if these things were connected.

The itch clawed at my skin, breaking me out of my thoughts. I had to get as far away from the camp as soon as possible. I'd already left it too late. I didn't want to leave while Anna was still mad at me, but I didn't have a choice. If she was pissed off with me now, there was no telling how upset she'd be if I tore apart the entire camp in a wolven frenzy.

Ruth batted her eyelashes at me. "Would you like me to bring you some breakfast, Luke?"

I glared at her. "No thanks. I've lost my appetite. Shouldn't you be on site?"

Ruth glanced down at her watch. "Yikes. It's late. I'll see you down there later?"

"No, you won't. I'll be away from camp for a couple of days."

"Why?"

"Because I have more important things to do than babysit a team of archaeologists," I snapped. "I have paths to maintain, environmental programs to monitor, and I'd like to eat something that didn't have to be scraped from the bottom of a pot."

"Oh." Ruth looked crushed. But after a moment, her face brightened again. "Well, I hope your time away is ... productive. When you get back, can you take me in for some private wilderness training, too?"

"You don't need it. A girl as well adept at saving whales as you can survive practically anywhere." I gave her a wave with my hand in what I hoped was a dismissive fashion. As I lifted my hand, I noticed a line of grey hair sprouting from my forearm. My fingers tingled as the nails curled over into claws. I shoved my hand behind my back. "So ... bye. Don't forget to wear your hard hat." I yanked the tent flap shut before Ruth could say anything else. My heart pounded double speed. I grabbed another shirt. My claw tore a hole across the shoulder as I pulled it on. *Fuck fuck fuck. I had to go.*

As much as I longed to stay near Anna, and the caves, I had to get away *now,* before they all saw me shifting into my wolf form. I pulled on my trousers, not even bothering to do up the fly, and draped my hood over my head to hide the grey bristles sprouting from my cheeks. I shoved my clawed paw into my pocket, and lifted the tent flap. Ruth had gone. I bent my head down and sprinted for the truck, not looking back as I fled from my mate.

9

ANNA

*A*s I searched through my bags for a change of clothes, Luke's words buzzed in my mind. The sentences turning over and over like a skipping record.

I'm just teaching Miss Sinclair wilderness survival ... wilderness survival ...

Ruth *knew*. She knew what had happened to Ben. Everyone at the university knew. Ben had been a popular guy, president of the Student Society and the Ecology Club. His death had been in all the papers. Reporters had interviewed me. I'd even been in the *Daily Post*. STUDENT HEARTBROKEN AFTER BOYFRIEND FALLS TO GRISLY DEATH. People asked me so many questions, as though I'd been able to read Ben's thoughts in his last moments. Why had Ben decided to cross the crevice without equipment? Why had it taken the forest rangers so long to find him? Had I got some kind of bad feeling when he'd left for the weekend, some kind of premonition of his doom?

The idea of it was ridiculous, but I often found myself turning our last conversation over in my head, wondering if I should have sensed the grim reaper over his shoulder, if I should have inspected his equipment or specifically warned him not to do any freeform rock climbing. But Ben was an experienced hiker and climber, and he was going with a mate. I didn't think any more of it.

And now I couldn't stop thinking about it.

Luke didn't know about Ben or how he'd died. I wasn't ready to tell him. But that didn't stop the guilt from gnawing at me as I'd woken up and felt that warm body beside me. The familiarity of waking up next to someone ... I'd thought it was Ben, before my mind registered what had happened last night, and where I was.

Guilt gnawed at my stomach. I felt as though I'd cheated on Ben, which was ridiculous. He was dead and I had to move on. But that knowledge didn't change how I *felt*. And Luke's comments to Ruth only rubbed salt in the wound. I knew I'd reacted viscerally, but it was the *way* he'd said it, so *mocking*, as though wilderness survival was this basic skill that everyone should have, as though people didn't make mistakes ... mistakes that cost their lives.

I tugged on some polka-dot thermals and a work shirt, and pulled a hoodie on over top. I knew I was being stupid, and unfair, but I was still reeling from everything that had happened. Losing my bracelet, finding the paintings, discovering Luke was a werewolf, and then last night ... last night ...

You're angry at Luke because you feel guilty, the voice in my head scolded me. *You didn't even think of Ben, your poor boyfriend who died a horrible, excruciating death only a few months ago. He's barely even in the ground and you're jumping into bed with a werewolf. And that's really why you're angry.*

Dammit. I couldn't think about all this now. I wiped the tears forming in the corners of my eyes, grabbed my trowel and raced down to the site, checking all my buttons were done up and my hair smoothed as much as possible.

I could tell from the way Frances eyed me when I jogged

over to the caves that Ruth had told her what she'd seen. My whole face burned with a fierce heat as I came to a stop in front of my professor, who stared at me with a strange look on her face.

"Hello, Anna," she said, a wry tone in her voice. "I'm glad you could join us. Ruth was saying Luke has been giving you some additional health and safety training."

"Yes. In wilderness survival. It wasn't meant to interfere with our work but I ... er, overslept." I said, a lame excuse both of us knew was a lie. Frances pressed a memory stick on a chain into my hand.

"That's fine. I need you to go to Crookshollow village and email these photos to Barry. He's waiting on them for the press release. They're hi res, so you'll probably need to upload them to the file database and send him the link."

"I thought you'd want to do that," I said. "You said yesterday you wanted to go to town to send some emails and have a proper shower."

"The BBC are showing up this morning." Frances beamed. I noticed she was wearing a line of wobbly eyeliner around her eyes, and her lips were done in a deep red. She was ready for her close-up.

"But I'm the one who discovered the paintings!" I cried. "Shouldn't I be talking to the BBC?"

"Frances is the director of the excavation," Ruth said, moving in to stand beside the professor. She tucked her blonde hair behind her ear. "It doesn't matter who discovered the site. What's important here is the research. These paintings are an incredible discovery; it will be an honour to write my thesis on them."

"*What?*"

"Ruth will be working alongside me for the preliminary research period," Frances explained, her words cutting through my skin like a dagger. "It's important that she be present for all media sessions so her name becomes associated with the site as well."

"But—" I spluttered, angry tears forming in the corners of my eyes, "—why is Ruth working with you and not me? I thought I'd get to—"

"Don't be ridiculous. You didn't honestly think just because you happened to stumble upon these paintings first, that you'd get dibs on them over a PhD student?" Ruth sneered. "I've already completed my master's. I'm the one in the best position to get the work done and have a proper paper published about the discovery. This is not some first-year essay assignment, Anna. It's serious archaeological discovery. We can't leave it in the hands of a bloody *student*."

"Ruth," Frances scolded. "That's not—"

"Maybe if you didn't spend so much time swanning about with that ranger, learning all about *wilderness survival,* you'd have figured out how things work around here," Ruth added in a bitchy tone.

My blood boiled. I wanted to tear Ruth's throat out. But what could I do? Ruth was right – she was a PhD student, and I'd just handed her the perfect doctoral thesis topic on a fucking plate. Her throwing me under the bus was just a fun side effect.

I turned on my heel and stalked back towards the camp, my fingers crushing the USB stick into my palm.

"Anna, wait." It was Frances. I sucked in a breath, trying in vain to compose my face. I turned around.

Frances tucked a strand of hair behind her ear, accidentally smudging the corner of her eyeliner. "I can see you're upset. Ruth was very rude. I'm sorry she gave you the impression that—"

"So it's not true?" I said. "You haven't already made plans with her?"

"She spoke to me as soon as we confirmed the discovery. So yes, she'll be helping me with the initial publication of the paintings. Now, don't worry about it. There is plenty of work to be done, enough work for several graduates," Frances said trying to soothe me. "I imagine we'll be studying the caves for *at least* three more seasons. I am sure by the time you're ready for your doctoral thesis, Anna, there will be a project here for you, as well. But for now, I really need those photos."

"Fine." I shoved the stick into my pocket. "I'm on it. I'll be back around lunchtime. I can even pick up some Cornish pasties for everyone if you like."

"Don't worry about that, I'm planning to cook fennel and black pudding soup for the whole team and the film crew." Frances beamed. "It's my mother's special recipe."

I resisted the urge to gag. "In that case, don't worry about me. I'll go see my mum, if that's okay, and have lunch with her."

"That's fine. Thank you, Anna. You really are a tremendous help." Frances patted my head, as though I were a puppy, and then jogged back to the caves.

I stormed back to the camp, catching sight of Luke just as he was getting into his truck. I ran towards him. I needed to apologise. It wasn't his fault I felt guilty ... and I was desperate to feel the heavy warmth of his arms around me, to hear him say something completely evil that would take away the sting of this horrible morning. But his face shot with panic, and he held up a hand, indicating I shouldn't come further. His other hand was shoved deep into his jacket.

"Where are you going?" I called out to him.

"Away," he replied, his voice coming out strained. He glanced up, and I gasped in shock. His cheeks were covered with thick grey fur, his nose already starting to morph into a snout.

Of course. The full moon must be right around the corner. That meant Luke could no longer control his shift. It looked as though he was only seconds away from becoming a wolf. *He must be leaving to go deeper into the forest, until his wolf form is no longer controlling him.*

Which meant I had two days on site without him. Two long days with Ruth tormenting me. It would be hell, but maybe it would help me sort my feelings out.

Luke slammed the driver's side door closed, turning on the truck and throwing it into gear. I jogged alongside the road when his truck bumped past me. "Anna!" Luke wound the window down, his face now completely covered in fur, his nose twisting before my eyes. "Are you still mad at me because of what I said to Ruth in the camp? I swear, I didn't mean it. I didn't know it would hurt you. I just wanted to save you from embarrassment."

"I'm not mad about that." My fingers brushed against the USB stick in my pocket. A fresh surge of anger rushed through my veins. "It was sweet, actually. I'm so sorry about the way I acted. My reaction had nothing to do with you. I will explain later, I promise."

"You don't owe me an explanation. I didn't mean to upset you."

"I'm sorry I told Frances about the paintings," I burst out. "I shouldn't have done that. She's got film crews coming and funding applications already filled out. People are going to be swarming all over the site."

"It's done now." Luke looked pained. His hand tightened around the steering wheel. "I can't wait much longer. The shift—"

"Ruth is taking all the credit for finding the paintings," I said, my voice wavering as a lump rose in my throat. "And Professor Doyle is letting her."

Luke closed his eyes. "Anna. I promise you that I will help you, but right now I have to go."

"Okay. Luke..."

"Yes?"

"Don't kill anything small and cute."

He smiled. "I make no promises."

I watched him drive away, my stomach somersaulting. As his truck turned the corner, I looked away, tears pooling in the corners of my eyes. Luke made my body sing, and my heart clench tight. But feeling this way felt like a betrayal to Ben. I still saw his face when I closed my eyes, his friendly smile, his kind brown eyes, his blotched, broken skin when I'd gone to identify him at the morgue.

The grief was still so fresh, still blanketing my mind in this haze of impossible sadness. Here, in the forest, where Ben had loved to spend his time, I sensed him in everything. He was the rustle of leaves in the trees. He was the crunch of twigs beneath my boots. He was the fresh smell of rain trickling through the foliage and the twittering of birds as they went about their business.

And amidst it all, was Luke. He smelled like wildness personified, like adrenaline pulsing through your veins, like the wind in your hair while you ran. He wasn't *of* the forest, he was the *king* of the forest. It was sexy as hell, but was it what I really wanted? Was I into Luke because he was so different from Ben, because he exuded this raw masculine authority, because he was exactly what I needed, or because he was the *last* thing I needed?

I blinked away my tears. I was a wreck. I needed to sort myself out, figure out what I wanted. And I needed to do it away from the trees and the birds and everything that screamed Ben's name.

At least I had this trip to town to look forward to. I told myself I didn't want to be on the stupid news anyway, watching Ruth smirking and preening for the camera. Instead, I would take my sweet time, enjoy a long shower and a real coffee and a Cornish pasty little sojourn from the mud and the cold. I lowered myself into my Mini, and turned the ignition. The tiny car spluttered to life, and I turned it onto the dirt track that met up with the main road.

After five miles of bouncing like a milkshake in the yard, I met up with the road. There was a couple on a motorbike in front of me, but they pulled over so I could putter past. I waved at them in thanks. The driver – a handsome man with long black hair streaming out behind him – didn't acknowledge me, but the Asian girl sitting behind him gave me a friendly wave and a smile through her visor.

The drive back into Crookshollow took me nearly an hour. I was thoroughly sick of being in the car, and it was still another twenty minutes to Crooks Crossing, where my mother's flat was. I had an idea. My closest university friend, Derek, lived in a flat in Crookshollow. He was studying English mythology as part of his English and History degree. He'd have a shower and a computer I could use, and if anyone knew anything about were-wolves, it would be him.

Crookshollow had this reputation of being the most occult village in England. Apparently, more witches had been hung there during the 17th and 18th centuries than anywhere else in the country. I wasn't sure that was something to be proud of, but the town embraced its sordid history. On the way to Derek's place I drove down the high street, past crystal shops and signs advertising tarot readings. At the end of the street, the gleaming Halt Institute towered over the surrounding buildings – a modern architectural monstrosity that housed the witchcraft museum, an art gallery, and a few local fashion boutiques.

Derek's car wasn't parked on the street outside his flat, but that wasn't unusual – sometimes he had to park around the corner if all the spaces were taken. I knocked on the door. No one answered. *Odd.* He wouldn't usually be at university this early. Derek wasn't a functioning human until at least 2pm, mostly because he stayed up until all hours of the night gaming. I did tend to attract geeky friends.

I banged on the door, hoping to wake him up. I should've called first. It had never even occurred to me. After two weeks in the forest with no reception, I was getting used to not being able to contact people via my mobile. If it was good enough for neolithic hunter gatherers, then I could survive for a few short weeks.

Finally, the door swung open. Rodney, Derek's flatmate, scowled at me, his eyes heavy with sleep. A towel was wrapped around his hips, and his hair stuck out at all angles.

"Derek's not here," he snapped at me. "He's gone to see his parents for a couple of days, to work on that family history project of his."

"Oh, sorry." I stepped back. "Did he take his mobile with him?"

"Probably," Rodney yelled back as he slammed the door in my face. "You really smell!"

"Thank you!"

So Derek wouldn't be any help until he got back. That was okay. Derek had already been a huge help to me. I'd leaned on him pretty heavily after Ben died, mainly because I couldn't talk to Mum in her catatonic state. I spent so many nights at his flat, sleeping in his arms, sobbing into his pillow. Derek had been nothing but kind to me, and I must've been confusing him by clinging to him the way I had.

He kissed me one night, while he was holding me in bed. I kissed him back, even though I felt nothing for him romantically. It was just comforting to be wanted again, after losing someone who meant so much to me. But it was wrong to lead Derek on, so I pulled away. He confessed he had feelings for me.

I told him I only saw him as a friend. We hugged and I cried some more and things had been mostly fine ever since. Sometimes I'd catch him looking at me a certain way, and I knew he still had a few lingering feelings, but he was actively dating and I hoped he'd soon meet someone who would rock his world. He deserved it. Derek was a good dude.

But him not being home put me in the unfortunate position of having to get back in the car and drive to my mum's flat if I wanted a shower.

I wasn't exactly looking forward to seeing my mum. I'd been living with her ever since Dad died, which was five years ago now, when I was in the sixth form at Crookshollow High. We got on well most of the time, but she relied on me heavily, always wanting me to cook and clean and spend my weekends with her. She was the reason I'd given up my place at Cambridge to stay in Loamshire. The rare times I left her alone for a couple of days, I'd come home to find her weeping on the sofa, Dad's photo album open on her lap. But those occasions were getting rarer now.

In the last year, she'd started taking art classes at the Halt Institute and going out to coffee with friends. I was starting to hope that I could leave her alone and do my postgraduate studies somewhere else. Ben had even encouraged me to apply to Cambridge. But then he'd gone and died, and she'd reverted back to her old ways.

In many ways, Mum had taken Ben's death harder than me. She seemed to regard it as a curse, a vicious cycle she'd brought on just by existing. She'd dropped out of her art class and the only person she spent any time with was Cynthia, her tarot reader friend who left our flat stinking of patchouli and cigarette smoke. I'd barely convinced Mum that she would be okay if I left her on her own while I was on the excavation, and I didn't want to think about the reaction I'd get as soon as I got through the door. After everything that had happened with Luke, I wasn't ready to deal with her just yet.

What I needed was a distraction. I had the whole morning to myself in the village. I might as well put it to good use.

I turned the Mini around and headed back down the Crookshollow high street. An idea occurred to me. A crazy idea, but then, everything had gone pretty crazy ever since Luke had shown up on site. I yanked the Mini into a car park, locked up, and walked up to the first occult shop I saw.

I read the gothic sign above the door. *Astarte.* This looked like just the place I needed. I glanced along the street, but I didn't recognise anyone wandering around. It wouldn't do for one of my university friends to see me heading into a new-age store. It would destroy my archaeologist street cred.

As soon as I opened the door, a wave of incense hit my nostrils. Choking on the sickly smell, I stepped inside. The shop was dim, with gauzy curtains covered in silver stars obscuring the front window. The place was lit with candles burning along the countertop and on the various wobbly shelves stacked around the small room. Every surface was crammed with books, candles, crystals, packets of cards, and statues of Egyptian gods.

The woman behind the counter – an old lady with a stooped back and a plait of thick black hair over her shoulder – waved at me, then went back to work. There was only one other customer in the shop – a handsome man about my age with wild ginger hair and broad shoulders. He was scratching urgently at his neck, while arguing with the shopkeeper over a quantity of tiny white pills spread out on the counter. As I walked around the shop, picking up the books and flipping through them, I eavesdropped on their conversation.

"—I need ten of these pills. Not tomorrow. Not next week. *Today.*"

"Look, you're not the only person who's come in here for

these," the old woman replied, her voice stern. "I can give you these six, but that's the best I can do until next week."

"Fine." The man gritted his teeth, took a handful of the pills, dropped a wad of cash on the counter and stormed out.

"Customers." The old woman looked up and grinned at me, a kind smile of crooked teeth. "They think you can work miracles and just magic up some more stock, although I suppose in a shop like this, it's to be expected. What can I do for you, dear?"

"I, uh ..." I didn't really know what to say. "I was hoping you could work a miracle for me."

She smiled wider. "As long as you don't need any Lycan pills, I'm all yours."

"Lycan pills?"

The lady waved her hand dismissively. "It's a herbal remedy. For hair growth. They're not a big seller, but I have my regulars who need them."

"To cure baldness?"

"Not exactly." She glanced at my hair appraisingly. "Your hair looks fine. So what miracle are you in the market for?"

"I'm looking for ... information on werewolves." I scratched my head. This conversation was ridiculous. I couldn't believe I was doing this. I was a rational person. I believed in the scientific method. I knew crystals didn't have healing properties. Why was I in an occult store talking to a crone? "I mean ... werewolf myths."

"I have a few books on the subject. But why don't you just ask your friend?"

"Huh?"

"Please, dear. I may be an old lady, but I can smell werewolf a mile off, and you reek of it."

"I ... what?" I glanced around the shop, but it was empty. I lowered my voice. "You know about werewolves?"

"Of course." She tapped the bottle on the counter. "You

didn't think I'd run a store like this and not know a thing or two about shapeshifters? I'm Clara, by the way. My own sons are shifters, you know."

"Really?" This conversation had only been going on for a few minutes, and already it had veered into Bizarro World.

Clara nodded. "They didn't get it from me. I'm purely human. But their father was a vulpine – that's a fox shifter – and both my sons inherited his genes. Shifters are much more common than you realise, although werewolves are pretty scarce in England these days. So what is it you want to know about werewolves? You might as well ask me. I can probably tell you more than any book."

"I don't ..." I took a deep breath. "I guess I want to know about their mates."

"How so?"

"What does it mean when someone ... when they call you their mate?"

"In most circumstances, it means you are a very lucky girl." Clara grinned. "Shifters – especially wolves – are caregivers. They're fiercely protective of their mates, and will do absolutely anything for them, including taking a bullet, if it came to that. Is that a bite I see on your neck?"

I pulled the collar of my shirt down so she could see the red mark across my collarbone.

"Ah. I see you have an immediate need of this information. Werewolf mating is very simple, by shifter standards. Werewolves are usually male, and they are instantly attracted to human women who possess the wolven genes. Many werewolves speak of a magnetic pull or an energy coursing through their veins – when they meet a women and instantly know they're meant to spend the rest of their lives together. Some women feel the same attraction."

"That sounds far-fetched." I rubbed my arms, remembering

the way my body tingled and coursed with heat when I was near Luke. Was that what she was talking about? Was that feeling more than just attraction?

"Does it? Love at first sight happens all the time, among human couples. There are several scientific papers on the subject, and many believe it has evolved as a physiological response to environmental pressures. Why should it not express itself as a physical trait?"

Woah. Clara spoke my language. She gave me a coy smile. "I get lots of sceptics in here, young lady. I've learned the best way to talk to them is to find a way to relate, instead of getting into an argument."

"I can't imagine anyone arguing with you." I grinned. I liked this crone. "So do you know many werewolves?"

"No. As I said, there aren't many left in England now. Most of them stick to countries that already have a wolf population. It makes their lives easier if they're ever seen outside in their wolven form. I do have a couple of regular customers, but this week has been one of my busiest ever, with all these new wolves in town. Like that last customer, for example."

"He was a werewolf? How can you tell?"

"The smell. It's obvious once you get used to it." Clara sniffed. "Plus, he was after these pills."

She tossed the jar into my hand. I read the handwritten label. "Lycan pills: take twice daily leading up to the full moon."

"Many wolves find the pills help them shorten the length of time they're under the moon's spell, and help them to control their wolfish urges. I make these myself, and I usually have enough on hand for my usual clients, but the new wolves this week have wiped me out, as you may have heard."

"When did these new wolves show up in town?" Luke had said he was protecting the site against any potential threats. It would be too big a coincidence for more werewolves to show up in Crookshollow just as the caves were being excavated.

"There's a ranger in the forest. He arrived two days ago. " Clara gave me a look. "I gather that's your man."

"Luke. That's him. How do you know he's a ranger?"

"He told me. We had a lovely chat. He's a wonderful lad, a little rough around the edges, but his heart is pure. His family have a long history in Crookshollow. It's nice to see a Lowe return here."

"You know all about the Lowe pack? About what happened?"

She nodded. "Yes, but that's ancient history, of course. There would be few here in Crookshollow now who would remember the death of that child, and of those left, probably none that cared, unless there was a descendant of Robert Peyton who still carried his anti-shifter fervour."

"That seems unlikely. What about other wolves?"

"I had my regulars, and that man this morning. I've never seen him before, either. I would stay away from him if I were you."

My stomach twisted with nerves. "How come?"

"He smelled your Lowe wolf on you, and likely sensed your genes. He knows you're a viable mate, and that another wolf has laid claim to you – a wolf whose family name has long been disgraced. He might try to claim you for his own."

"Can he do that? Don't I get a say in the matter?"

"It wasn't uncommon in the past for rival packs to clash over viable female mates. Most of that behaviour is verboten these days, feminist wolf movement and all that, but some wolves still stick to the old ways. He struck me as the latter type."

My stomach clenched. I'd come to the village to escape this werewolf stuff for a few hours, to give myself some time to think. The last thing I needed was to get stuck in the middle of a territorial wolf battle over my own vagina. "What do I do? Is there some kind of … anti-wolf spray I can use?"

"I'm afraid no magic is powerful enough to repel the primal energy of a lycanthrope." Clara grinned, tapping a stack of black card decks on the counter. "I *can* sell you a deck of Crookshollow tarot cards, though. Each card has different pictures of famous spiritual landmarks of Crookshollow. They've also got playing instructions inside."

"Playing instructions?"

"Tarot cards were originally designed as playing cards." Clara set a deck down in front of me. "If you're out in the middle of the forest, perhaps you could use a bit of entertainment."

"Thanks." I paid for a set, and Clara threw in a pamphlet about shapeshifters. "A lot of this is New Age codswallop," she said, jabbing a wrinkled finger at the howling wolf and full moon on the cover. "But if you want some good general information on shifters, it's a good place to start."

"Thank you."

"You're welcome. I just hope what I've told you hasn't confused you even more."

"Confused me?"

Clara's kind eyes bore into mine. "I was in exactly your position once, my dear. I loved a shapeshifter, but I had to temper the decision to follow my heart against a world of doubt."

"I … I've known Luke only a couple of days," I said. "It's too early to say that I love him."

"If you say so." She turned back to the counter, and started rearranging quartz pyramids with thin fingers. "If you have any more questions, you can come back here and I'll try to help you."

"Thank you." I rushed out the door, my mind reeling. I'd gone into Astarte hoping for some clarity, but instead I felt more confused and scared than ever.

I WENT home to the flat. My mother lay on the sofa, staring unblinking at the ceiling, an open scrapbook clutched in her hands.

"Hi, Mum." I kissed her on the forehead. "I brought you a Cornish pasty, and a new tarot deck. I thought you and Cynthia might like to try reading my fortune."

She didn't reply, her eyes barely registering my presence. My gaze fell on the scrapbook, and I gave a start as I realised the photographs weren't of my dad. They were of me and Ben – shots of us grinning from under the family Christmas tree, hiking along Hadrian's Wall last summer, marching in a student protest against the Iraq War. From every image, Ben's lively face grinned up at me. My heart pounded. Why was she doing this to herself?

"Anna." Mum blinked. Fresh tears rolled down her face. She reached up and embraced me with thin, weak arms. "Are you okay? Have you come home to stay with me?"

"I'm just here to take a shower and grab some stuff. I'm living on site for the next three weeks, remember?"

"Oh." Her face fell. She clearly didn't remember at all.

"Why don't you call Cynthia to come over? She could help you finish that Monet puzzle you started." The box still sat on the kitchen table, the border completed, a few splashes of colour dotted in the centre. It didn't look as though she'd fitted any more pieces since I'd last been home.

Mum's eyes fluttered shut. She pressed the scrapbook tight to her chest. "No. I don't think so."

I sighed. "That's fine. I'm just going to take a shower, and then I'll fix you some tea."

The one advantage of having a mother catatonic with grief was that I didn't have to listen to her complain about my smell. I took a long shower, using an entire bar of soap, and tried not to let my mother's behaviour get to me. As I soaped down my body for the fourth time, my sadness at seeing her like that flipped over to anger. When I was eighteen and we lost Dad, I had to hold things together while she fell apart. I had to cook and clean the house and pay the bills and deal with the lawyer and the funeral home. And I did it all while the pain of losing my father rubbed my heart raw. I did it for her, so she could fall apart and retreat into her own private grief.

Which probably explained how I was able to keep going after Ben died. Keeping busy was the only way I knew how to deal with the pain. The university suggested I take a semester off, but I dug my heels in and ended up with the top grades in the whole department. I'd kept on doing everything I had been doing before, while my mum faded back into the same private world.

Seeing her sprawled out on the sofa made my body burn with rage. *I* was the one who'd lost my partner this time, and yet, I wasn't able to lie around and weep and mourn him. I had to hold myself in check to deal with her. And what did her pain achieve? What were her tears in aid of? Dad and Ben had been robbed of their lives, and Mum was wasting hers away. I didn't want to do that.

After changing into some clean clothes, I made Mum some tea, did a load of my filthy, muddy laundry, and logged on to my computer to send off the images to the university. I tried to ring Derek to ask him about werewolf myths, but he wasn't picking up his phone. Lately, Derek had been weirdly obsessed with writing out his family history. He'd been working on the project since second year, and he had collected all kinds of titbits about his ancestors all the way back to the 1700s. Apparently, someone in his family was quite a famous witch hunter. As a mythology student, that was the kind of thing Derek loved. When he went away on his research trips, he got so engrossed, he was unreachable. I hoped he'd come up for air and return my message soon.

"I'm leaving now," I told my mother, as I picked up my clothes from the dryer.

"Okay." She didn't look up from the sofa.

"Please eat your pasty."

"I will." She made no move to grab the paper bag.

"I'll probably be back again in a few days." I lingered in the doorway, wanting to say so much more, but not sure where to start.

"Yes," she said. "Can you pick up some takeaways for dinner?"

I sighed. "I won't be home for dinner," I said through gritted teeth.

"Oh."

I hung on the door, letting the frigid wind blow inside, hoping she'd say something else. *Goodbye, daughter. Enjoy the dig. I hope you have a great time. Did you discover anything wonderful? Did you meet any sexy werewolves?* But she didn't.

I pulled the door shut behind me, locking her inside. I debated calling Cynthia and telling her to come and sit with Mum, but thought better of it. Mum probably wouldn't even answer the door.

Behind the wheel of the Mini, my mind whirred through everything I'd found out from Clara. This other wolf, he had to be there because of the caves. Were things going to get dangerous? As I neared the forest, my stomach flipped with nerves. I wasn't sure what I would find when I got back, and I worried about Luke out there alone, not aware that there were other wolves in the territory.

When I finally reached the site and pulled up beside Frances's battered jeep, I noticed two unfamiliar vans – white paint, with the BBC logo emblazoned on the side. Frances's media campaign was already well underway. I dumped my bag in my tent. On my sleeping bag was a small square of paper. I unfolded it, and read a message scrawled across it in black ink.

Anna

   I have to see you again. Meet me at the old oak at midnight. I promise you won't be hurt.

   Luke

My hand trembled as I stuffed the note into my pocket. How had Luke even written a note in wolf form? He must've doubled back to deliver it before he changed. That was a huge risk.

Would I go? I didn't have a choice. I needed to tell Luke what I'd seen. Even if he was in his wolf form, I hoped he'd be able to understand my words and be on his guard.

My chest tightened. If something happened to him ... I didn't want to think about it.

I can't lose another person I love. I just can't—

Love? The word pulled me up short. Why had I thought that? I didn't love Luke. I *couldn't.* I'd known Luke for all of three days, and for a large portion of that time, he'd been downright rotten to me. I had a more deep and meaningful relationship with the guy who delivers our pizza. I liked him, sure. He was damn hot, and thinking about him made butterflies flutter in my stomach. But not love. It couldn't be love.

Then why are you planning to meet him again at midnight, despite the danger?

"Shut up, brain," I said aloud, as I folded my clean clothes into my bag. *Great, now I was talking to myself.* I was sleeping with a werewolf and talking to myself. At this rate, I'd be locked in an asylum by the end of the week.

With a film crew on site, I had to look at least halfway decent, especially if I wanted to upstage Ruth. I was already wearing a clean jumper and jeans, so I quickly ran a brush through my hair and dabbed on a little makeup, squinting into my tiny compact mirror as I jabbed at my eyes with an eyebrow pencil. No wonder Frances had messed hers up so badly. If anyone ever invented a camping makeup kit, they'd make a fortune.

I stalked over to the caves, arriving just as the film crew started rolling. They had set up giant shade sails in order to keep the rain off the equipment and the cave entrance. Frances was standing behind the director. She waved at me to be quiet. I slowed my walk, moving carefully so as not to step on too many twigs or dead leaves, and came to stand alongside her.

Ruth stood in front of the cave, smiling her infuriatingly chipper smile as she described the rock formations and the geology of the area. She'd probably spent the entire morning fixing her hair and makeup: her short blonde bob was impeccably set, not a single hair out of place. Her eyes were done with a little wing, and a hint of pink highlighted her lips. She looked as though she belonged on a toothpaste commercial, instead of in the middle of an English forest in the driving rain.

Halfway through her spiel, the director called cut in order to reposition the cameras. Ruth checked her face in a compact mirror. My stomach seethed with jealousy. It should have been me out there, talking about the site.

"Why is Ruth in front of the camera?" I hissed to Frances.

"I thought she might like a chance to be involved," she replied. "Ruth is so excited about this discovery. Cave paintings are her specialty, you know. Her master's dissertation was on the Lascaux caves."

Cave paintings are her specialty, and yet she hasn't figured out that those are less than a hundred years old, I thought but didn't say.

The camera started rolling again. I watched Ruth gesturing

to the rocks as she explained how the caves had formed from water running through the mountain ranges. Water ran down over the edge of the sail and dribbled down the back of my sweater, cold water sliding over my skin.

I've had it, I said to myself, as a large drip landed in the centre of my head. *I've had it with being taken advantage of, with missing out on opportunities because I'm too nice to speak up. I'm sick of being busy surviving the various tragedies of my life and looking after everyone else. It's time I looked after me.*

Somehow or other, without hurting Luke or endangering his claim on his rightful territory, I was going to expose the paintings as a sham. If I couldn't get credit for discovering the greatest archaeological find in England's history, then I damn well was going to get the credit for exposing it as a fraud.

10

LUKE

I sped deep into the forest for as long as I dared, heading through an area that wasn't frequented by hikers. My paws shook violently as I gripped the wheel. I cursed myself for going back and leaving that note for Anna. No one had seen me, but it had cost me precious time. I gritted my teeth as my wolf form pushed against my skin, begging to be fully unleashed. Grey hair bristled all over my body, and I'd had to kick my boots off as my feet melded into paws. It took all my concentration to keep the truck on the road. Sweat poured down my face, and my whole body raged with an itch that would only subside once I gave in fully to my wolven side.

Up ahead, the road ended in a small gravel clearing. A sign pointed out the local flora and fauna, and arrows showed the direction of the next hut. There were no paths here – hikers had to use a compass and map to find their way. The only people who came out here were conservation groups studying birds or squirrels or tree lizards, and this was the wrong time of year for any of that.

I kicked the door open. It took me three tries to get my

shaking paws to cooperate in unhooking my safety belt. I rolled
out of the car, my skin crawling with agony.

You're such an idiot.

I half-ran, half-hobbled into the trees, my chest heaving. I
wanted to get as much distance between myself and the car
before the change. Once I'd transformed near a rest-stop in the
Black Forest and shredded the tires on some poor German family's Volkswagen. I needed the truck in one piece so I could get
back to the site.

You should never have left Anna that note.

I didn't have time for any more thought. The wolf won over. I
crashed through the trees, my paws sliding across the icy earth.
My shirt tore as my spine bent double. The itch consumed me.
My blood boiled in my veins. I dropped to my knees, my fingers
digging into the dirt as the change took hold of me.

I cried out as my skin tore away, my bones rearranging themselves, slipping from their disks and snapping in the opposite
directions. More fur burst through my skin, like a thousand tiny
needles piercing my flesh. My vision darkened, colours fading
into dulled hues as objects in my periphery suddenly coming
into sharp focus. I threw back my head, and howled.

I was wolf once more.

WHEN ONE FIRST changes into one's wolf form, the first order of
the day is always breakfast.

I caught the scent of a rabbit that had crossed in front of me,
and followed it for a mile until I managed to track down the
creature itself. One swift bite to the jugular, and I had satisfied
the growling hunger in my stomach.

My thoughts muddied as instinct thrummed through my
body. But unlike my previous shifts, if I focused on Anna, I

found myself able to retain my independent, human thought. So I found myself a sheltered spot in the hollow of a rotting tree trunk, and thought of her.

Last night ... it meant so much more to me than just sex. My body burning for her, the image of her face blazing across my vision. I could barely concentrate on the task I'd given myself.

Now that I was in my wolf form, I knew that I wouldn't attack her. The idea of it turned my stomach. But still, asking her to meet me was a risk. She could be followed, and we could both be found out. But I needed Anna to see me for what I truly was, to understand that the wolf was a part of me, in the same way whatever was bothering her this morning was a part of her. If I scared her off, that was probably a good thing. If I didn't, well, we'd deal with that together.

I ached for her. Anna was everything to me now, and I couldn't bear even a single day without seeing her, even if it had to be as a wolf.

Anna was my mate, and nothing or no one was going to separate us.

11

ANNA

I *have to see you again. Meet me at the old oak at midnight.*
I promise you won't be hurt.

Once again, I stood beside the rotting carcass of the fallen oak, freezing my extremities off, waiting for a wolf who was late. Once again, Ben swirled through my thoughts, his voice whistling through the trees and caressing my skin with frigid, dead fingers. Once again, I wondered if I should have myself committed, because I was clearly going nuts.

A twig snapped. I whirled around, scanning the treeline. My breath caught in my throat.

I shouldn't be here. This is crazy.

I should *be here,* I told myself, annoyed that I was still looking back to the past. *Ben is dead. He isn't coming back. Why shouldn't I be falling for a werewolf?*

"Luke?" I called out, rubbing my mittened hands together in a vain attempt to keep them from falling off. "Luke, is that you?"

Another twig broke. I focused on a knot of trees at the top of the ridge, around thirty metres from where I stood. A wolf stepped out from behind one of the trees, its grey coat shining in the moonlight, a line of reddish fur down its spine I didn't remember from last time Luke changed. He was beautiful.

The wolf crouched in the dead leaves, paws facing me, mouth hanging open and pink tongue panting against its chin. It had its eyes almost closed, just two slits eyeing me up in an almost sinister way.

Even though I knew it was Luke, seeing a wolf so close still gave me an uneasy feeling. "Hey." I gave a little wave, not really certain what I should do. Should I get closer? Did he even understand my words?

The wolf sat up, its back straight and front paws pressed together. It nodded its head slightly, acknowledging my presence.

"Um ... so I'm really cold, and I'm not exactly sure why you asked me to come out here. I hope you're keeping well."

The wolf nodded its head.

"And you've been keeping out of trouble."

Another nod.

"But you ate something small and furry, didn't you?"

A sheepish nod this time. I wished he'd open his eyes.

I shifted weight to my other foot. This was weird. I wasn't sure what I was supposed to say. "So, um ... I went to town today. Frances made me email off some photographs for the press release. While I was there, I went to this occult store on the high street, and the woman there ... she makes pills for lycanthropes ... that's you, a lycanthrope. I learned that today. And yeah ... she said another wolf is in the area. I actually walked past him – he's got reddish hair, a bit like that colour along the spine of your pelt, actually ... do you call it a pelt?"

Luke tilted his head to one side.

"So ... I don't think it's a coincidence. He could be here because of the caves. You have to be careful—"

The wolf snapped its head up, baring its teeth. Its eyes bore into mine, the deep brown irises of a killer locking focus on its prey.

That's not Luke.

My stomach plummeted to my knees. *Shit.*

The wolf pounced, galloping towards me on strong paws. Time seemed to slow. Its shoulder muscles rippled as it narrowed the space between us. My throat closed. Its jaws pulled back, revealing those rows of sharp teeth.

Run.

I willed my legs to move. I turned and raced back towards the camp. I seemed to move in slow motion, my legs dragging through the air as though I were trying to run through syrup. I thrust my hands out in front of me, plunging through the trees without a clue where I was heading. The torchlight swung wildly around me, lighting the forest like a fire. The wolf pounded behind me, panting as it closed in on me. In the distance, someone was screaming. It took me a few moments to realise that someone was me.

The wolf's feet pounded against the dirt. Leaves crunched. It panted with anticipation. I could practically feel the heat of its breath against my cheek. Any moment now—

Something crashed through the undergrowth beside me. I screamed, and ducked left, grabbing a tree trunk to prevent myself from keeling over. Behind me, I heard a thump, and the wolf's snarls turned into a whimper.

I dared a look over my shoulder. My attacker was on locked in a vicious battle against another wolf, this one with a grey pelt and glowing green eyes. The two rolled across the ground, jaws snapping and claws slicing.

Luke!

The second wolf – Luke – overpowered the first, pinning its shoulders to the ground, jaws snapping in its face. I choked back a scream, expecting him to tear the first wolf's face off. Luke bent down, and took a bite out of the wolf's shoulder. Blood gushed from the wound, and the wolf howled with pain and rage. Luke stepped back, growling, his teeth bared and tail twitching. The other wolf rolled to its feet and raced off into the trees, disappearing into the night.

Luke stalked in a wide circle around me, growling into the forest, sniffing frantically over the ground. After doing three circuits around the general area, he sat down and looked up, his eyes wide as they met mine. He panted in a friendly way, his tongue hanging out over his teeth.

"Luke." I sank to my knees, struggling to catch my breath. I held my hand to my chest, trying to calm my thundering heart.

He trotted towards me, head down, back stooped in an unthreatening way. I couldn't believe I had mixed him up with the other wolf. Luke's coat was pure grey, darker across his back, fading to an almost snowy white under his belly. He was smaller than the other wolf, but leaner, his sleek wolven body loping towards me with an even gait.

My heart pounded as he walked right up to me. His snout nuzzled my hand. My breath caught in my throat as I ran my mitten through his fur, sinking deep into the soft, silky strands. Luke licked my cheek, and I giggled.

"Thank you for saving me." I wrapped my arms around his thick, muscled neck and buried my face in his fur. Luke placed a paw on my shoulder, and whimpered.

"I don't know how much you can understand me."

Luke inclined his head again.

"So you do understand? Nod for yes, shake for no."

Luke nodded once.

"Okay. That's good." I breathed deep. The wolf even *smelled* like Luke – that deep, primal scent that drove me over the edge. At the moment, it was the most beautiful smell in the world.

"Luke," I whispered into his fur. "It's been such an intense day for me. There's a film crew here and Ruth is acting like she's Renee Zellweger. Listen, I'm so sorry for the way I reacted this morning. I know you know my dad died. He was killed in a factory accident. But what you don't know is that five months ago, my boyfriend was killed here in the forest. He'd gone hiking with a mate and they'd decided to do some bouldering across one of the rocky ravines further downstream. Ben slipped and fell into a crevice. He broke several bones and cracked his head. The friend couldn't get him out and by the time he got back with help, Ben was dead."

Tears sprung in my eyes. Luke licked them away, his rough tongue like sandpaper against my skin.

"Last night ... it was the first time since Ben. And it was amazing. I *really* like you, Luke, but it's hard for me being here, in the forest, without him. My mother has retreated back into herself, the way she did after Dad died. I'm having to hold everything together for her and I'm struggling. When you were talking about wilderness survival, it just got to be a little too much for me. I felt guilty, and I took that out on you. It wasn't your fault. You didn't know."

Luke nuzzled into my neck, his smell calming me. I squeezed him tighter, his powerful body reassuring me, easing away my pain.

"Wow," I laughed, as tears rolled over my cheeks. "I never thought I'd say this, but it's so much easier talking to a wolf than another human. It's nice for once to know someone is listening to me."

Luke's long tongue slobbered across my whole face, leaving a trail of sticky saliva across my cheek and neck. I laughed and pushed his snout away.

"Luke ... I ... I don't want to sleep alone tonight." The memory of that wolf's cruel eyes tugged at me. I rested my chin against his shoulder, reassured by the muscles rippling beneath his fur. There was no way anyone could hurt me with Luke by my side.

Luke stood up again, breaking our embrace. He disappeared into the trees, his grey pelt gleaming under the pale moon. "Where are you going?" I called after him, not wanting to lose him. Luke turned back to me and barked once, as if to say, "What are you waiting for?" then kept trotting on into the darkness.

What *was* I waiting for? I glanced up into the trees, where the bare branches swayed in the wind. An owl hooted. Ben's voice faded into the cold of the night.

I got to my feet and followed Luke. He circled around the outside of the camp, and a few minutes later, we came to a stop in the trees beside my tent. I scanned the rest of the camp, but couldn't see any lights on or torches flickering in tents.

"I think we're safe," I said, holding open my tent flap. Luke darted inside and I zipped the tent up tight.

Last night, we had folded our naked bodies together in Luke's bed, limbs entwined and the scent of sex hanging thick in the air. Tonight, there would be none of that.

The trees rustled over my head, stray branches brushing against the canvas. Luke's chest rose and fell. He was taking such a huge risk being here, not just that he might be discovered, but that he might frighten me away. In fact, the opposite was true. I was in awe of this tremendous gift he'd given me, the trust he'd placed in me by coming to me in his wolf form. Being so close to him like this, I felt so safe. I wanted to give him a gift in return.

"I want so badly to escape Loamshire," I said, the words falling from my mouth before I even realised it. "I am the anywhere-but-here girl. I've had this intense loathing for the place ever since I was a teen. I got good marks and wore glasses and liked science fiction and anime and gaming, and the other kids ... they were mean. I didn't have many friends.

"The one thing that got me through high school and my dad's death was knowing that by the time I got my A-levels, this town would be eating my dust. I applied for university as soon as the enrolment opened up. I had my scholarship essays all written. All my life, I've wanted to explore ancient ruins and to have adventures and finally, it was going to happen.

"My mother has been in bad shape ever since Dad's death. She was getting better, but when I got my acceptance to Cambridge, she got worse again. She didn't leave her bed for days." Tears stung the corners of my eyes. "I gave up my spot to stay here and look after her. I put all my dreams on hold and went to Loamshire University and tried to make the best of it. And then I met Ben, and he loved to have adventures, and he made friends easily, and he was just so in tune with the world. Being with him ... I felt as though I were getting to live a bit of my own dream, you know?" I shook my head. "You probably don't know. I'm sorry.

"Now, I'm finishing up my degree, but with Ben gone, Mum is getting bad again. She can barely feed herself, and I don't want to think what would happen if I left her in charge of paying the bills. She needs me so badly, and the worst thing is, I resent her. I hate myself for it, because she's my mother, but I don't understand why she can't just get off the sofa and move on with her life. I did it. I'm still doing it. And it's hard, but at least it's not a cop-out. Just because Dad and Ben were robbed of their lives, does that mean I should be robbed of mine, as well?"

Luke tilted his head to the side, and he placed his heavy paw on top of my hand. I smiled, despite the tears.

"Time is ticking for me to accept postgraduate spots. I've been accepted to Yale, Auckland, and Cambridge. All of them are in exciting, far-off places that aren't here, but when I think about telling my mum I'm leaving ... I just can't see it." I sighed.

"I'm going to be in Crookshollow forever, trapped here by the ghosts of the dead."

Luke pressed his nose against my hand and whimpered. That was exactly how I felt when I thought about the stack of acceptance letters burning through my desk at home. His weight pressed against me, warm and reassuring, and my anxiety about the future faded. Calm washed over me. It would work itself out.

I had Luke now. With his strong body and sharp mind on my side, I knew that somehow or other another, I would figure things out.

"Goodnight, Luke." I kissed the soft fur on top his head. He butted my chin with his wet nose, then curled up beside me, a reassuring weight against my side. He rested his chin on his paws, his eyes wide open, trained on the tent flap.

I settled back into the pillows, weariness overcoming me. It had been a long, weird day, and had ended with me running for my life. But with Luke here with me, I couldn't even muster up an ounce of fear.

I am safe.

LUKE STAYED beside me the entire night, his body heat keeping me warmer than any thermal sleeping bag. At some point, I woke up and rolled over, coming up against a warm wall of soft fur. I lay awake, watching his chest rise and fall as he breathed, in awe of the beautiful creature that trusted me so completely.

He'd said he was dangerous in his wolf form, but he was as gentle as a kitten. A giant kitten with razor sharp fangs and claws. I stroked him, my hand sinking into his soft fur. The bite mark he'd left on my neck burned with heat. I couldn't wait until he returned to his human form so we could have another night together.

"Hey Luke," I murmured into his fur. He nuzzled my hand as I reached for my phone to check the time. "It's just on 6am. You should probably get out of here, or one of the others might see you leaving."

He shook his head furiously, and planted a firm paw on my stomach.

I laughed. "I'd like you to stay, too. You have no idea how much. But if Frances sees me bunking off my archaeological duties to hang out with a wolf, we're going to have even more problems on our hands. Not to mention, the film crew hanging out on site."

Luke shook his head again.

"I'll be fine." I promised, pushing his paw off and pulling off the shirt I slept in. I put my arms through my bra and did that up, then pulled my pink thermals over top. "This wolf is hardly going to attack the site in broad daylight, especially now that he knows you're nearby. And I promise I won't go anywhere else without you. I know you won't be far from me if I need you."

Luke stared at me for several moments, then slowly nodded his head.

"Atta boy." I rubbed behind his ears. Luke got to his feet and shook his body down. I admired the toned muscles of his legs, the beautiful shape of his jaw, the powerful slope of his back. Even in wolf form, he was a stunning creature.

I opened the flap, and a gust of cold air blasted my face. Luke stepped outside, his beautiful tail swooshing behind him. I watched as he darted off towards the bushes.

"Luke?" I shoved my head out into the frigid air. He turned his head, those wide green eyes swimming in my vision.

"Be careful."

Luke nodded, and trotted away, his tail disappearing into the dark trees.

It was strange, but even though he hadn't spoken a word to

me, and even though he was a wolf and so we couldn't have sex again, last night had felt even more intimate than the previous one. I felt as though I were seeing a side of Luke he didn't show many people. And I had been able to tell him things I couldn't tell anyone else, things that had been stirring in my mind for a while now, about Mum and postgraduate study and my future. When I slept, I hadn't dreamed of Ben, or Dad. When Luke was with me, I had peace.

I just wished he could stay here on site with me, in person. For all the bravado I'd put on for him, I was afraid of this new wolf and what he might do. I didn't want to run into any more surprises. But I suspected I hadn't seen the last of the new wolf.

12

LUKE

*S*hit.

As I darted around the edge of the camp, behind the caravan where Frances was burning a pan of bacon, the new wolf's scent trail crossed mine. It was fresh. He'd been here recently.

My mouth still tasted metallic, from the other wolf's blood. I hadn't been able to clean away the taste of it. My eyelids drooped as I sniffed out the edges of the trail. I hadn't slept last night, too concerned with guarding Anna from intruders. He would have been hiding upwind, where the rain and wind would have carried away his smell.

I wanted to stick to Anna like a bee to a fucking gorgeous flower, but she was right – she'd be relatively safe with all the other people on site. The film crew had stayed overnight, and he'd hardly attack with them around. Besides, by sticking around, I was running the risk of attacking someone, or being seen. On the other hand, the wolf couldn't have gone that far. I might never have the chance at such a fresh trail again. With one last, lingering look towards Anna's tent, I bounded off into the trees.

I followed the wolf's trail deep into the forest, but lost it about eight kilometres along the ridge. Not because the trail ran cold, but because the track was muddied by another scent trail … a distinctly wolfish trail. There was a third wolf in the area.

I should have gone outside and dealt to the first wolf last night, I cursed myself. Now I had two shifters to deal with, and from the way these trails met up, it looked as though they could be working together. The wolf who'd attacked me had come to this spot, and then followed along the new wolf's trail, which was hours old.

Another wolf.

This thing was getting really dangerous. My father had told me there were other packs who wanted the caves and paintings to remain hidden. The alpha of the Bleddyn pack had wanted to marry my grandmother, but she'd chosen my grandfather instead. If they knew the caves had been discovered and my grandmother's paintings brought to light, they might come here to claim the territory they thought to be rightfully theirs.

And then there would be the wolves who wanted to act on behalf of shifters everywhere, in order to keep the true origin of the paintings a secret. It wouldn't take much digging for an archaeologist or a reporter to uncover the local legends about the caves, and then werewolf stories would appear in every tabloid paper across the country. There were packs who would kill everyone involved to keep that from happening.

Dad, I wish you were here. I slumped down under a tree, feeling defeated. I licked my coat, grooming away some of the mud that had dried there. *I don't know what to do about all this. It's too late now to destroy the paintings. How am I going to hold on to our ancestral home?*

And there was another problem nagging at me. *Anna.* She lit my body and mind on fire in a way I hadn't dared to hope for.

After Dad died, I never dreamed I'd feel happiness again, but when I was with Anna, I felt stronger, more powerful, more in control. The grief didn't sting my veins with quite the same intensity. And she *understood*. She'd been through it all before, twice. She knew better than anyone the pain of losing someone close to you, of how you saw them in everything and heard them in your sleep. Of how you walked through every encounter like a zombie, your mind far away in the world of the dead. Of how you got excited to see them or call them, only to be hit again with the force of the memory.

Anna told me last night about how badly she wanted to leave Crookshollow, to study and work in another country and have the life she'd wanted for so long. More than anything, I wanted her to have that life, because she deserved it. And even if she didn't realise it, I could see the weight of her mother's pain weighing her down, burning out her flame until there was nothing left.

She had to leave, and I had to be the one to convince her to leave. She was too kind to leave her mother of her own accord. But I couldn't leave with her. Not with my family's past on display for the world to see, and certainly not with other wolves sniffing around. This was my family legacy, my heMargaretge. To me, being in this forest was like coming home. But to Anna, it was a prison. How could I be with her when we both wanted different things?

Grief gripped me. I would've talked to my father about Anna. He would have loved her. They could have stayed up for hours talking about books and archaeology together. He would've locked his own bright green eyes on mine, and when I'd finished laying out the issue, he'd give me a practical, no-bullshit plan for what I had to do.

But he wasn't here. And without his plan, I was lost.

You have to make your own plan.

Sighing, I got to my feet, and stepped onto the trail, following the path of my two wolven visitors deeper into the woods.

13

ANNA

*F*rances had all but abandoned our neolithic cave floor. I was almost relieved. The thought of going back to tagging fox bones and stone chips after everything that had happened filled me with dread. Instead, she and Ruth spent most of the day down in the caves, delicate brushes in their hands, clearing away dirt and dust on the paintings, ready for the professional photographer from the university who would be arriving tomorrow. The cave was narrow and wouldn't accommodate more than two people at once, or at least that was how Ruth had gleefully explained it when she ordered me to remain behind in the camp.

Fine by me. Rainclouds rolled over the forest, sending down enough water to restart a biblical flood. Instead of sloshing around in the cold caves, I sat in the caravan, wrapped up in woollen jersey, scarf and gloves, reading Heinlein while sipping my third hot tea of the day.

It was my job to speak to the reporters from the *Daily Post*, who would be arriving sometime that morning. In the meantime, I was enjoying one of the rare periods of downtime on site.

At least, I was trying to enjoy it. I scanned the page before realising not only did I have no idea what I'd just read, but I'd actually been holding the book upside down. Luke's face hovered in my vision. I glanced out the window to the forest. Was he out there somewhere? Was he all right? Had he met that other wolf, and worse yet, what would become of him when he did?

What was it like to date a guy who turned into a wolf and fled into the forest every single month? Was this my destiny, to lie awake at night and wonder if Luke was safe, had he been set upon by another pack, or shot by a hunter, or got his leg caught in a trap? Luke was so beautiful, it was easy to forget he was a wolf, one of the most feared creatures known to humankind.

Is that the life I wanted for myself – to be constantly fearing for Luke's safety, to not know where he was at all times? I'd only just started to claw my way back to the world from the clutches of grief. If I lost Luke … that would undo me.

This is ridiculous. I tossed the book down on the table. *You're acting as though Luke is yours. He's not. You've had one night together, and it was amazing. But now he's running around as a wolf and you haven't even discussed if you're exclusive. For all you know he could be shagging his way through the forest right now …*

Then why do I feel as though we were somehow bound together, that nothing that had happened was any kind of accident? I touched the spot on my neck where he'd bitten me. Clara's words echoed in my mind. Were Luke and I fated to be together? The thought both terrified and excited me.

A sound outside the window startled me out of my thoughts. An enormous SUV skidded along the dirt track into the camp, mud splattering up the doors, smearing across the pristine paint job that had clearly never seen a dirt track in its life. A woman wearing a skin-tight pencil skirt and stiletto heels climbed down from the cab. She frowned as her heel sank into the muddy earth. I leaned out the caravan door and tossed her a pair of spare boots.

Putting her stiletto heels back into the SUV, she shoved the boots onto her stockinged feet and clomped angrily up the caravan steps, her coat over her face to ward off the driving rain.

"This suit is *silk,*" she snapped as she slumped down at the counter, scowling at me as though I controlled the downpour. Her voice buzzed in my head. It sounded familiar, but I couldn't place it. A sheepish looking man in a flannel shirt followed after her, carrying a large camera. *The Daily Post.* I should have guessed.

I made them both coffee while the woman – who introduced herself as Misty – wrung water out of her skirt onto the caravan floor, set up her dictaphone, and bitched about the remoteness of our site. I learned she normally covered arts and lifestyle news, attending gallery openings and catwalk shows and theatre previews. Her life sounded glamorous and exciting.

Misty had been up in Crookshollow reviewing a Ryan Raynard art exhibition when she'd got the call to cover our story as soon as possible, before one of her competitors got the scoop. While I talked her through the discovery and some basic facts about cave paintings, her photographer snapped away in the background. I don't know what interest he had in the card table covered with site notes or the pyramid of empty coffee cans on the filthy kitchen bench, but maybe he was going for some kind of artistic still-life thing.

Misty stared hard at my face. "I recognise you ..." She frowned. "Yes, that's it. You were the girl whose boyfriend died in the forest a few months ago. He fell on some rocks and got busted up real bad. I wrote a piece about it."

A lump formed in my throat. I remembered where I'd heard Misty's voice. She'd hounded me over the phone for three days until I relented and gave her a two-sentence statement, which she'd spun into a full article about my fragile emotional state. I didn't want to talk to any more reporters about Ben, especially not now. "Yeah. That's me. So, anyway, the site is dated to the neolithic period, which is—"

"Why are you here? I mean, surely the forest is full of bad memories for you?"

I shrugged. "Of course. But I can't let Ben's death stop me living my life and doing what I want to do. He would've loved knowing I was out here, digging up the past. But can we please not talk about him anymore?"

"Oh, of *course*. I'm *so* sorry." Misty didn't look that sorry. She suddenly seemed keenly interested in the site and all the minutiae of dig life. She asked me a lot of questions about living in tents and what I ate and how much dirt I had to shift each day. "Is conducting a dig in an ancient cave dangerous?" Misty asked.

"It can be. Caves carry inherent dangers like slips or falling hazards, but these caves are pretty solid. We have a strict site safety protocol, and a local forest ranger oversees us to make sure we're adhering to guidelines. There haven't been any accidents so far."

I knew her paper was famous for tabloid-style stories, so I expected this article would be more about "The Real Indiana Jones" than any kind of actual reporting about the discovery. My stomach twisted in knots when I caught the photographer snapping a picture of me. "I don't want you to use that," I told him.

"Oh, he won't." Misty smiled. "I promise. Shall we go see the site now?"

"Sure." I brightened at the thought of handing them off to Ruth. "Right this way."

At the caves, I left them in Ruth's hands and went back to the camp. Inside the caravan, I poured myself another cup of tea and shoved two slices of bread into the toaster, willing my nerves to unwind. The memory stick Frances had given me yesterday lay on top of the counter.

I'd barely glanced at the photographs yesterday, as I'd been preoccupied with Mum. Now, they started to play on my mind. I had a mission to complete. I hadn't been able to even look at the paintings since I'd discovered them, so keen was Frances to keep me away from her prized discovery. But thanks to Luke, I knew a lot more about the paintings than they did.

As I reached for the stick, I felt eyes boring into my back. I whirled around, expecting to see Misty at the doorway, her silk blouse clinging provocatively to her chest. But there was no one there.

Odd. The gnawing sensation of being watched didn't leave me. *Was it Luke?* I pushed open the door of the caravan and scanned the treeline for a beautiful grey wolf, but couldn't see Luke anywhere. But then, he wasn't supposed to be seen, especially not while the place was crawling with press. Was he nearby, watching me, protecting me? The thought was reassuring.

I sat back down again, feeling much better. From the table, the USB stick stared back at me. It was the key to bringing down Frances and Ruth. And I had made a promise to myself I wasn't going to be sidelined any longer. But still, I didn't reach for it. Was I being vindictive because I was jealous of Ruth's attention? Was this really the archaeologist I wanted to be, ready to publicly take down my colleagues at any cost?

I thought about Luke's connection to the paintings. To him, they were more than pictures on a wall – they told his family history. It occurred to me that if Luke's grandmother had painted the murder of her family, she might have hidden other messages into the paintings – things relating to Luke's family. Wouldn't it be amazing if I could give him some details about his history?

That was a much more noble goal. I grinned. It wouldn't hurt to take a look, for Luke's sake, of course.

I pulled Frances's laptop towards myself, and booted it up. Gingerly, I slid the USB drive into its slot, and navigated to the album. As the bright images filled the frame on the screen, my admiration for Luke's grandmother soared. They were remarkable in their accuracy and their mimicking of ancient art. Even with four years of archaeological training and the knowledge they were fake, I was almost fooled. Only when the carbon dating samples came back from the lab would Frances get any clue the site was only a few decades old. And I had to find a clue before then, otherwise my work would count for naught.

My toast popped. Ignoring it, I opened up the archaeological graphics software, and used the tools to import all the photographs. Next, I used the software's "paste and stitch" tool to line up the images next to each other to create one panoramic view of both walls of the cave. I then bent the image around a convex shape to simulate the walls of the cave. This gave me a three-dimensional mockup of the site.

I grinned as I used the mouse to navigate through my handiwork, zooming in on certain sections. Frances would be impressed. She didn't even know how to attach images to emails, let alone make something like this.

Looking at them in context filled me with awe. The painted section stretched for at least fifteen feet. The drawings covered every inch of the walls and unfurled across the ceiling, and a large section of wall at the end of the frieze had been smoothed clean – a future canvas, waiting to be filled, perhaps?

I used an overlay lens to draw white dotted lines across the images, dividing the paintings into "panels" depicting separate scenes. The scenes were easy to discern, as the same pack of wolves – two adults and three cubs – appeared in most of them. The early scenes were elaborate paintings of life in the forest –

the cubs suckling from their mother. The father wolf chasing down a hare, birds in the trees serenading a sunbathing cub. Then came the scene where the wolves transformed into humans, standing on their hind legs, their human features in various stages of appearance. A moon rose in the distance.

I had to give Luke's grandmother credit, she had done a remarkable job. The paintings were drawn in a style so close to early drawings it would be impossible to tell these from an authentic neolithic frieze. And from what I could see of the pigments used, these appeared authentic, too. The wall would certainly prove a convincing fake to anyone stumbling upon it, which may have been exactly what she'd intended.

The last two scenes drew my attention. They were drawn with haste – the lines crooked – and were clearly unfinished. They used one colour only, the black ochre that came from soot. The wolves were drawn in outline, no colour or details added, as opposed to the other scenes, where they are drawn in hues of grey and brown and red.

Hang on ... what's that?

I leaned closer, examining the image in detail. In it, a crowd of humans waved flaming sticks and long spears. Their mouths were open as though they were shouting. The one at the front wore a long garment that had been coloured in with a black scrawl. A cross hung around his neck. It was a priest, and there was only one family of priests in Crookshollow. Robert Peyton, leading his mob of angry villagers into the forest to destroy the wolves.

They didn't have priests in neolithic England, but I needed something more. His outfit could be argued to be some kind of tribal costume. I continued to squint at the paintings.

Behind the mob – drawn small and squeezed between two of the figures so it was difficult to spot – there was another robed man with a cross at his throat. In his arm, he cradled a child, and in his other hand, he tore off the child's arm, while the babe's mouth hung open in a silent O of shock.

Holy shit.

Luke's grandmother hadn't just drawn a message to try to warn her husband and sons, she'd tried to tell the truth. The baby wasn't killed by a wolf. It was killed by someone in the village, someone wearing a cross.

The baby was murdered by a Peyton.

14

LUKE

I chased the dual scent trail deep into the forest, where it crossed with those of a herd of deer and a hunting dog, and then I lost it completely. By then the scent was hours old, and it had been muddied by other animals and a hunting party and the onslaught of rain.

Dammit. I collapsed under a tree, tucking my paws beneath me and furiously licking the mud from my coat in a vain attempt to hide my frustration. The chase had taken most of the day – the sunlight had all but faded away, blanketing the forest in a grey dusk.

Something else had been bothering me, particularly about the wolf that had attacked Anna last night. He smelled familiar to me, as though I'd encountered him before. But I didn't recognise him. Dad and I had met very few other wolves – that was the whole point of hiding in the Black Forest – and he definitely wasn't one of them; the red streak down his back was distinctive, I'd never have forgotten it. So then where had I seen him before? *Déjà vu* tugged at the corners of my mind, but every time I thought I grasped the recognition, it pulled back, out of my reach.

I needed to start back towards the camp, so I could watch over Anna through the night. That wolf had sensed my mark on her. He knew she was my mate. And that meant he would probably be back to attempt to take her for his own again.

I started back, picking my path through the trees. After a half mile, I came to a small stream. I followed this down the valley, picking up the scent of a path I'd made earlier when I'd been patrolling this area. As I skirted the edge of the stream as it wound its way through the limestone bed, carving out a path through ancient rock, a powerful scent wafted across my nose.

The wolf from last night. He was here.

I scanned the rocks, searching for him. My gaze settled on a tiny crevice between two jagged rocks. Two beady eyes glowed from inside, their gaze locked on mine, filled with menace.

His scent covered the area, smeared across every rock and branch. I'd found where he'd been hiding. I set my paws wide, flattening my back and raising my tail. I pulled my lips back, revealing my teeth. His head emerged from the gloom, the red streak along his back glowing in the dwindling light. He bared his teeth at me, his jaw muscles bulging with rage.

Werewolves communicate telepathically in their wolf form, although usually bared teeth and an aggressive stance would get the point across sufficiently. But this wolf and I had some things to discuss.

"What are you doing here?" I growled.

The wolf didn't reply. Its eyes burned into mine. It growled low in its throat.

"You don't belong here," I tried again. "This is my territory. My mark is all over this part of the forest. Fight me for it if you must, but you'll lose."

"I've come for what's mine." His voice boomed inside my head, the force of his will so strong it almost knocked me backward. I dug my claws into the rock, and stood my ground.

"What do you mean, what's yours? You have no claim here."

"I want the caves," he said. "I saw you bring a crowbar into the caves. You intend to destroy what is mine."

"You've been watching me?" How had I not sensed him? He must've been standing downwind. In all the bad weather we'd been having, it could just be possible to disguise a scent. Maybe he'd smeared his coat with mud to hide himself further.

The wolf didn't offer an explanation. He inclined his head. "I want the girl, too."

"You attacked her. She is my mate. That is an unacceptable insult."

"I didn't intend to hurt her. I was only going to drag her away, but she wasn't having it. She has a real wild spirit. She would make fine cubs."

"She's not yours to mate with. She has already been claimed." My whole body pulsed with anger. *Who did this guy think he was?*

The wolf pulled back its lips into a smirk. "I hardly think I have to worry about you. She will choose the strongest of us as father to her cubs, and that will be me."

"Hardly." He wasn't getting his paws anywhere near Anna, not if I had anything to say about it. "I will challenge you for her if necessary, but you will lose."

He jumped down from the ledge, and paced in a wide circle around me, his back flattened and ears pulled back. "You're getting in my way. This is your only warning. Remember, I know where your mate is, and you cannot be with her all the time."

With that, the wolf turned, and darted into the forest. I bounded after him, diving into the stream and swimming to the other side. The current dragged me downstream, and by the time I crawled up on the opposite bank, the wolf was out of sight. I put my nose to the ground, caught his trail, and bounded after him.

My chest tightened with fear as I realised where he was going. He was heading straight back to the camp.

Anna. I poured on the speed. I had to get to her as soon as possible, before it was too late.

FOR HOURS, I pounded through the forest, my limbs screaming in protest as I drove my body to the brink of exhaustion. Three times I crossed the path of the other wolf, but I wasn't getting any closer to him. He must have some serious speed in order to stay so far ahead of me.

I emerged on the edge of the camp just as the moon rose above the tops of the trees. Lights were on in the caravan, but a quick peek in the window revealed only Frances was still up, poring over images of the cave paintings. I did a circuit of the camp, my nose twitching every time I caught a whiff of the wolf on the breeze. But the wolf himself stayed out of sight.

Anna's tent lay intact, the flap open just enough for me to crawl through. I got down on my front paws and wriggled through the gap, wiping my paws on the fly as best I could.

"... is that you, Luke?" Anna murmured from beneath the layers of blankets. My heart soared to see her there, alive and intact, her brown hair falling over her gorgeous eyes.

In reply, I nuzzled her face with my snout. My legs were shaking from the effort of standing. I gave up trying, and collapsed beside her on the bed.

"You're all wet," she protested, but she made no move to push me away. Instead, she wrapped her arms around me. Even though I was cold and exhausted, her touch gave me a new kind of strength. I nuzzled into her shoulder, breathing the scent of her in deep. Anna was alive, and she was mine. That was all that mattered. No giant red-tinted wolves would change that.

15

ANNA

*H*e's here.

Relief washed over me. I'd gone to bed early, my mind still reeling with what I'd seen in the paintings. But ever since then, I'd been lying in my sleeping bag staring at the ceiling, floating between sleep and waking, my mind wandering to Luke out in the forest all alone, with that other wolf on his tail. I'd imagined him dead, fallen off a rocky ledge like Ben, dashed to pieces upon the jagged rocks below. I'd imagined having to go to the morgue to identify his body, running my fingers over his cold skin, trying to explain to the coroner why my boyfriend had a tail.

And now here he was, soaking wet and panting hard. He looked as though he'd run a marathon to get here. *He came back to me.*

"I'm so glad to see you." I buried my face in his fur, breathing in the rich, earthy scent of him, the pure masculine power of his body. He made no move to shy away, instead placing one of his huge, powerful paws on my back. I pressed my cheek against his ribcage, feeling the rise and fall of his ragged breath.

"Luke ... I discovered something today. I can't believe the

others haven't seen it yet – it so clearly dates the paintings to a more modern era. But I guess when you have BBC documentaries and tenure in your sight, you only see what you want to see."

Up and down, in and out. He rested his snout against my shoulder, letting out a deep, rumbling sigh. I stroked his fur, enjoying the softness drawing through my fingers.

"Your grandmother must have known who really killed that baby. She painted it into the images. It was a priest. He was tearing the child to pieces, making it look as though it had been attacked by a wild animal. It was one of the Peytons. They killed the baby in order to incite the town against your family. It's right there in the painting. Your family was completely innocent."

Luke's weight pressed against me. He made no noise of movement to acknowledge what I'd just told him. I jabbed him in the ribs.

"Luke, did you hear me? Your family is innocent. All the shame your father carried around, all the dishonour the Lowe pack suffered, it was for nothing. And one way or another, I'm going to help you prove it."

Luke's chest rose and fell, rose and fell. From his snout came a loud snore.

I sighed, cradling his huge head in my arm. "Fine. We'll talk about it in the morning. Goodnight, my handsome wolf."

As I drifted off to sleep, I thought I heard a faint voice inside my head, a voice that was not my own. It whispered, "Goodnight, Anna. I love you."

16

LUKE

*D*reams assailed me in technicolour, the frenzied images of past hunts, of running with my dad from park rangers and hunters, of hiding in caves and hollowed-out trees. Always moving, always on the run from something, my father's face always long and sad.

Beep-beep beep-beep.

Something shrill roused me from my dreams. I shook myself awake, glancing around for the source of the noise. Anna's mobile phone. I batted it with my snout in a vain attempt to shut it up. One of the disadvantages of being stuck in my wolf form – no opposable thumbs.

"Urrrgh." Anna rolled over, throwing one arm out and clicking off her phone without even opening her eyes. I felt a flicker of shame at myself. I'd fallen asleep. I was supposed to be guarding Anna, but I'd been so exhausted from the previous night, and all the running ... but Anna was okay. She was still alive. That's all that mattered. I vowed to never let my guard down again.

Anna stroked my cheek. "Hey, Luke."

Her voice sounded husky from sleep. Her eyes fluttered

open, the long lashes sticking together. Her lips pursed into a perfect bow. Goddamn it, I couldn't wait until I was out of my wolf form, and I could throw her on the bed and take her the way I wanted to.

Instead, all I could do was nuzzle her hand and give her my puppy-dog eyes and hope she would go and fetch me some bacon from the kitchen.

Anna leaned forward and tugged off her sleeping shirt, leaving her naked breasts on display. I growled low in my throat as the sight of those glorious orbs sent a wave of desire through me. *Soon, soon.* It wasn't much longer before Anna and I could resume our relationship where we'd left off – naked and tangled up in each other's limbs.

I placed my paw on her thigh. Her skin felt so smooth and supple.

"Luke, you have to go." Anna clasped her bra behind her back, and pulled her pink thermals over the top. "Frances and the others will be awake soon. You know they can't see a wolf hanging around the camp."

I nodded my head. She was right, of course. The idea of leaving her wrenched at my chest, but today I wouldn't go off in search of the wolf. I'd be staying as close to the caves as I could, watching and waiting. That wolf was nearby and I wouldn't let him come near her again.

"Go, go, go." Anna shoved me out the tent door. I took one look across the camp, scanning the trees for movement. I sniffed the air. He'd come close, last night, within a few metres of the tent. But my presence must've held him back. Once again, I mentally flayed myself for falling asleep. The flap on Frances's tent moved. I dared one last, long look back at Anna, her beautiful face drawn with concern.

She kissed the top of my head. "I'm fine. Now *go.*"

I darted into the trees just as Frances emerged from her tent and stumbled in the vague direction of coffee. I guessed by the fact she wasn't screaming in terror that she hadn't seen me.

As soon as I saw Anna arrive successfully in the caravan, I ran up along the ridge, following the night's trail left by my wolf visitor. I didn't want to go too far from the camp, but I needed to have some idea where he'd gone.

After a couple of miles I traced him back to the stream, and a small cave in the rocks. His path didn't lead away again, so he must still be inside. I didn't follow him into the cave, not wanting another confrontation just yet. His scent drenched the rocks and trees – I'd found his lair.

There was no sense in hanging around there. I followed the rocky seam back through the forest, towards my family cave. When I reached a rocky outcrop overlooking the cave entrance where another film crew had gathered, I sat down and folded my paws in front of me. I tried to shift back into my human form, but I couldn't. The moon was still full.

NASA defines the full moon as lasting only a few moments, when the earth is directly, mathematically in between the sun and the moon. However, I was a werewolf, which meant that technicalities didn't apply.

I watched the camera crew set up their equipment. Frances dashed back and forth, helping the men carry their heavy lights down into the cave. Ruth sat on one of the rocks, balancing an umbrella awkwardly in the crook of her arm while she tried to touch up her makeup in a compact with the other. I followed Anna as she weaved through them all, answering questions, handing out trowels to use as props, and genuinely being her usual accommodating, gorgeous self.

A smell wafted across my nose, sharp and pungent, it carried the distinct aroma of wolf. But it wasn't the same wolf as yesterday. This was the second wolf, the one whose path both and the red wolf and I had followed yesterday. He was here.

Shit.

I leapt to my feet, every sense on high alert. I shoved my nose in the air, trying to figure out where he was. The stench of him told me he was close, probably right up on me, but I couldn't see him hiding among the rocks. *How had he got so close without me sensing him earlier? It didn't make any sense—*

I heard the sound before I felt the hit. A sharp intake of breath. The crunch of a paw against the rock. And then something hard slammed into my body, and I tumbled through the air. I scrambled for purchase, but found nothing except fur and teeth.

We bounced down the rock face, claws digging into each other. My back cracked against the rocks. I rolled and slammed hard on my shoulder. Pain shot through my body. My grip loosened. The wolf dug its claws into my back.

For the first time, I got a good look at him. His fur was dark, an almost black stripe across his thick back, fading around to a dull grey over his enormous belly. His long face peered down at me, eyes so dark they were practically black bore into mine with a look of cold, calculating evil. This wolf didn't just want to fight me over territory, he wanted to grind my bones between his teeth.

"You were warned to stay away." The wolf hissed inside my head as he flipped me over and slammed my body against the jagged rocks. My body screamed. Red welts flew across my vision. "You should have listened. More will die if you don't listen."

More will die.

Panic rose in my chest as the wolf's claws circled my neck, and he slammed my head down on the rocks. My brain bounced inside my skull, which now throbbed with a terrifying urgency. *Who was this guy? What did he mean by, "More will die"? Has he killed someone? Is Anna okay? And when had he warned me? Does he mean the warning the other wolf gave me? Were they working together? Was the other wolf nearby?*

With two of them on me, I'd be a goner. I had to make a move. I drew up all my remaining strength and threw all of it into leaping up. The wolf yelped in surprise as he tumbled off my back. Ignoring the pounding in my skull, I pounced, knocking his back against the rocks. I snapped my jaws in his face. He snapped right back. I ducked away from his gnashing teeth, swiping my claws across his cheek. He howled with rage and lunged for me. I leapt back, releasing my claws from his fur. His claws tore chunks of fur from my shoulders as they were wrenched free, but at least I was no longer in danger of a bite.

I couldn't take this guy. He was more than half again my size, and he was angry as fuck. I needed to get away. But how could I lose him?

I leapt down the rocks, landing on all fours. The impact shuddered through my legs, but I had no time to recover. I made a run for it, plummeting down the rocky ledge into the trees. *Get to the stream. He can't follow me in the stream.*

My feet pounded against the dirt. This was the second time in as many days I'd found myself running from a wolf. This was not ideal. I much preferred biting to running.

Behind me, trees rustled, paws slammed into the wet earth. A voice in my head screamed. "You cannot escape me, Lowe!"

The stream loomed ahead, the banks swelling from the recent rain. I sucked in my breath and plunged in. Freezing water rushed over me. The open wounds on my shoulder stung, and my head throbbed in the sudden cold. I paddled along with the current, allowing it to drag me downstream as quickly as it could take me.

I glanced over my shoulder, but the water threw me around so much I couldn't focus on the shore behind me. I couldn't see where the big black wolf had got to. I couldn't smell him, either. All I could see, taste and hear was the rushing, churning water.

The icy water stabbed at me like thousands of tiny needles. I bumped my way through jagged rocks and over frothing rapids, plunging underwater and spinning wildly as I fought to gain control. I still couldn't see the wolf anywhere, and his voice had gone from my mind. I couldn't smell anything but water and fish.

Only when the pain became unbearable did I decide to leave the safety of the water. I dragged myself up onto the bank, allowing myself only a moment to catch my breath and shake off as much of the frigid water as I could, before plunging into the forest again.

As I ran, I sniffed the air, but my senses had grown dull. I couldn't make out the trails of animals that had scurried across the forest floor, nor smell the whiff of fresh carrion from a recent predator kill. Colours grew brighter, more luminous. That could only mean one thing.

My front legs cracked and buckled, and I plunged face-first into the dirt. I tried to get up, but my knees bent back on themselves, and I fell back into the mud. My paws sought for purchase, and as I tried to grip the nearest tree, my claws shrunk back and my toes grew out, becoming hands once more. My pelt retreated back into my skin, and the wildness in my veins dimmed, fading to a dull roar.

The full moon was over. I was no longer stuck as a wolf. Now I was a naked man in the middle of the forest, miles from my mate, with no weapon, map or compass, and at least two very angry wolves on my trail.

Great.

I squinted up at the sky, hunting for a peek of the sun through the thick trees and cloud. I estimated the time based on its height and the amount of time since I'd left Anna's tent as around 9:30am. I walked over the map of this area of the forest in my head, locating the road I'd parked on in relation to the river. With a vague direction in mind, I shifted back into my wolf form, and started to trot.

Weariness seeped into my veins. I'd barely slept in two days, and all the worry over Anna's safety had fried my brain to mush.

I hit the road an hour later, and dashed along through the trees, my eyes darting everywhere, imagining I saw a wolf lurking behind every trunk or nestled in the crook of each low-hanging branch. After a few miles, I could just make out the outline of my jeep, parked at the end of the dirt road. It was still there. I transformed back into my human form. My bare feet stung as they slapped against the freezing mud. I looked forward to the fresh clothing I'd stored in the back. And the chance to sit down.

I slowed to a walk and circled around the edge of the clearing, sniffing every trunk for a sign of the wolves. I caught the faintest whiff of the red wolf, but the scent was either old or far away. I was safe, for now.

I stepped out of the trees, and made my way towards the vehicle. I'd barely gone two steps when the scent hit me full on.

Werewolf.

My blood turned cold. One of them – the red wolf – was coming straight towards me through the trees. Branches snapped. Leaves rustled. The deep growls of a hungry, angry wolf rumbled through my body. I couldn't see him, but I could hear him, smell him. He'd be on me in a moment. And I was in the open, in my human form, with no weapon – completely vulnerable.

In the split second I had to make a decision, I opted not to change into my wolf form. I was exhausted after my run-in with the black wolf, and I doubted I'd win in a fight. Instead, I went for the crowbar I kept in the truck. I dived for the wheel arch of the jeep, my hands fumbling for the keys I'd hidden underneath. I grabbed at the hook I hung them on, but they weren't there.

"Looking for these?" a deep voice said.

I whirled around. A man stood at the edge of the clearing, holding up my keys. Unlike me, he was already dressed, in dark jeans and a canvas work shirt, the buttons only done up halfway, revealing a muscular chest covered with tattoos. Long red hair hung over his penetrating brown eyes. It was the red wolf, all right. He smirked at me, and tossed my keys up into the air, catching them in his fist.

"Go on," he said, still dangling the keys from his fingers. "I won't stop you."

I growled, tossing up whether I should change back into my wolf form and attack him. It was sorely tempting, but I needed to find out more about him. And the only way to do that would be to somehow get him talking. I prepared myself, ready to shift in a moment if he advanced on me. "What do you want?"

He took a step forward, entering the clearing. He raised his head and sniffed the air, his nose wrinkling. "Your mate has stood here," he said. "I can smell her scent all over these trees."

"She hasn't been here," I said. But when I inhaled, I could sense her, too.

"Oh, really?" He smirked. "You didn't take her here in that dump truck of yours, a little wilderness adventure?"

Perhaps it was her scent on my own body. But that should have washed off in the river. *Has he done something to her?* The black wolf's words echoed through me. *More will die.*

"If you've done anything to hurt Anna—"

"Relax." He held up a hand in mock surrender. "I haven't touched her. Yet."

"Stay away from her," I warned. I kept my eyes glued on him, but I shuffled along the side of the truck, inching towards the cab. I had a hunting knife in the driver's side door. If he pulled anything, I could smash the window and grab it.

"No can do, I'm afraid, Luke. She's an important part of my plan."

"What do you want? How do you know my name?"

"I've been watching you ever since you arrived. I know your first name, your shoe size, and more about you than you think. And as for what I want, I've already told you. These caves belong to my family. I'm here to take back the territory that is mine, and that includes the girl. If that means I have to fight you, then so be it."

My blood boiled. Who did this guy think he was? *"My* family has claim over this place. So you can just take your little wolf arse back to whatever backwater jungle you crawled out of and go back to cuddling monkeys or whatever it is you do with your time."

The wolf puffed out his chest, his eyes flashing with anger. "Be careful with words you cannot take back. My name is Caleb Lowe. I'm the son of Amos Lowe. My father died protecting these caves. By rights, they belong to me."

I stared at the man in disbelief. "You mean to tell me, we're … cousins?"

"We are?" That stopped him short.

I pointed to my chest. "Luke Lowe, son of Walter Lowe. I thought I was the only surviving member of the Lowe pack."

"This doesn't make sense." The wolf rubbed his forehead, his eyes narrowed. *"I'm* the only surviving Lowe."

"I'm as surprised as you are." I gestured to the door of the car. "Can I put some pants on?"

"And have you pull some weapon on me? Not going to happen, Luke. What you need to do is explain how it is that your father came to not be dead, and how you found the caves."

"I take it you know what happened at the caves all those years ago, with the villagers—"

"—and the fire and brimstone and torches and pitchforks." Caleb made a stabbing motion with his fist. "I know. My mother told me the whole story. What she didn't tell me about was you."

"Your mother? But how—"

"We'll get to me. You first, little cousin."

I bristled at the insult, but decided it best not to challenge Caleb while I was ... tackle out. "Fine. My—I should say, *our* grandmother saw the villagers coming. She was a powerful psychic. At the time she had her vision, she was sleeping in the cave with my father. Our grandfather had taken the two older cubs out to hunt, but my father wasn't yet old enough to join them. When the vision overcame her, grandmother wrote a warning into the painting on the cave wall, in the hopes the others – who were still not back from their hunt – might see it upon their return and join them in hiding. She then ran into the forest with my father, covered them both in mud and leaves to mask their scent, and they hid in the trunk of a rotting oak. The villagers came, found the caves empty, and started searching the woods, creating all kinds of noise that drew my grandfather back. He couldn't sense his wife or son anywhere nearby. Assuming the villages had already killed them, he set upon them with my brothers, and their rage cost three human lives before the villagers managed to overpower the wolves."

"Shit," Caleb cursed. "How do you know all this?"

"My father told me. He said the scene from that day was permanently etched into his mind. His mother saw it too, and she became distraught. She fled their hiding place and went to confront the mob. They were shocked to see her – a human woman – risking her life to help her wolf husband, but their shock turned to fear and anger as they realised she complicit in the death of this innocent child. In their fury, the villagers killer her, too. My father watched from his hiding place as they stove her head in. But they didn't find him. He was the only survivor."

"I never knew he survived," Caleb growled. "If I had, I would have found you much earlier."

"Why, so you could beat me up and steal all my toys?"

Caleb snorted. "We're family. Together we could have re-established our pack."

"I'm not establishing anything except who you are and how you're related to me. And who's the black wolf with you? Is he related to me, also? Why is he warning me that more people will die?"

At the mention of the black wolf, Caleb's body stiffened. "He's definitely not with me, and he's definitely dangerous. He's attacked me once, and I barely escaped with my life." He pointed to an angry gash along the side of his torso. "If he says he's killed ... I believe it. The black wolf wants to claim the caves, too. He has powers I didn't even know were possible. Somehow, he can mask his scent for short distances. The other day I tracked him for several miles across the forest, but he evaded me in the end. The track was a dud. I think he'd planted it to try and lure me away. And you too, since you followed me." Caleb frowned.

"So then what's your story? Are you some kind of immaculate conception?"

"Nothing as dramatic is that, cousin. My mother was already with child when Robert Peyton led the villagers to the caves. Amos was preparing to leave the family pack in order to establish a pack of his own with my mother. If he'd been able to do that, the Lowe name would have lived on. But he never got that chance. When my mother Maria heard what had happened in the forest, she packed up a little food and warm clothing and ran away to Scotland, where no one knew the name of Lowe or the curse that followed us. I was born in Aberdeen, and my mother married the alpha there and had two more sons. He has never accepted me as his own, favouring his own children within the pack. I hated it there. I was sixteen when I left the pack and lived wild." Caleb glanced around him at the trees, and my beaten-up truck. "I see we have that in common, Ranger Luke."

"Indeed." I wanted to believe this guy. If what he said was true, it meant I had family – a cousin, an aunt. It was a tenuous connection to the past, to the kind of life my father had always wanted but could never hope to attain. But every fibre of my body screamed *danger.* I couldn't afford to trust Caleb, not with Anna in the picture.

"Maria made sure to tell me of my history, my birthright. I've visited these caves several times over the years, but I knew I needed a mate before I came back to establish my pack. No one else seemed to want Crookshollow, so I let it be. But when I saw the archaeological excavation in the paper, I came here as fast as I could. I intended to stop the team digging up all that shit about our family again. And luckily, a perfectly serviceable mate happened to be right here. It couldn't be more perfect."

"We are *cousins,* Caleb." I gritted my teeth. "We both have an equal right to this place. And Anna has already been claimed, by me."

Caleb gave me a sad grin. "It's a pleasure to meet you, Luke. It's nice to know that I have some family left in the world. But I'm still going to have to ask you to step aside. As the son of the elder brother, I am the alpha here."

I laughed. "You can't be serious."

"Oh, but I am. I want this territory. My whole life I've wanted to establish a new Lowe pack, my own pack, as a fitting legacy for my father. And it has to be here, to reclaim the territories lost. With few wolves left in England, I'm sure to quickly dominate this region, maybe one day even challenge the Scottish pack. And with a strong mate like Anna by my side—"

"Excuse me." His words made my skin crawl. "You want *my* mate? That's not the way this works, and you know it. Anna is mine. You cannot simply take her."

"Of course I know the way it works. Each of us has one mate who is ours alone, whose DNA is compatible and whose companionship completes us. But that doesn't mean she can't be of use in my pack. Wolves have shared mates for many centuries, when the needs of the pack required it. Anna is a powerful vessel, and she will make strong cubs. I have searching the length of this country and have not found my own mate, nor another girl as suitable as her. So I *will* have her. If you wish to keep her as well, then you may join my pack as the beta. Together, we will be stronger. But if you do not give her to me, I will fight you for her. And I will win."

"Excuse me." Anna's voice cut through our conversation. "It's rude to talk about people behind their backs."

I whirled around. Anna stepped out from behind a tree, coming to stand in the middle of the clearing, directly between Caleb and me. She stared at us both defiantly.

"You're alive!" My heart soared. I took a step towards her. She held up her hand.

"Of course I am."

"How did you get here?" I demanded, taking another step. Anna shot me a furious look.

"Don't come any closer just yet. I'm not sure I want either of you anywhere near me. As for how I got here, I followed Luke's tire tracks in the road. There aren't that many paths in this part of the forest. It was easy enough to find." Anna jabbed her thumb over her shoulder. "I'm parked a hundred metres down the road there. You two are so busy pissing at each other, you didn't even hear me pull up."

"You came all this way just to tell me you want me, princess." Caleb smirked. "I'm very humbled."

"Talk to Anna like that again, and I'll wipe that smirk off your face," I warned.

"Stop it, both of you!" Anna yelled. I winced as her voice echoed through the trees. "There are more important things we need to discuss."

"Is that why you're here? Did something happen?" The black wolf's warning pulsed in my mind. *More will die. More will die ...*

"I read in the paper that the full moon was officially over, and Frances didn't need me on site, so I came here to surprise you with what I discovered. Only I'm the one who got the surprise."

"Anna, I—"

"I don't even want to hear it. This whole conversation has been disgusting. I'm not just some breeding factory you can trade like businessmen arguing over stock options. I have my own needs and desires." Anna glared at me with such venom, the hair on my neck stood on end. I could feel my cock shrink back up into my body. She turned her gaze to Caleb. "You've just discovered you have a real living relative, and the first thing you do is challenge him to a fight? Hardly the protective, family-first alpha I'd expect."

Caleb started to say something, but Anna held up her hand for silence.

"I'm not anybody's mate to be traded," she said firmly. "Let's clear that up right now. And that goes for *both* of you." She glared at me. Shame burned my face. "I haven't agreed to be anybody's mate, despite what may have happened in the heat of the moment. Now, can you two stop this ridiculous macho competitive thing for a minute. We need to work together."

"Who put you in charge?" Caleb sneered at her. I knew that

he did not intend to stop, not at all. "And why do we have to work together?"

"I put myself in charge, because I'm clearly the only one mature enough to handle the responsibility. And we're working together because I've discovered something about your family, from the paintings your grandmother left behind in the cave. A wolf didn't kill that child. It was a priest, and my suspicions is, it was one of the men in the Peyton family."

"You mean, the Lowe were innocent all along?" I demanded. I couldn't believe it. My mind whirled with emotions. My family was innocent of the crime. My father had carried the guilt of his family shame for nothing. He had suffered greatly, wondering which of his brothers had attacked the child. He'd gone to his grave believing his family carried a dark secret. But it wasn't true, and I could never tell him that. A lump rose in my throat, but I pushed it back down. My veins hummed with anger, with a wild sense of injustice.

All that guilt my father had carried around for so many years. The shame of bearing the Lowe name ... it had all been for nothing.

Anna nodded. "I told you this last night, but from your expression, I realise you'd fallen asleep."

"This is true?" Caleb demanded. "You're not making this up?"

"I'm an archaeologist, not a storyteller. I'm sure I'm right, I just need to try and prove it."

"Why?" Caleb's eyes narrowed. "What's in it for you?"

"You mean besides helping you two clear your family name?" Anna looked at him, and then to me, her face confused for a moment. "I realise you wolves aren't inclined to believe that humans can have altruistic motives. But there is something—" she paused.

"A-hah," Caleb stepped forward. "I knew there was a but."

"Those paintings aren't tens of thousands of years old, like my professor and her dippy graduate think. And I intend to prove it, without revealing your secret to the world. But in order to do that, I need to figure out exactly what's going on. Now," Anna walked over to Caleb and held out her hand. "Keys."

"Don't you touch her," I growled. Caleb shook me a filthy look, but he dropped my keys into Anna's hand. She walked over to me.

"Much as I like you like this," she said grinning, running her hand over my bare shoulder, "it's time to get dressed."

"I love it when you get bossy," I growled. I pressed my mouth to hers, pulling her body against mine. My cock stiffened as she kissed me back, her hands gripping my shoulders. As her tongue slid over mine, all my desire for her welled up inside of me. It had been two long, agonizing days without her skin next to mine. I needed to remedy that, as soon as possible.

I spun Anna around, pressing her back against the side of my truck. My hands skimmed her body, rubbing her stiffening nipples through the thick fabric of her shirt and thermal vest. I gripped the bottom of her shirt, preparing to tear her clothes off and take her right there—

"Luke, no," Anna protested, her hands clamping down over mine. "As much as I want this, we can't do it here."

"Why not?"

"For one thing, I might be very tempted to join in." Caleb piped up from behind me. My body shook with fury. Why couldn't he just go away?

"And we have a little trip to make." Anna held up the keys. I took them from her and unlocked the door, hunting around the back seat until I found my clothes and boots. I pulled on my jeans, stuffing my very insistent cock down the waistband. Anna patted my arm.

"Later tonight," she said, her smile inviting. "Maybe."

"I don't know if I'll last that long," I growled back.

"I'll make it worth your while." Anna's touch lingered on my arm. The familiar sparks of our connection fired off between us.

"You two make me sick." Caleb grabbed the passenger side door, and climbed in. "Where are we going?"

"The two of you are going back to the site, to guard the cave against any other wolves who might show up there." Anna slid out from under my arm and stalked off towards the road. "I am heading into Crookshollow. I have some research to do."

17

ANNA

"*A*nna—" Luke rapped on my car window. I knew he'd followed me back to the Mini, but I was too pissed off to turn around and look at him. Pissed off at him, yes, but also pissed off at myself. I couldn't believe how I'd acted before, falling into Luke's arms as soon as he touched me. I wasn't supposed to do that. I was supposed to yell at him until he understood that he couldn't treat me like some chattel. But one look into his green eyes and I melted like an ice cream in the Brighton sun. Embarrassed, I stared down at my jeans and turned the key again. *Damn car picked a fine time not to start.*

"Anna!" Luke growled. "Open this door so we can talk."

"Not now." I kept my head down. I didn't want him to see how red my face was. "Take Caleb back to the camp."

"And just parade him around in front of everyone? What do I tell Frances?"

"Tell her he's your long-lost werewolf cousin who tried to kill you last night and wants me to shag him even though I've never met him. I don't know, Luke. Make something up."

"I'm not leaving you. There's another wolf out there. He says he's already killed—"

Another wolf. This just kept getting better. I gripped the wheel. "That's not my problem. I'm not in the mood to be near you right now."

"You're mad."

"Damn right." The engine turned over once, but puttered out again. I ground my teeth together. *This is ridiculous.*

"Because Caleb and I were fighting over you?"

I nodded furiously, still avoiding looking at him. Actually, it had been kind of flattering. I'd never had two guys that hot both wanting to sleep with me before. But that didn't make what he'd been doing right. "And because you were standing there talking about my life, my future, as though I didn't matter."

"But you were flirting before." He sounded dejected. *Good.*

"You were naked. And your cousin was there. It wasn't appropriate for me to express just how angry I am."

"What we did in front of him wasn't very *appropriate,* either. You're very confusing."

"Haven't you ever been with a woman before?" I turned the key again. The Mini spluttered to life.

"Can't we just talk?"

"Nope." I backed away, my head over my shoulder. I yanked the wheel hard around. Luke leapt back as the Mini bumped over the rutted road, veering dangerously close to the wide ditch. At the last second it righted itself, and I clattered off in the direction of Crookshollow, Luke's forlorn face haunting me from the rearview mirror.

Fuck him for acting like a caveman. I couldn't believe the way they were carrying on, fighting over me like I was the last piece of steak on the BBQ. I figured the best way to solve their issue was to make them work together to guard their family legacy. Plus, it would be good to get some distance from Luke, now that he was a human again. My body still pulsed with desire for him. I wanted nothing more than to turn the car around and go back to him, beg him to take me hard across the bonnet. But then I'd just be telling him that acting like that was completely okay, and it wasn't.

I was only just starting to gain control of my life after Dad and Ben. I wouldn't let anyone take that away from me. Not even Luke. Not even if I secretly, deep down, desperately wanted to be his mate.

I tried to force Luke out of my mind. I replaced his gorgeous face with Ruth's stuck-up smirk. I drove back towards Crookshollow village, drumming my fingers on the steering wheel and imagining the look on her face when I revealed that the paintings weren't neolithic.

As soon as I exited the canopy of the forest and my phone beeped to inform me I had reception again, I pulled over and texted Derek. He texted back immediately, inviting me to come on over.

For once, the weather was worse in Crookshollow village than it was in the forest. Rain pounded down in sheets. There was hardly anyone on the road, and the high street was practically deserted, many of the shops shut up for the day. I pulled into a car park in front of Derek's flat, yanked my hood over my head, and ran for the door.

"Anna!" He embraced me, his muscles straining. Derek was a total fitness addict. He was always at the gym or going for a run or participating in one of those bootcamps where you swung on ropes like Tarzan. That meant his hugs could be quite intense.

"Derek ... I can't breathe." I flailed my arms uselessly as he squeezed the air from my lungs.

Derek released me. "You smell awful," he said, grinning as he ran his fingers through his short, wavy black hair.

"I really wish everyone would stop pointing that out."

"It's hard to miss. Do you want a shower?"

I flopped down on his overstuffed sofa, glancing up at the

giant print of Zeus in his war chariot that hung over Derek's bookcase. Derek's whole flat was covered with prints of famous mythological figures and celestial bodies. Mine was covered with postcards and magazine cutouts of places I wanted to travel to, ruins I wanted to explore. We were quite similar, in many ways. I guess it wasn't a big surprise that he'd liked me. "No thanks. I'll do it back at my flat. I will take a cup of tea, though."

"Or a glass of wine?"

"What about both?"

Derek laughed, and headed for the kitchen. I heard the kettle start to boil and the clink of wine glasses.

I stretched out on the sofa and kicked my shoes off, the way I'd always done when visiting Derek's cramped bachelor flat. Living with three other guys, no one would ever notice the stench wafting from my thick wool socks. "I just wondered if you could help me with some research?"

"Sure thing," Derek called back. "Is this about the cave paintings?"

"How do you know about those?"

"They've been all over the news. It's quite an exciting discovery. I bet Ruth must be thrilled."

"Ruth?"

"You know, being the first person to discover the paintings." Derek cleared a space on the table and set down a steaming cup of tea and a wine glass filled to the brim. "I bet she'll get her name in all kinds of archaeology textbooks now."

"I was the one who found them!" I screamed, beating my head against Derek's sofa in frustration. Derek laughed, and pushed the glass of wine towards me.

"I can see you need this more than you need the tea. Not that you're bitter or anything." He slumped down next to me, placing his arm casually around my shoulders. "All I can say is, welcome to the world of academia. But don't worry, you got your name in at least one article."

"Huh?"

"Check the front page of the *Daily Post* website."

A terrible sinking feeling grew in my stomach as I clicked on my phone and navigated to the tabloid website.

WIDOW OF DEAD HIKER KEEPING HIS RECKLESS LEGACY ALIVE

Article by Misty Sharpe

Anna Sinclair, 22, girlfriend of hiker Ben Brownstone who died horrifically when he fell down a waterfall in Crookshollow Forest five months ago, hasn't wasted any time getting back into the devil-may-care lifestyle. We interviewed Sinclair from a remote site in that same forest, where she is working with a team on a dangerous treasure-hunting expedition in a cave. When asked if the caves were dangerous, Sinclair exclaimed excitedly that there were slips and falling hazards, and expressed her regret that an onsite forest ranger was making them adhere to safety guidelines.

Adrenaline-junkie Sinclair took us down to view the recently-uncovered cave paintings, despite the fact neither this reporter, nor her photographer were wearing appropriate shoes. She dismissed our concerns about the safety of the caves, saying she wouldn't let a little thing like the death of her boyfriend stop her living her life. She then asked us not to print that particular statement ...

No. My throat closed over. *This can't be happening.*

I scanned the rest of the article, horrified that they had turned what was supposed to be a report about the find into a piece about how I was dishonouring Ben's memory by committing the same foolhardy mistakes as he had.

"I can't believe it." I slammed my phone down on the table. "They twisted around everything I said. And some of it they just plain made up!"

"It's the *Daily Post,* what do you expect?"

"My professors are going to read it. I'll never be allowed on another archaeological site again." I buried my face in my hands.

"It'll be fine." Derek squeezed my arm. His tone was reassuring, kind, the way he'd been with me through the whole time I was dealing with Ben's death. "Forget that article. It will be wrapped around people's fish and chips by tomorrow. Now, what did you want my help with? Archaeologists and mythology students don't usually have joint interests."

"I want to know about werewolves. Specifically, werewolf myths associated with England."

"Any particular reason?"

"I believe the cave paintings aren't as old as Frances and Ruth believe they are. I just need to prove it academically, without having to fork out my entire year's scholarship for the carbon dating lab fee. One of the friezes depicts a man transforming into a wolf, and there is a lot of other wolf imagery. I need to look at some other examples of this type of imagery and mythology and put forward a case for the actual period the paintings are dated to."

"So, basically, a contextual art thesis?"

I nodded. "It might work with the clothing, or a particular type of flora and fauna shown, but I thought the mythology was a good place to begin. I need to build a really solid case to take down Ruth."

"I'm happy to help." Derek went to his bookshelf and started pulling out books, setting aside a small stack. "These will do for a start. I believe I've even got a book on animal depictions throughout British prehistoric artwork ... ah, here it is." He dumped a heavy volume on my lap.

"Thanks, Derek." I fingered the gilded edges of the book. It looked old and expensive and important. "Are you sure you don't mind me borrowing these? You don't need them for an essay or anything?"

"They're all yours. But, you know, the easiest thing would be if you just took me up to look at the paintings."

"I don't know ... Frances has a pretty tight grip on access. I don't know if she'd let you on there unless you had a BBC camera strapped to your back or a *Time Team* trowel in your hand."

"Come on, Anna. I could totally help you expedite this process."

"Okay, sure. I'll bring you some photographs next time."

"I mean the real thing." Derek gave me an intense gaze. "Take me to see the paintings."

I stopped short. "Oh. I don't know ..."

"Come on, Anna. What harm can it do? I've visited you on sites before. I'm not exactly going to fall into a pit of scorpions."

Was that a good idea, with all the craziness out on site right now? Luke's face flashed into my mind. He'd said something today about another wolf, a wolf who had killed. I knew Luke would be pissed off if I brought Derek to the site, knowing the black wolf was watching us. But Derek knew a lot more about this kind of stuff than I did, and he might be able to point out some more features of the paintings we hadn't noticed. It definitely didn't hurt to try.

Luke will just have to deal. He's not running this show. I am.

I flipped open my phone and checked the list of call times for various news outlets Frances had given me. "Why don't you drive out tomorrow, around nine am? We've got a film crew arriving about ten, so that should give you plenty of time to look at the paintings before they start swinging around their lights. Bring a camera and a notebook and brush your hair. I'll tell Frances you're from *National Geographic* and we won't have a problem."

"I'll be there. This is exciting!" Derek clinked glasses with me. I slugged back my wine, and chased it down with the lukewarm tea. We caught up on all the university gossip for another hour or so, until my pores started to sweat from all the dirt lodged inside them. Time for a shower.

TWENTY MINUTES later I was at Mum's flat, rapping on the door. "It's me, Anna," I called out, a lump of panic rising in my throat as I banged on the door and no one answered. "Let me in!"

Had she slipped in the shower? Was she lying at the bottom of the stairs? Had she forgotten to eat for three days straight and died of starvation? This was all my fault for leaving her—

After five minutes of non-stop banging, our neighbour Mrs. Barnaby yelled out the window for me to stop the racket. "She's not home," she snapped. "I saw her leave about an hour ago, with that young friend of hers."

"Cynthia?"

In reply, Mrs. Barnaby tossed my mother's spare key at me, and slammed the door in my face.

That was a relief. I unlocked the door. The place looked a little cleaner than I remembered. There was a bit of food in the fridge, and the scrapbook wasn't lying open on the sofa. I smiled when I noticed Cynthia's handbag sitting on the kitchen counter, my new tarot deck peeking out from the side pocket. *That Cynthia. She may believe in tarot cards, but if she's finally got Mum to come around again, she's my favourite person.*

With Mum's whereabouts still unaccounted for, I decided it

was time for that shower. I shoved my clothes into the laundry and climbed into the shower, letting the hot water soak away my fears from the day.

I was still angry with Luke over the way he'd spoken about me with Caleb, but now that I had some distance from the forest, I wondered if I might have overreacted, just a tiny bit. I was concerned about how attached I'd got to him so quickly, and like my mum retreating from reality in order to protect herself from more pain, I was looking for any excuse to retreat from Luke, because in my head I was worried that he'd be killed, and I'd have to live with the grief of losing another man in my life.

And he said there is another wolf, a wolf who has killed ...

This was stupid. I couldn't live my life being afraid of death all the time. The way my body had reacted when Luke touched me ... that was what I needed. That was the reality I should be grounding myself in. Ben had been fond of saying, "Life's too short." That's why he spent so much time hiking and rock climbing and not doing his schoolwork. Ben didn't even own a mobile phone. He thought life was too short to spend it staring at a screen.

Well, maybe life *was* too short for me to give up on Luke. I'd been lucky to have loved Ben, but he was gone now. And Luke ... he was very definitely *not* gone. He made my body feel like no one else, and he made me want to be bold and bright and adventurous. I hadn't felt that way in a long time.

This is all so complicated. I wish someone could just tell me what to do. But that was the old Anna talking, the one who accommodated everyone else's needs at the expense of herself. The one who didn't go to Cambridge and who swapped her field school at a Sicilian villa for the damp, miserable Crookshollow Forest. I wasn't sure I was that girl anymore.

I stepped out of the shower, wrapped myself in a towel, and crossed the hall to my bedroom to find some clean clothes. I was rooting through my drawers for some underwear when I felt a strong finger slide along the side of my neck.

"I love a girl who's wet for me," a husky voice whispered against my ear.

I jumped a mile in the air, my heart jackhammering against my chest. My towel slipped down my torso. I spun around. "Luke!"

"Anna." His fingers traced the line of my collarbone, the touch turning my fear to passion.

"Don't scare me like that," I scolded him. "I'm really not in the mood."

"Your nipples say otherwise." Luke touched a finger to my breast, my nipple hardening under his caress. A small moan escaped my throat. My body remained rigid, on high alert, every sense tingling with sweet anticipation. The humming energy surged around us, drawing us together like magnets.

"I am still angry with you," I managed to choke out, but the words sounded unsure. I'd forgotten what I was angry about.

"That's why I came." Luke moved closer to me, his chest pressing against mine. Heat pulsed through his shirt, searing my naked skin. His fingers danced over the edge of my neck, around my nipples, teasing me with the lightest touch. "I was going to surprise you in the shower, but I decided under the circum-stances, it was a bit sleazy."

"And waiting in my bedroom for me is less so?" I said, finding my self-control at last. I yanked my towel up over my chest and tried to duck away from him, but he stepped towards me, cutting off my path to the dresser. The only way around Luke would be to go across the bed, and under the circum-stances I thought that might give the wrong message.

Besides, my skin burned from his touch. I didn't want him to stop. Not really.

"Point taken." Luke gripped my shoulder, his face suddenly

serious. "I didn't mean to flirt. It's just hard to resist when you're all naked and damp and gorgeous. I really *did* come to talk, and to make sure you were okay. I was worried about you. I didn't like the way we left things, especially not when there's at least two dangerous wolves out there."

"So you thought you'd break into my house and scare me? How did you get in, anyway?"

"You left the front door unlocked. I needed to check you were safe."

"I'm fine, Luke. I'm a little annoyed. I don't like being talked about as though I'm some sow you're haggling over at a market."

"I get that, and I'm sorry. It's the wolf in me. He comes to the surface sometimes, especially so soon after the full moon. All that adrenaline and instinct haven't quite left my veins yet. We're very possessive, especially of our mates. It can sound a little primal if you're not used to it, but no offense was meant."

"You keep saying that word. *Mate.* What does it mean? I mean, I know what it *means.* But what is a mate to you?"

Luke paused. "I'm not sure I should tell you. I think it might be something you'll add to that list of things you don't like."

"That's for me to decide. Before we go any further, I want to know exactly what I am to you."

"Werewolves retain many of the primal animal instincts of their wolf half. One of those instincts is to breed and carry on the genetic line, passing on our wolfish genes to the next generation. The wolf genes are passed through the male line, but only females with certain genes can give birth to a werewolf."

"That makes sense." Clara hadn't told me that.

"We're guided to these females by scent. A potential mate gives off a very distinctive odour. They're very rare, and it's not unheard of for a wolf to go through their entire life without finding a mate, especially when the genes are recessive and can disappear from a line. Wolves believe there is only one mate for them in the world, and that mate is drawn to them, just as much as they are drawn to her." Luke's eyes bore into mine. "That's why we both ended up at this site. It's fate, the universe, whatever you call it, trying to draw us together."

"But we didn't know each other! I didn't even know I had this ... wolf gene."

"Yes, but you weren't meant to go to this excavation, were you? I remember you saying neolithic archaeology wasn't your thing."

I thought back to my conversation with Professor Hicks. "You mean Becky Masters wanting my place on the Sicily dig was no accident?"

"Huh?"

Briefly I explained about Becky's accident and how I'd ended up taking her place on the Crookshollow dig. "I don't particularly like Becky, but I hate the idea that I was somehow responsible for landing her in hospital."

"It wasn't your fault at all." Luke grinned. "The universe finally saw a chance to get us together, and events fell into place to make it so. It happens to so many wolves. It happened to my grandparents, too."

"You mean ... you think we're destined to be together?"

Luke nodded solemnly. "I do. Does that scare you?"

"Yes," I whispered, reaching up with my hand and running my fingers over his cheek, tracing the line of stubble along his jaw. "No. maybe ... I don't know. It *feels* right, and that scares me. I can't explain why, but I believe it."

"You don't know how pleased I am to hear that," Luke growled, and claimed my mouth in a fierce kiss. Heat surged through my body as his tongue slid over mine. My core throbbed with desire – it had been too long since he'd been inside me. I wanted him bad.

I broke the kiss after a few moments, panting hard. "I still have questions."

"Can they wait?" Luke bent to kiss me again.

I shook my head, even though my body screamed in protest at being wrenched away from Luke yet again. "If I'm your mate, then why does Caleb think he can 'claim' me?"

"As the son of my father's older brother, Caleb would technically be alpha of any new Lowe pack. That means he has mating rights over the females in the pack, even if they are mated to another. That right isn't usually exercised, but Caleb seems particularly keen on you." Luke leaned forward and stroked my naked thigh, just below where the towel stopped. "I can't say I blame him."

My whole body shuddered, but I needed to know more before I let him tear my towel away. "But I'm not in this pack. I haven't agreed to be part of any pack."

"To wolves like Caleb, what you think doesn't count." Luke knitted his fingers between mine. "That's why I'll have to fight him, to establish the order of our pack. Once I've established myself as an equal rival, he won't come after you. He'll have to treat you with all the respect due to a member of his own family."

"I don't want you to fight him. Did you see his arms? They're like tree trunks. He could snap your neck as easily as opening a jar of pickles."

"I'm not afraid of him, or his pickle jar–opening abilities." Luke flexed the muscles in his arm. "I can take him."

"He's your cousin. Maybe you could try being nice to him?"

"That's not how wolves work. Besides, I don't trust him."

"Why not?"

Luke shrugged. "All sorts of reasons. Why has he only just shown up in my life now, when the paintings came to light? How could he have been out there all those years without my father learning about him? Why did he never try to find *us*?"

"That same reason you never tried to find him. He thought he was the only one—"

"I don't want to talk about Caleb anymore," Luke growled. He cupped my chin in his strong hand and pulled my face to his. "I have something else on my mind."

"What's that?"

Luke's lips slammed against mine, all his desire welling up into the kiss. His lips forced mine apart, his tongue bombarding me. I wrapped my arms around him, and all thoughts of Caleb and mating and the caves flew from my mind. My core throbbed as I gave in to the urgency and hunger of our kiss.

As our kiss heated up, Luke walked me backward into the bathroom. "I like the idea of you all dripping wet," he whispered, as he reached behind me and turned the shower back on.

I leaned in to kiss him and he tore the towel away from me. Steam rolled off the shower, making my skin warm and slick. Luke slid his hands down my torso, his fingers leaving trails of fire across my sensitive skin. He ran a single finger between my legs, right along my slit, and my core thundered with pleasure. God, I wanted him, right now.

"Hey, both of us have to be naked." I lunged for him, and grabbed the edge of his t-shirt, pulling it over his head. I slid my hands over his muscled torso, enjoying the way his tattoos moved as he did, the colours shifting.

"Pants next," I said, grabbing for his belt. I fumbled with the buckle as Luke's tongue attacked mine. I could already feel his cock straining against the fly of his jeans.

"As you wish." Luke tugged down his jeans, kicking them away. From beneath his boxers, his cock stood proud. I pulled them off, bending over him as he stepped out. The head of his cock bobbed just in front of my eyes.

The length of it still shocked me. It was so big it looked like it belonged on the set of a porn film. I'd never been with a guy who was so huge before, nor looked at a cock and wanted to touch it so bad, to wrap my mouth around it and feel him jerk against my lips. I reached out tentatively with my tongue and touched it to the tip.

Luke groaned. The sound made my core surge with pleasure. I felt powerful. I took the head into my mouth, enjoying the taste of him. Warm and earthy and slightly salty. I'd never given much head before – Ben found it hard to relax and enjoy it, and I'd done it to other guys I'd been with more out of a sense of obligation, but with Luke, I couldn't wait to put my hands all over his cock.

I stroked him slowly, alternating my mouth and my hands. Luke's fingers entwined in my hair. "Anna ..." he groaned. God, I loved it when he said my name.

I slid my tongue down the length of his shaft, marvelling at how big it was. My hands pumped it faster as my tongue circled the tip, pressing into the little v just below the head. Luke curled his fingers in my hair, his breath hitching as his leg muscles clenched. Knowing I had this effect on him made my whole body flush with heat.

"No more of this," Luke breathed. With a grunt of effort, he grabbed me under the shoulders, lifted me off my feet, and placed me under the shower.

The rush of hot water over my flushed body made me shudder with delight, but not nearly as much as when Luke climbed in beside me and wrapped his arms around me, his tongue darting into my mouth.

Luke pulled me towards him, the warmth of skin against skin burning through my body, lighting every nerve ending on fire. He guided me under the stream of water, adjusting the head so it dribbled a light pattering of water over both our bodies.

"Oh dear," he said, picking up the soap and loofah from the shelf where I kept them. "You are a very dirty girl."

"I just had a shower."

"Go with it." Luke rubbed the soap over the loofah, building up a nice lather. He alternated strokes with the loofah with his hands, drumming his fingers against my body. His touch sent shivers of delight through me as he soaped along my shoulder-blades, lathering across my chest, just brushing the tips of my nipples. I moaned. Of course I would go with it.

"I'm filthy. I need more soap." I leaned my back against the side of the shower, bracing myself as he lathered me from head to toe. He unhooked the shower nozzle and used that to wash off the soap, licking and kissing.

I moaned as he trained the shower head against my nipple. The jets pounded against my sensitive flesh, bringing a whole new range of sensations. The heat, the pressure ... it was part pleasure, part pain, all wonderful. Luke moved the head to the other nipple, alternating the water pressure with sucking and blowing until I was begging him for more.

"As you wish." He trailed the head across my stomach, slowly, slowly inching lower. And then, he took it away, leaving me dripping.

"Luke—" I growled with frustration, my core throbbing with need.

The shower head was thrust between my legs, and the jets of hot water hit my most sensitive parts. I bucked against the wall as the pressure built up inside me. Who could believe he could do this to my body with just water?

Luke moved the shower head down my legs, teasing the sensitive skin between my thighs as he pushed a finger inside me. I moaned, bucking my hips forward, not even caring that I was begging for more. He pushed a second finger inside, then brought the head back up, pressing it hard against my clit.

"Luke ... I ... I ..." Breathing was hard.

"Yes?" He angled the head away and pressed a finger against my clit, moving it in slow circles, giving me soft when I desperately wanted hard. Just when I thought I couldn't take it, he pressed the head between my legs again, hitting me with the full force of the jets.

That threw me over the edge. The world exploded. I melted away, my body turning into molten lava and flowing down the drain. Red welts formed behind my eyes, and for a moment I lost myself.

When I came back, I was on my knees in the shower, clinging to Luke's legs. He stared down at me, stroking my damp hair, a self-satisfied smirk across his face.

"I know I'm good." He grinned. "But I didn't know I was *that* good."

"It's my turn now." I'd wipe that self-satisfied smirk from his face. I grabbed the loofah from the corner of the shower and stood up, holding him for support as my legs were wobbling dangerously. I lathered it up, running it over his chest, following the line of soap with my hands, the way he had done. As the water washed the soap away, I kissed a trail along his chest. He kept his eyes locked on me, his expression intense.

As I ran the loofah over his throbbing cock, he sighed, "Anna." He gripped my shoulder.

I took the shower head and crossed it over his shoulders, down his chest, up the insides of his legs, anywhere but where he most wanted it to go. Two could play this game.

When he let out a frustrated groan, I knew I had him. I aimed the warm jets directly on the tip of his cock, letting the warm water wash off the soap. He dug his fingers into my shoulders. When his cock was thoroughly clean, I aimed the spray at the wall and I took him into my mouth. First the head, which I circled with my tongue, and then the shaft, deeper and deeper, pushing him down as far as he could go.

Luke wound his fingers through my hair, his eyes boring into mine as he watched me take him in again. His facial muscles twitched as the pleasure coursed through him.

He tasted clean and warm and totally, utterly masculine. As my mouth rolled over his cock, it hardened between my lips. Hard for me.

Luke kept watching me. I'd never seen a guy do that before. The eye contact was so hot, sucking Luke was making my body ache for him again. Between my legs, I throbbed with need for him.

I pumped him faster, using my hand along the length of his shaft, as my tongue licked and sucked at the tip.

"Anna," he moaned. "Please. I'm so close. I want to be inside you."

My whole body flushed with pleasure. Right now, nothing would make me more satisfied.

I removed my lips from him, and stood up carefully, not wanting to slip. Luke leaned out of the shower to grab the condom from the pocket of his jeans, and he rolled it on. His lips found mine, his tongue probing deep, hungry for me. He wrapped his powerful arms around me, smothering me with his warmth. The water pelted us as the shower head flailed around beneath us, completely abandoned. We no longer needed the heat.

Luke lifted me with ease, pressing my back against the tiles. I wrapped my legs around his torso, pulling him closer. He lined himself up, and with one thrust, he entered me, his shaft filling me to the hilt. I groaned with pleasure as we fitted together like two puzzle pieces that had found their mates. I dug my heels into his back, driving him deeper inside me. He sighed with pleasure.

"You feel so good, Anna." He braced himself against the tiles with one hand, the other gripping my arse. He began to thrust up into me. Slowly at first, our bodies moving together. Luke built up a steady rhythm, his body fitting perfectly into mine.

Warmth flooded my body, seeping through Luke's touch, and rising up within me. I'd never had a guy before who made me feel like this, as though the very act of sex was something I claimed for myself. I loved the power of his body, watching his muscles expand and contract with concentration as he thrust into me.

The pleasure built inside me, the warmth bubbling over like a kettle boiling. I dug my fingers into Luke's shoulders. He buried his face into my neck, his teeth digging into my neck, finding the same spot where he'd bitten me before. The pain arced through my body, becoming one with the pleasure welling within. I fell over the edge, my body wracked with heat. Fire seared my limbs, lighting every nerve, firing off wave after wave of pleasure.

My muscles clenched around Luke's cock. He thrust harder, his fingers digging into my arse. A low growl rose in his throat. Every muscle in his body clenched – a snake coiled in wait.

As he came, he sank his teeth into my shoulder. The pain raced through me, becoming one with the ecstasy in my veins, driving me to a new level of pleasure.

Luke collapsed against me, his body shuddering, his breath panting against my neck. He withdrew slowly, his arms still supporting me.

"Woah," he said, his eyelids heavy.

"Yeah. Woah is right."

Slowly, Luke lowered me to my feet, then leaned back against the shower wall. I turned off the water and replaced the shower head, then pulled open the door. Water pooled across the floor, the shower mat and all our clothing was completely soaked. We'd managed to fling soapy lather across the ceiling, and on the mirror. I didn't want to clean up. I wanted the mess to stay there forever, to remind me of what had happened.

I wrapped myself in a towel, and handed one to Luke. Without him inside me, my body felt empty, bereft, but still warm from his touch. I was drenched in the scent of him, high on his taste and the power he gave to me.

Luke took my hand in his and kissed my knuckles. "Are you still angry with me?"

"Absolutely furious," I replied, as I sank into his arms.

NOTHING MADE me hungry like good sex. Which meant that right now, I was *ravenous*.

Unfortunately, I mused to myself as I searched the kitchen cupboards for a frying pan and pulled ingredients out of the fridge, if I'm going to be with Luke, I'll probably put on a hundred pounds.

Funny, but I didn't even care. What we'd just done in the shower ... phew. My body still tingled from head to toe at the memory of it. Maybe being his mate wouldn't be so bad after all ...

Our clothes had been utterly saturated in our antics. I'd placed everything in the dryer, and put on some leggings and a pretty wool dress from my own closet. Luke wandered around with only his towel wrapped around his hips, which I didn't have a problem with at all.

While I fixed us bacon and mushroom pasta, Luke walked around the small flat, staring at the photographs of archaeological sites covering the walls, my father's books stacked in the bookcase. He paused for a long time in front of the portrait of my father that hung above the fireplace.

"You have his eyes," Luke said, his voice husky. I knew he was thinking about his own father. "He looks like a very kind man."

"He was," I said. "He was gruff and distant and sometimes I got the feeling he didn't really know what he was supposed to do with a daughter. But he was very kind."

"Can I ask how he died?"

"He worked in a factory in Crooks Crossing. It was an old place and all the company managers lived down in London, so there wasn't a strong management presence and the place was kind of run down. A lot of the equipment broke or failed, and they were always in the paper after worker accidents. One day, my dad was working on a machine and some critical part fell off, jamming the mechanism. He needed to fix it quick, as product was still coming down the line. So he lifted the guard and reached inside." I cleared my throat. "The piece dislodged, and the mechanism basically sucked him inside."

"Shit." Luke crossed the room and scooped me up in his arms. "That's rough. I'm so sorry, Anna. How old were you?"

"Eighteen." I rested my head against his shoulder. "It's fine. It's old news now. I don't want to upset you by talking about it—"

"You don't upset me," Luke murmured into my hair. "I find you inspiring. I'm still learning how to live with this grief thing. But seeing what you've done after losing not only your father but a boyfriend, too ... you're much braver than I."

"Hardly." Luke's words and the warmth of his arms brought on a rush of emotion. A lump rose in my throat.

"Hey, I'm sorry. I didn't mean to upset you. I ... admire you, Anna. And not just because you're fucking hot. And now I understand why you're such a stickler for safety. You know first-hand what can happen when things go wrong."

I sniffed. "The pasta's boiling."

"Right." Luke pulled away, his kind eyes searching mine. But I didn't want to break down right then. I wanted to keep on floating in postcoital bliss. So I pushed thoughts of my dad and Ben and what could happen to Luke to the back of my mind, turned back to the kitchen and focused on stirring the sauce.

Luke continued his perambulations around the room. Occasionally, he sniffed the air. "Something smells off in here."

"That's no way to talk about my cooking."

He frowned. "That's not what I meant. It smells like an animal in heat."

"It's probably just my mum's friend, Cynthia. She does tarot card readings at a shop downtown, and they burn all sorts of incense. The smell follows her like a cloud. She'd be just the kind of lady to wear a scent called *Eau de Wolf*. Oh, that reminds me." While the pasta boiled, I dragged the huge book Derek had given me from my satchel beside the door, and held it out to him. "My friend Derek gave me this. He's a mythology student and I think it might help me create a case to discredit Ruth—"

As soon as the book touched his hands, Luke flung it across the room. It hit the wall and bounced off, landing on the floor with a defiant THUD.

Luke stared down at his hands, his breath shallow.

"What is it?" I touched his shoulder. He flinched away.

"It's another wolf," Luke hissed, bringing his hand to his face and sniffing deeper. "A very ancient, powerful wolf."

"Here?" Fear tightened my chest. I stared around the room with fresh, frightened eyes, searching for a chair out of place, a window cracked open, a cupboard ajar. Had a wolf come to my house? Could he still be waiting somewhere, lurking in the shadows ready to attack?

"Luke, has someone been in my house?"

"They must've been while we were in the shower. That's the only explanation." Luke sniffed the air again. "The scent isn't strong. But it's all over that book. That's what I was smelling before."

"You could smell a wolf who had touched a book, which was sitting in my bag?" He'd told me his senses were stronger, more attuned, but I had no idea just how much.

Luke nodded, his eyes wild. He jabbed his finger at the side door, leading out to the alley where we kept the bins. "Anna, did you leave that ajar?"

"What?" I glanced at the door. He was right, it was slightly open, a few droplets of rain driving through the gap and splattering on the floorboards.

I thought back to when I'd arrived at the house, retracing my steps from the bedroom to the kitchen to the door to the car. My hands had been full with Derek's books. I had my keys in my mouth. I'd thrown everything down and gone to look for Mum. I hadn't been anywhere near that door. "No. Did you come in there?"

"I went in the front, after you." Luke indicated the locked front door.

"Maybe Mum left it open accidentally?"

"Fuck." Luke slammed his hand down on the counter. I winced. I hated seeing him so worked up. It was making me even more afraid of what was out there. "This wasn't your mum being forgetful. It's him, Anna. It's the black wolf I've seen earlier. He's old, and powerful. He said he has killed before, and that more will die if I don't get out of his way."

Chills ran through my body. "Could he still be here?"

Luke shook his head. He sniffed the door handle, and around the door and the stool where I'd placed the books. "Whoever this wolf was, he's gone now. He didn't get very far into the room, and he didn't touch much, as far as I can tell. If the wolf was still here, I'd be able to smell him – even with his scent disguised – he couldn't hide for long in such a small space."

My blood turned cold as I realised something. "My mother

wasn't here. The neighbour said someone took her out. I thought it was Cynthia, but what if it was this wolf?"

"Don't worry, Anna. We'll find her." Luke pointed to the phone hanging from the kitchen wall. "Call your mum's friend, and anyone else she might be visiting. We may find her yet."

I grabbed the phone and dialled my mother's mobile phone. I hung up as soon as I heard it ringing from in the lounge. Panic tightened my throat. I dialled Cynthia next. She picked up on the first ring. "Oh, yes. Elaine's here with me, dear. I found this amazing five-thousand-piece puzzle of Tutankhamun's tomb paintings, and we've got the whole border nearly complete. And I've pulled your card for the month and must give you a warning—"

I thanked Cynthia and hung up. Luke had the book open on the table, and was thumbing through the pages, sniffing the edges and frowning.

He looked up when I had finished. "So she's safe, then?"

"Yeah. She's with Cynthia. It sounds as if she's had a small breakthrough. They're doing a puzzle together."

"That's wonderful." Luke frowned, and held up the book. "Anna, where did you get this from?"

"I told you, Derek gave it to me."

"He's your university friend, right? Where did he get it from?"

"I don't know." I grabbed my phone and wrote a frantic text to Derek. Luke clenched and unclenched his fists, his neck muscles bulging and tensing up. A few moments later, my phone beeped.

"He says it came from *Astarte*," I said. "It's the new-age shop downtown—"

"I know the one," Luke said. "I've been there before."

From the pocket of his jeans, he pulled out a small bottle. It looked familiar. I peered closer at it. Then I remembered where

I'd seen it before. It was identical to the one Clara had shown me when I'd visited the shop, the one Caleb had wanted but she wouldn't sell to him. I remembered her saying Luke had come in for the pills.

"That's right. You've already met Clara."

"She's quite something," Luke said. "And these pills are fantastic. My full moon shift lasted only two nights this time. I'm wondering if Clara might be able to tell us who has touched the book other than your friend."

"She can probably do more than that. Clara said there had been more wolves in the area than usual," I said. "When I visited her, she had run out of those pills because you'd bought them. She didn't have enough to sell to Caleb. Maybe there have been other wolves in the shop asking for the pills, too. She'd know who they were."

Luke grabbed my jacket off the back of the chair and tossed it to me. "Grab your mittens, babe. Let's go."

"But the pasta—" My stomach growled in protest.

"It will have to wait. We need to find out everything we can about this other wolf."

A FEW MINUTES LATER, we found ourselves standing outside *Astarte*. I couldn't believe I was back at this shop for the second time in a week. The sceptical scientist in me silently rebelled against the crystals and dreamcatchers hanging in the window, although I did have to smile at the sign by the door that read, "I tried yoga once, but found it a bit of a stretch."

I remembered Clara's unique sense of humour, and brightened. She was certainly a character. Besides, where was the sceptical scientist when you were having hot sex with a werewolf against your shower wall? My cheeks burned with the memory. I hoped Clara wouldn't be able to read that thought in my cards.

Luke grinned as he saw me hesitating. "You come to this store often, then?"

I shook my head, then pointed across the street at the *Bewitching Bites* bakery. "That place is much more my style. There were far too many hippy dippy new agey folk in my first year archaeology lectures, writing essays postulating the location of Atlantis and derailing lectures with discussions about whether aliens really built the pyramids. I find it all rather ridiculous."

"You're dating a werewolf. Isn't that ridiculous?"

"Maybe." I grinned back at him. "Depends if we're actually dating."

He squeezed my hand. "I'm game if you are."

"I haven't decided yet."

I pushed open the door to the shop. It must've been a slow day for crystals and Crookshollow ghost tour brochures, because the shop was completely deserted. From somewhere in the back, a little bell tinkled. The place looked just the way I remembered it – tiny tables and dark mahogany bookshelves lined the dimly-lit space, crammed full of candles and crystals and strange books. I coughed as a wave of sweet-smelling incense hit my nostrils.

Clara glided in from the back of the shop, carrying a stack of books that was almost as tall as she was. Her kind face broke into a grin as she saw us both.

"Yes?" she asked, her head tilting to the side. Luke rushed over and helped her set the books down on a small round table under the window.

"Hi there," I said, suddenly feeling a bit stupid. "Um, I don't know if you remember me—"

"Of course," Clara grinned, showing a row of crooked

teeth. She set down the books on the counter, and bustled over to us. She took my hand and rubbed it in her own, her wrinkled fingers cool to the touch. "You were the girl who'd just met a werewolf. And I see you've brought along your friend."

"Luke, this is Clara." I expected him to shake her hand, but instead he just glared intently at her across the counter.

"I remember you, too, young man," Clara said, her eyes sparkling. "I never forget a shifter."

"You have remarkable sight," Luke said.

"It is one of my gifts."

"Is your other consorting with dangerous wolves?"

"Luke!" I couldn't believe how rude he was being.

Clara chuckled. "Don't worry, pet. His behaviour is understandable, given the circumstances. Remember, I told you a wolf is always overprotective of his mate."

"I never said I was his mate."

"If you say so, dear. I take it you have found some kind of object."

I held out the book to her. "A powerful werewolf has touched this. I believe it was originally brought from you. We need to know how if any other wolves have come in wanting Lycan pills, and if there's any way to find this particular wolf."

"No other wolves have come in, apart from you, the grumpy guy from the other day, and my regulars."

"Can the book tell you anything about the wolf?"

Clara took the book in her hands and studied the title for a long time. She slid it back across the counter towards me. "I'm afraid you will not find him until he wants to be found. It is a skilled magical worker who has handled this book. I cannot get any kind of reading from this book, and nor did I get anything when I sold it. If this wolf is as powerful as you say, I would've remembered him. Not even my sight can pick up anything, except that the wolf who handled this book means you great harm. "

"My friend was the one who brought it," I said. "His name is Derek. He studies mythology. He probably comes in here to buy books a lot."

She looked startled for a moment. Then she yanked the book across the counter and flipped through the pages again. "Yes," she breathed. "It does smell a bit like Derek. I don't remember selling him this particular volume, but he does buy a lot of things from me."

"Someone broke into my house today, and they left their scent behind. Luke can smell it on the book."

"That's because he wanted you to," Clara said, laying the book out flat, and opening it to the middle. She pulled a small magnifying glass from the drawer below the till, and examined the spine and the edges of the pages. She pulled a thin pair of tweezers from the purse on her belt, and dug them into the binding. A few moments later she pulled out a thin quill. "Yes, this is a very skilled magical worker indeed."

"What's that?"

"Part of a spell," Clara said, sniffing the quill. "A charm, actually. You'd need to have this tested to confirm, of course, but I'm pretty sure it's poisoned."

"Someone's trying to poison me?" I gasped.

"Unlikely. This is part of a love spell. It's designed to 'poison' you against the one you love."

I glanced at Luke. His face shone red with rage. "So what do we do?" Luke demanded.

Clara slammed the book shut. "Nothing. At the moment."

"Well, you're a great help." Luke snatched the book off the table.

"Luke," I tugged on his shoulder. "What about Caleb?"

"Of course." Luke growled. "That scheming bastard. It must

be him. He hid his true scent from me. He convinced me he was my cousin, that we were family. And all this time he was here to destroy everything and take you for himself."

"No!" I grabbed his arm. "That's not what I meant. I don't think Caleb is this big bad wolf. What I mean is, he's all alone at the caves, and he has no idea how powerful this other wolf is."

Luke's face darkened. "Either way, we need to get back to the caves."

We raced out of the store without even saying goodbye to Clara. Luke threw the book onto the back seat of my Mini, and started climbing into the driver's seat. "Excuse me," I jabbed my finger at the passenger side.

"We don't have time for you to get all possessive about your car," Luke huffed. "I will drive us there faster. Simple fact."

"I'm allowed to be possessive about the car. It's *my* car. And as for speed," I twirled the keys around my finger. "You ain't seen nothing until you've seen what I can do in a Mini."

Luke relented. I climbed in, fastened my belt, and stomped on the gas. The Mini zoomed off down the high street and nailed the first corner. We took off towards the forest at breakneck speed. I felt a flash of satisfaction as I glanced over at the passenger seat and saw Luke gripping the dash with white knuckles.

"What's that?" he cried suddenly, when we were nearly at the dig.

"This, Luke Lowe, is how driving *should* be done."

"No, that up ahead." He was already undoing his belt. "Stop the car."

I pulled over on the side of the track, my heart beating as I noticed the police cars up ahead. An ambulance was parked on the other side of the road, its lights off. As I got out of the car, a young officer jogged towards us, motioning for us to go back.

"You can't be here." she said. "Please drive on."

Luke dug an ID card from his wallet. "I'm the ranger in the forest," he said, his voice stern. "What's happened? Someone should have called me."

She glanced down at Luke's ID, and frowned. "We did call you. Your phone went straight to voicemail. But since you're here now, you'll need to give a statement to the DS. There's been a murder."

A *murder*? My chest tightened. I thought of the other archaeologists, working in the cave, unaware of the werewolves lurking in the forest. "Who?" I demanded.

Her gaze flicked over to me. "We're not giving out information to the public at this stage."

"This is Anna Sinclair," Luke said, his hand resting protectively on the small of my back. "She's working on the excavation. Is it one of the archaeologists?"

"Anna Sinclair?" The officer frowned even harder. "Then you'll need to give a statement, too. Your name has come up in our inquiries."

"It has?"

"The victim was a reporter from the *Daily Post*. Her name was—" she consulted her clipboard, "—Misty Sharpe. It looks as though she were coming out to the archaeological site to conduct more research. She stopped here, parked her car, and then walked a few yards before someone tackled her and tore her throat out."

My head spun. Misty was dead? I'd only talked to her yesterday. Her ridiculous article was on the internet just this morning. How could she be *dead*? And who would have done such a thing? To have her throat torn out, like a wild animal ...

The officer gave me a pointed look. "She was coming here to talk to you, Miss Sinclair. Apparently, there was quite an article about you published this morning, and Misty was hoping for a follow-up. It seems you are ..." She consulted her notes. I could see she had a printout of Misty's article. "...hot-headed and unremorseful about your part in your boyfriend's mysterious death ..."

My face blazed. Death followed me everywhere, it seems. My mind swirled with memories of the police at my house, asking for information about Ben, telling my mother Dad was dead, escorting me to the morgue to identify the body. It was the same thing all over again. *This cannot be happening.*

But it was. While we gave our statements to the detective sergeant, leaving out the bit about the shower and the black wolf, a SOCO team buzzed around the site in their white coats and gloves. Four officers manoeuvred a stretcher into the ambulance. On the stretcher was a large, black bag. I couldn't believe that inside was Misty Sharpe, her stiletto heels no doubt still on her feet.

Misty was dead, and the police thought I had something to do with it. But I knew better. One thing was for certain. The discovery of the caves had brought more wolves to Crookshollow. And one of them had murder on his mind.

And that meant I could be next.

18

LUKE

I had to hand it to Anna. She really knew how to put her foot down. The Mini careened along the dirt road like it was on a NASCAR track. Her brow was creased in concentration, her entire being focused on putting as much space between us and the cops as possible. In no time at all, I could make out the white side of the caravan and the orange pup tents through the trees. My stomach clenched with nerves, every sense on high alert.

I knew Caleb had been lying to me. He'd already attacked Anna once, and he'd openly declared he was prepared to challenge me for her. And now some wolf was showing up at her house, leaving her books laced with poison? And a reporter who interviewed her has turned up dead? Caleb knew something about all this, and I needed to shake it out of him, by any means possible.

"Caleb!" I yelled, leaping out before Anna had even pulled to a stop.

No reply. From the caravan, I heard peals of laughter. *Ruth.* Ruth was laughing. Ruth didn't laugh. Laughing was impossible when you had a stick shoved that far up your own arse.

Maybe it wasn't a laugh. Maybe it was the sound of her choking on her own scorn. Maybe the black wolf had already got to them. I raced up the stairs of the caravan, heart hammering against my chest, and thrust open the door.

The site that greeted me stopped me short. "Um ..."

Caleb stood behind the stove, wearing a rolled-up topographic map as a chef's hat and an apron with a picture of a Tyrannosaurus Rex skeleton and the word *YOLO* on the front. He was flipping crepes in a large frying pan. Batter coated every surface of the kitchen, and bits of burned crepes clung to the ceiling like determined limpets. Around the counter sat Frances, Ruth and Max, all roaring with laughter as Caleb flipped a pancake over his shoulder without looking. It landed on one of the plates sitting on the counter, and Frances leaned forward to claim it as her own.

"What's going on?" I demanded, my eyes meeting Caleb's. Anna clambered up the stairs behind me and peered in underneath my arm.

"Oh, Luke," Ruth gasped between giggles. "Have you met Caleb? He's a reporter for the *Ecological Gazette*. He's writing a piece on the impact of archaeological discoveries on the natural environment, so he's going to be camping on site for a few days to observe us."

"I thought it would be just the kind of anti-archaeologist piece you'd approve of," Frances said between mouthfuls.

"The police were just here, asking questions about a murder that happened nearby. I'm just trying to cheer everyone up. Hi." Caleb stretched out a batter-covered hand. I shook it, frowning at him. *What was his game here?*

"Nice to meet you, Caleb." Anna reached around me, and shook his hand, staring up at him warmly. "Do you have one of those crepes for me?"

"Sure do." He loaded up the pan with a spoonful of batter,

splashing most of it over the sides. I wanted to tear the crepe from her hands, but I couldn't do that in front of the others. Soon, all the archaeologists were around the counter, chewing on their crepes.

"Would you like one, too, Ranger?" Caleb grinned cheekily at me. I blinked. His face had a certain familiarity to it. With his reddish hair, he reminded me a little of my dad, just younger and more evil.

"We need to talk," I hissed in Caleb's ear. He nodded as he slid a crepe onto a plate and handed it to me. I tossed it in the rubbish bin beside the bench. Anna glanced between us, then casually reminded Frances what time it was.

"Oh, we've got to get back!" The professor wiped the crumbs from around her mouth. "The crew will be wanting to interview Ruth again while the rain has stopped. Caleb," she threw a quick glance in my direction, "don't forget to wear the hard hat I gave you if you come back to the caves."

"I won't." Caleb tapped the brim of his hard hat, which was sitting on the bench beside the sink, splattered with flour and batter.

The archaeologists filed out of the caravan, leaving me alone with my supposed cousin and easy access to a knife rack. Caleb swiped off his paper hat, and nonchalantly poured himself a cup of tea.

"What is it, little cousin?" he sneered, as he brought the cup to his lips.

I growled, the wolf in me pressing against my skin, begging to be set free to tear him to shreds. But before I could confront him, Anna dropped the book on the table. "Can't you smell it?"

"Not really ... oh, shit." Caleb took a deep whiff of the cover, and his eyes grew wide. "I've smelled this wolf before."

"Of course you have," I growled. "It's *your* scent."

"Luke," Anna warned.

"Excuse me?" Caleb lowered his mug.

"I'm starting to think this black wolf is an illusion. It's the only explanation that fits all the facts. You've enchanted this book to be a love spell, so you can have Anna for yourself. I followed your scent in the forest, and it merged with this same scent on the book. That's because both scents are from the same wolf – you. That's why the scent appears and disappears, and why the black wolf hasn't been anywhere near the site, and why I've never seen you or him together. He's a glamour. I don't know how you're doing it all, but we have it on good authority the charm on the book is pretty powerful. You must have some considerable skill."

"Have you been smoking something, Ranger?" Caleb waved his hand in front of my eyes. "Because you're crazy. I'm just me. I'm not posing as a black wolf. I'm not running around murdering reporters. I've been here all day, keeping the team safe. You can ask them."

"I will. Come clean now, and I might not rip your throat out."

Caleb laughed. "This is fucking ridiculous. One wolf having two scents is impossible. Besides, I've seen the other wolf. So unless you think I can magically alter my appearance as well—"

"Well, can't you?"

"Of course I bloody can't! Look, of course I want Anna – she's fucking gorgeous and an ideal mate. Who wouldn't want her? But I'm not about to kill my only living relative in order to get her. You and I are more powerful together, little cousin. We need to find the black wolf, and take him out before he kills someone else. He's hiding down by the stream somewhere."

"I know where he is," I said, thinking of the cave I'd seen in the rocks.

"Good. Because I've been following the faint whiff of his trails over the forest for the last few days, and I couldn't find his lair. He's clearly disguising his scent. At first I thought it might be an old trail, but then I've seen him stalking around."

"And this wolf wants me?" Anna looked sick. "Why did he kill the reporter?"

"I don't know," I said, wrapping my arms around her, pulling her close. "But we have to be careful. I'm not letting you out of my sight."

"If this wolf claimed these lands for himself, then he'd naturally assume he'd be able to take you for his own," Caleb said.

"That's not going to happen." I gripped her hand, squeezing it. "We've been assuming he wouldn't attack in broad daylight, but the police said Ms. Sharpe was killed a couple of hours ago. He's more dangerous than we know. I'm assuming you couldn't convince Frances to call off the dig?"

"Not a chance."

"Then we need to guard the site, around-the-clock surveillance."

"Agreed," Anna said. "And if we are dealing with a magical wolf, we'll need some kind of magical protection."

"What do you mean?"

"I can't believe I'm even suggesting this, but perhaps Clara has some charms or spells or things that can help protect us." Anna glanced at her watch. "By the time I got back to town, she'd have closed the shop. But I'll head in first thing tomorrow."

Caleb picked up his hard hat. "I'm going back to the caves. I'll be able to watch out for the crew while I'm there."

"We're coming, too." I grabbed Anna's coat from the rack by the door and tossed it to her. There was no way I was letting Caleb back in those caves without being present. Anna may trust him, but I sure didn't.

～

CALEB and I spent the last few hours of daylight taking turns holding lights while Frances and Anna painstakingly brushed mud and debris off the cave paintings. Ruth was busy on the surface with another film crew.

After dinner, Anna sat down with her stack of books, and started on her research. A fervour to prove the paintings fake had taken hold of her – she said that if she could do that, then maybe that would get Frances to call off the dig, and that would get the whole crew to safety.

Not wanting to leave her side, I pulled over one of the books – a history of supernatural occurrences in Crookshollow – and flipped to the section on the Victorian era. My eyes fell on a chapter about the Peytons.

.... famed for their prowess as witch hunters, the Peyton family had a place of honour in the Crookshollow community. During the late Victorian period, patriarch Robert Peyton was Bishop of Loamshire and he led some of the last witch hunts on English soil, primarily against what he called "shifters of form who did poison the earth with their unnatural visage." The family was supposedly haunted by a cursed relative who could change his form into a wolf. They committed this unfortunate cousin to a mental asylum. Peyton and his family stabbed to death at least eighteen people they believed to be shapeshifters, including a family who lived in a cave in the woods near Crookshollow ...

Beside me, Anna was scribbling notes furiously. "I've got it," she whispered to me, jabbing her finger at one of the cave paintings on the screen. "You won't believe it, Luke. It was so simple."

"How?" I whispered back.

She pointed to one of the images, where my grandfather dragged a pig's carcass back to the cave, and his three children waited with open mouths for their supper. "This pig is pretty easily recognisable as an Oxford Sandy and Black pig," she said. "There's no other pig breed it could possibly be. But that particular breed wasn't introduced into the country until the seventeen hundreds."

"Much later than the neolithic, then?"

"Exactly." Her grin was infectious. "And when you couple that with the priests in the last image … it's obvious. Ruth is going to be spewing when I tell her. Did you find anything?"

I passed her the book and pointed to the paragraph on Peyton. "They sound like nasty people." She shuddered as she read the page.

"Yep. But did you notice what's interesting? They may have a shapeshifter in the family."

"You don't think that's just part of the legend?"

"All legends start from somewhere. Perhaps you should ask your friend the mythology major."

"I will. He's supposed to come out here tomorrow to look at the caves …" Anna paled. "Oh, I hope I haven't put him in danger."

"He'll be fine. We can drive out in the morning and wait for him. I'd like to meet this friend of yours."

"Okay. Thanks, Luke."

The sun had long since sunk below the horizon. The beer supply had run out and one by one the archaeologists loped off to bed. Anna glanced at Caleb and I. "I feel too wired to sleep," she said. "What should we do now?"

"You're going to your tent," I growled. "But you're not sleeping any time soon."

"So no one wants to play cards with me?" Caleb asked.

"Play with yourself. You're taking the first watch tonight. Come get me at 3am and I'll relieve you of duty."

"So you trust me now?"

"I don't. But Anna does, and that means something to me."

"It should." Anna grinned, wrapped her arms around me and kissing my lips.

As we walked across the camp, Anna snuggled tighter against my body. The warmth of her ignited my desire. My cock was already straining against my jeans. It had only been a few hours since we'd been in the shower together, but already I was desperate to be inside her.

Anna hung back while I circled her tent, sniffing the air for a hint of the black wolf's scent. Nothing. But I knew better than to assume he was gone for good. I pulled open the flap and peered inside, but no one was hiding in wait for us.

"After you." I pulled back the flap all the way. Anna ducked inside and I followed her, wrapping my hands around her beautiful round arse.

"Hey!" Anna protested, leaping away. But there wasn't far to go in the tiny tent. She fell back against her sleeping bag, and I climbed on top of her, my cock pressing urgently against her thigh.

Anna's lips found mine, her tongue sliding between my teeth. My hands cupped her face, bringing her closer. My body ached for her, wanting to be as close as possible, right now.

I reached up to unbutton her shirt, but Anna held my hand. "Let me do it," she whispered. "You've already ruined two of my favourite shirts."

I was going to protest, but then she started undoing the buttons, starting at her neck and working her way down. She appeared a little nervous, like a schoolgirl in the back seat of a car for the first time. That only added to my desire as she unhooked the last button and pulled her shirt open.

Her breasts were cupped inside a black bra. I reached behind her and unhooked it, sliding it and her shirt off her shoulders. I cupped one of her breasts in my hands, loving how perky and firm it was. She gasped as I closed my mouth around the nipple and sucked gently, her nails digging into my back.

As I sucked on her other breast, Anna fumbled for my

buttons. I shrugged my shirt off my shoulders, and pressed my body against hers, loving the skin against skin, the way her hard nipples rubbed against my chest.

Anna kicked off her jeans, and pulled mine off, too. I tugged down her underwear and thrust my face between her legs. I parted her lips with my tongue, inhaling the sweet smell of her. She moaned as I ran my tongue along her, finding her clit and circling it slowly. Anna's nails dug deep into my shoulders as her first orgasm claimed her.

While her body was still shuddering with pleasure, I climbed on top of her, put on the condom, and entered her. Her wetness enveloped me, our bodies fitting together perfectly. I moved slowly against her, the pressure rising in my stomach as my own pleasure built. Anna gasped and clawed at my back.

"You feel so good." My cock slid in and out of her, our bodies fitting together perfectly. I buried my head into her shoulder, dragging my teeth along her neck. Pressure tugged at my core, the wolf inside me struggling to escape, to unleash all my wildness.

"Luke," she gasped, her walls tightening around me. I pumped harder, enjoying the way my length slid right into her, the way she bucked her hips up to meet each thrust. She wanted me just as much as I needed her. "Oh, Luke."

Anna clenched around me, her body shuddering as an orgasm tore through her. Her eyes fluttered shut, her head fell back, her breath hitching. Her walls contracted around my cock, squeezing me tight. I thrust faster, loving seeing her lose control.

Feeling her come sent me over the edge. The pressure building inside me spilled over. I saw stars as I came, the bright lights of a thousand distant galaxies shimmering in a brilliant supernovae.

We collapsed against each other, utterly spent. I wrapped her in my arms, enjoying the warmth of her body stretched across the furs. For a few precious minutes, we enjoyed the bliss of our bodies, but then the fear and uncertainty started to creep back.

Anna wrapped her arms around my neck. Her limbs went stiff. "Luke, I'm scared." Anna's lip trembled.

"Don't be." I wrapped my arm under her neck, stroking her cheek with my other hand. "I'm here, and so is Caleb. We won't let anything happen to you."

I won't let anything happen to you, I thought, as I kept my eyes glued on the door. *Especially not anything named Caleb.*

I wasn't going to let that red-headed lout fool me again. He wasn't going to get Anna. Of that I would make certain.

I woke up from a dream about death to find Luke still lying beside me, his eyes wide open. "Did you sleep at all?" I asked.

"No. But you're okay, and that's what's important. No black wolves in sight."

"Where's Caleb?" Why had Luke not slept? Hadn't Caleb relieved him of his duty?

"Outside," Luke growled. "But I needed to watch him, too."

"You don't still suspect him, do you? You're being paranoid. Caleb is your cousin, and apart from attacking me that one time, he's been a perfect gentleman."

"I have to be suspicious. He's a wolf on my territory, and he's close enough to you to do real harm. Just let me be a protective alpha, would you?"

"I guess. Does that mean you're coming with me into Crookshollow today? It would mean leaving the site unguarded."

"Do you have to go?"

I glanced over at my phone. "Yeah. I need to talk to Clara about some charms to protect us, and get to my friend Derek before he leaves for the forest."

"What? Why?"

"Remember, I told you my friend the mythology nut was coming out here today to look at the caves? But after what happened to Misty on the road, I don't want him anywhere near this place. But I can't just call him and tell him not to come." I tapped my useless phone screen.

"Shit. Okay. Guess we're going to town." Luke glanced at me with hard eyes. "You really trust Caleb?"

"I really do."

"Fine. But if we come back here and Ruth has been torn to shreds, try to refrain from doing a victory dance on her corpse."

"I make no promises." I grinned at his dark humour, hoping like hell there would be no more death.

"Derek, have you noticed anything strange this week?"

"You mean, apart from the fact you're spending more time at my house drinking all my tea than out on that archaeological find of the century?"

I drained the rest of my cup, and punched his arm. "Be serious, please. And be serious while you put the kettle on again. I need another."

I felt a bit guilty leaving Luke hunched down in the car while I drank tea with Derek, but it couldn't be helped. True to his word, Luke wouldn't let me go to town alone, but I didn't want him inside while I spoke to Derek – I was worried Luke's presence would throw off our usual rapport. I hadn't told Derek about Luke, and I didn't want to suddenly surprise him, knowing the way he still felt about me. Plus, I hadn't told Luke about Derek's feelings, and I didn't want a macho showdown. We had more important things to worry about.

"I was being serious, you know. About you noticing anything strange."

Derek went to the kitchen and got the kettle going, then sat back down across from me, patting my leg in a friendly way. "Strange how?"

"I don't know. A feeling of being watched, someone hanging around your house. Someone who is not me asking you odd questions. Just anything odd or out of the ordinary."

"What's this about, Anna?" Derek leaned forward, his eyes sparkling. He loved a good mystery, and here I was, being rather mysterious. "Does this have something to do with that reporter who died?"

"Yeah, and about why you can't come on the site any more. It's very ... complicated," I said, thinking fast. "And ... top secret. There are some interesting facts about the cave paintings that haven't been released in the media. I think that might be why that reporter was killed, someone thought she was getting too close to the truth."

"What kind of facts? You're not in danger, are you, Anna?"

Oh, just a maniacal werewolf who wants to mate with me. Nothing particularly dangerous at all. I shrugged. "I ... I think I am, but I'm being well looked after. I can't say too much at the moment, but suffice it to say the paintings may not be as old or as special as first thought."

"That sounds like something from a spy film."

"I know. And it gets worse. I think, before she died, the reporter had been following me – I was at home the other day after coming here and I think she might have snuck inside while I left the door open. And because I was around at your place first, I'm worried they might come after you next."

"I'm intrigued. And slightly terrified. You've got to be careful, Anna." Behind us, the kettle popped. Derek sprung to his feet, taking my empty cup with him to the kitchen. "Do you want some mousetraps with your tea?"

"Yes, please." I'd left site before breakfast, and I was starving.

While Derek prepared the tea, sliced cheese and tomato and heated the grill, I shuffled through the papers on his coffee table. He was really making headway on his family history project, probably because the deadline on his master's thesis was approaching rapidly and he was desperate for distractions. He'd laid out his family tree across the table on a big sheet of white card – all the different generations labelled with dates and spouses and children. Post-it notes stuck out from every surface, and lines were crossed out or dotted over. There were some lines with question marks where he obviously hadn't found the right data, and others had notes referring to certain documents he'd photocopies from archives. I scanned the names above Derek. There were his parents – Theodore and Alice – and his grandparents, and he'd traced the line right back to—

I stopped short, my breath freezing in my throat. It can't be the same person. It must be a coincidence.

There, on the paper, listed as Derek's great-grandfather on his father's side, was Robert Peyton, the man who had killed Luke's family.

"Derek?" My voice came out high-pitched.

"Yes?" he called over the sizzle of bubbling cheese.

"This chart says you're related to the Peyton family."

"Yeah. Isn't it cool?" Derek came back to the table with two steaming mugs of tea and a plate of mousetraps. He pushed a thin book across the table towards me. "They're quite an old Crookshollow family. Apparently, they used to have quite the reputation as righteous witch hunters. My great-grandfather Robert was Bishop of Loamshire."

"I've heard some stories about them. Someone in the village was saying they had something to do with the caves—"

My phone vibrated, startling us both. I grabbed it and held it to my ear.

It was Frances. She was screaming incoherently. I held the phone away from my ear as Frances's screeching cut away to static.

"Frances, what's wrong? Where are you? How are you getting phone reception?"

The phone crackled some more, and then Ruth's voice came landed in my ear. "Anna? You've got to come ... immediately. The site's been ... royed."

"What?" I didn't think I'd heard her right. The line was terrible. They must still be somewhere near the site.

"Come back now! The police are on their way, and they'll need to take your statement." Ruth's voice was choked with sobs. "Someone has been here with a crowbar. The cave paintings have been completely destroyed."

20

LUKE

This time, I was the one driving. My powerful truck made quick work of the dirt roads, and we even passed the police on the way out to the site. Anna gripped the edges of her seat so tight, her knuckles turned white.

As we pulled up in the truck and ran over to the caves together, my hand clasped tight around Anna's, Ruth glared at us, as though we had something to do with this mess. Frances sat by the cave entrance, her face in her hands.

"What happened?" Anna huffed as she drew up beside the other archaeologists.

"It's like I told you on the phone," Ruth said, her voice hoarse. "You guys left. We had breakfast and did a quick Skype interview in the caravan, then came out here to get some more work done. But when we entered the tunnel, we noticed all the debris lying around, and the paintings were gone. Someone has hacked off all the images. There's nothing left but dust and chips on the floor of the tunnel."

Frances let out a strangled sob.

"Shit." Anna's knees wobbled. She sank to the ground beside Frances, her face terrified. "Who would do such a thing?"

Her words were directed at Ruth, but the question was for me. I answered it in my head. *Caleb.* I'd left him alone here, and tried to forget about all my misgivings about him, because Anna trusted him. I'd even checked with Ruth before we'd left, and she confirmed he hadn't left their side for a moment yesterday. But then he'd gone and done this – even though he swore he wasn't going to any more – and had destroyed forever the last link I had to my family, my history. Hatred and anger burned in my veins.

"No one saw anything?" Anna asked. "You guys aren't hurt?"

Ruth shook her head. "We were all over in the caravan. But I can't help but think, what if we'd been here when ..." She shuddered.

Anna was already sliding through the cave entrance. I jumped down after her.

"Where are you going?" Ruth called down. "You can't disturb anything. The police are on their way—"

Anna ignored her. She picked up one of the torches from the edge of the abandoned neolithic site, and clicked it on. I followed her through the crevice, and down to the tunnel entrance. The whole cave reeked of wolf – the black wolf's smell, which I knew now was Caleb's true scent.

"Shit," Anna whispered, aiming the torch light into the tunnel.

I sucked in a breath as the full magnitude of the damage came into view. The walls of the tunnel had been cruelly hacked to pieces, leaving jagged ribbons of colour. Piles of rocky debris littered the tunnel. Dust wafted through the stale air. I coughed as the smell invaded my nostrils, choking out my other senses.

The only thing left was a single crude piece of graffiti that hadn't been there before – a stick figure of a woman with dark hair and glasses, a knife sticking out of her chest. The woman was meant to be Anna.

"I'll fucking kill him." My hands closed into fists. The wolf within me growled in agreement.

"Luke, I think you're mistaken about Caleb—"

"I've seen enough," I snapped. "This is a direct threat to your life. I'll make him pay."

"But we don't even know that's me ..." Anna yelped as I grabbed her hand and dragged her back out through the cave. "Luke, hey, where are you going? Let me go!"

I pulled Anna back through the cave entrance and up into the forest, when I sucked in several fresh breaths. "Where's Caleb?" I snarled at Ruth.

"He's gone for a walk," she replied. "He thought he'd have a look around the outside of the camp, see if he could see anyone hiding there, or footprints or anything. At least he's looking out for our safety. Isn't that supposed to be your job, *Ranger*?"

I didn't have time to get into a verbal sparring match with Ruth. I grabbed Anna by the hand. There was no way I was going to let her out of my sight until I had subdued Caleb.

"Luke, what are you doing?" Anna cried, as she struggled to keep up with me. I charged into the trees, yelling Caleb's name.

"Dammit, Luke." Anna punched my shoulder. "Answer me."

"I'm looking for that *cousin* of mine," I snarled. "He's responsible for this. We're going to settle this, once and for all."

"You're looking at the wrong wolf, Luke. Ruth said Caleb was in the caravan with them. He can't have done this."

"Ruth likes Caleb. She'll say anything to protect him," I snarled back.

"He didn't do it. You have to get that into your thick head if we're ever going to solve this."

"Listen to your princess, Lucas."

I whirled around. Caleb stood in the middle of the forest path, his unbuttoned shirt flapping in the stiff breeze. At least this time, he wasn't smirking. He looked tired, drawn out. But most of all, he looking fucking guilty.

"You." I hissed at Caleb. "You did this."

He shook his head. "I assure you ... this was all the black wolf's doing."

"You just couldn't take it, could you?" I growled. "You couldn't handle the fact that Anna chose me. So you kill that reporter, and destroy the paintings, and threaten her. Well, if you want Anna, you'll have to get through me, and I tell you right now that—"

"Is that any way to talk to your cousin?"

"You're no cousin of mine."

Caleb took a step closer. I bared my teeth. My hands balled into fists. The wolf bubbled below the surface, prickling against my skin. My nails dug into my flesh, becoming sharp claws. Bristly hair sprouted through my arms.

Caleb shook his head, his eyes dark with fury. As he took another step towards me, I saw his own fur bursting through his skin. "You seem quick to cast blame away from yourself, cousin. What reason would I have for killing the reporter? How does she fit into my nefarious plan? I could just as easily ask the same questions of you. Weren't you the one who tried to destroy the paintings only a few days ago? Don't you keep a crowbar in the back of that filthy truck?"

"I'm going to kill you!" I yelled, slashing my claws at his face. Caleb ducked back, just as my fingers sliced through the air inches from him. Caleb growled in response, his lips turning back into a scowl.

"Guys!" Anna leapt between us. I halted, pulling back my wolf just as he threatened to burst forth. "Don't be like this. Caleb, Luke couldn't have done this. He was with me at the time. We were in Crookshollow."

"See?" I glowered at Caleb.

"But Luke, I don't think Caleb did this either," Anna spoke directly to me. "It doesn't make any sense. His whole purpose here is to establish his own pack. How can he do that when he destroys the only evidence of his claim to this place? Or when he's got police swarming all over the forest?"

"Well, then who else did this?" I demanded.

"It was the other wolf," Caleb whispered. "The black wolf."

"I thought we'd established the black wolf couldn't possibly exist."

"No," Caleb snapped. "*You* established that, because you're so desperate to believe that I'm the culprit here. I know the black wolf exists, because I've seen him with my own eyes. His scent is all over that cave."

"You mean *your* scent."

"I don't have to listen to this shit." Caleb fell forward, and with a crack, his spine bent, his contorted, growing shorter and thinner, his fingers shrinking as his nails grew into long claws. A few moments later, Caleb's red wolf stood before us, his lips pulled back into an angry scowl. He gave a defiant bark, stepped out of his pile of tattered clothing, and ran off into the forest.

"Caleb, come back!" Anna yelled after him. She took a step into the trees after him, but I grabbed her arm.

"What are you doing? He's dangerous."

"You are ridiculous," Anna snapped, wrenching her arm away.

"What, me?" What was she talking about? "He's the one who—"

"He's family, Luke. Do you have any idea how lucky you are to have found family when you most needed it? Instead of embracing it, you're accusing him of all these despicable things."

"It had to have been him. He's attacked you before—"

"That was before he knew you were family. He's telling you the truth, Luke. Your version of reality where Caleb is the bad guy makes no sense. But you're just too stubborn to see it." She turned to follow Caleb. "You just want to believe he's the bad guy because it's too painful trusting someone else."

"Anna, wait—" I reached for her again.

She shrugged me off, tears streaming down her cheeks. "Don't touch me. Don't follow me. I ... I can't even stand to look at you right now."

"But the wolf—"

"Don't worry," Anna called as she jogged away. Even though she was turned away from me, I caught the hitch of her voice as a sob escaped her throat. "As far as you're concerned, he doesn't exist."

21

ANNA

I stalked into the forest, fuming at Luke. He was being ridiculous. This stupid vendetta he had against Caleb was endangering us all. He needed to work together with his cousin, and if me being angry at him would get him to cooperate, then it was worth it.

However, he was right about one thing. I shouldn't be out here by myself. "Caleb?" I called out. "It's me, Anna. Luke's not with me. Can you come out, please?"

A few moments later, I heard a rustling in the undergrowth to my left. I jumped back, my heart in my chest, as a wolf's head poked out from the brown leaves, its pink tongue panting heavily. I relaxed as I recognised Caleb's brown eyes and reddish-tinged fur.

"Hey." I bent down and patted his head. "I'm glad you're here. Would you like to walk a bit? I could do with clearing my head. And I definitely *do* believe there's another wolf out here."

He nodded his head slightly, and the two of us headed back down the path. We walked in silence for several minutes, a smattering of rain falling through the branches and hitting my shoulders in large, cold droplets. Out here, sound dissipated, becoming larger, more full, each rain droplet and bird call and crunch of the leaves a thing of exquisite beauty, part of the orchestra of nature. I breathed deep, the peace calming my nerves.

We emerged into a small clearing, near the edge of one of the streams that trickled through the rocky seams. Through a gap in the trees, the grey clouds bulged, heavy with water, waiting for the opportune time to let it drop on us. A steep, slippery face sloped down towards the water, and further along the stream I noticed a tall outcrop of rocks, a small dark hole inside them. I could see that in parts, the stream was almost – but not quite – narrow enough to jump over. My heart hammered against my chest as I realised this was exactly the scenario Ben had been in when he died. He'd been further north, and the stream had been wider, but the slippery rocks, the jutting, jagged edges like teeth, ready to swallow me whole …

I sat down on the rock, far back from the edge, and tried to drive away the thoughts of the past. I had far too much to deal with in the present. I patted the stone beside me. "Caleb, change back, and let's talk."

He did as I asked, his fur retreating into his skin, his snout retracting into his face, the nose and lips separating, becoming the chiselled features of Caleb's handsome face. He rolled over and stretched out on his back, clicking his fingers and exposing his naked body.

"I'm here. What do you want?" he snarled at me. He didn't bother to hide himself, his gleaming body on full display.

"I'm sorry about Luke." I stepped up to him and met his eyes. If he was going to try and intimidate me, I was going to bite back. "This whole experience has been hard for him."

"Luke doesn't trust me," Caleb said flatly.

"Of course he doesn't," I said. "He's lived his whole life believing he was the only child of the original Lowe clan. He's been alone, apart from his dad, for as long as he can remember. And now here you are, on his territory, trying to steal his girl."

"I wouldn't have tried to take you in the first place if I'd have known he was my cousin," Caleb growled. "Besides, it's become obvious to me you're not my type."

"I know that. But he doesn't. His father died just recently. Did he tell you that?"

Caleb shook his head.

"Well, I'm telling you now. Luke is still grieving, and one thing I know about grief is that it hits different people in different ways. Some people retreat into themselves, and become a shadow of who they are. Other become healers, they take care of everyone else around them, because it's easier than facing their own pain." I gulped as a lump rose in my throat. I didn't want to cry now. "And some people – people like Luke – dedicate themselves to a mission, to one last crusade in honour of their loved one, because pursuing a goal in that person's name is a way of keeping them alive."

"That sounds familiar." Caleb grinned.

I nodded. "But one thing that pretty much all grieving people have in common is a paralysing fear of losing those they love. As humans, we always feel so invincible, but as soon as you lose someone, you realise how tenuous your happiness truly is. More than anything you want to shield yourself from ever feeling that kind of pain ever again. You start to pull back from people you love, but it's hard, because you already care about them. But when someone new comes into your life – especially someone who has some tie to the person you lost – you push them away, because it's easier to do that now than to come to care for them and lose them all over again."

Caleb grimaced. "This conversation has veered way into an area I'm not comfortable with."

"I don't want to hear a damn word about real men not talking about their feelings. It's utter shite and you know it."

"What *do* you want me to do about this?"

"I want you to talk to Luke. Find a way to make him trust you. Otherwise, he's just going to keep finding reasons to doubt you, and he'll either drive you away from here, or kill you, or become so distracted that he gets killed by this other wolf. None of these are things I want to happen. He has to learn to trust again, to love again. It's the only way he'll ever be truly free."

Behind me, a loud bark clipped the air.

Caleb and I whirled around. Luke sat upright on the edge of the trees, a front paw raised in a kind of tentative greeting. My heart pounded against my chest. He'd heard the entire conversation.

I jabbed Caleb in the side.

"Luke ..." he began, then cleared his throat. "I guess ... I'm sorry about jumping on Anna before. I didn't know she was family. I'm not trying to kill her, or you, or take her from you. I swear. I told you about my stepfather, how he treated me, how he drove me away. All I want is a pack of my own, and I think you and I, together, could form that pack. But for now, all we really need is for you to trust me. Don't waste your energy watching me, waiting for me to screw you over. I got your back, man – focus on the real enemy."

Luke glanced up at his cousin. I couldn't read the look in his eyes. Then his gaze flicked over to me. He turned tail, and bounded away into the woods.

"Luke!" I leapt to my feet and dashed after him. Behind me, Caleb called out, but I ignored him. I needed to find Luke.

He slowed down to a fast walk, and I was able to follow him through the trees. "Where are you taking me?"

In response, Luke flicked his head over his shoulder, licking his lips.

Luke ran all the way back to the camp. Night was falling steadily, casting its gloom over the campsite. Judging by the amount of cars parked across the road, the police had arrived. All the lights in the caravan were on, and I could see people moving around inside. Luke nudged the flap of my tent, and I lifted it up for him. He darted inside, and I followed.

"Why did we come here? You're acting very strange." I asked.

Luke sat on the bed, and changed back into his human form. "Unlike Caleb, I didn't want to be naked in the middle of the forest." He grinned, grabbing my hands and pulling me down beside him.

"This is serious. That wolf is still out there. Do you get that now?"

"I am deadly serious." Luke wrapped me in his arms and kissed me fiercely.

I melted into the kiss, the warmth of his mouth against mine lighting up my whole body. The ache in my core flared to life, and all my conflicting thoughts went fuzzy. "But ... shouldn't we do something ... the wolf ..."

"He'll be far away from here right now, with all the police around." Luke pulled my shirt off my shoulders. "Right now, the only thing I can think about is being inside you."

My protests melted away under the fire of his kiss.

LUKE AND I SLEPT FITFULLY. Every few hours, some sound outside the tent tore us from our dreams, and we huddled together, listening hard in case it was the wolf. But the wolf didn't come back.

As the sun started to rise I heard the police return. They wandered around the forest, talking in to their radios. I couldn't stay in bed any longer, and threw back the covers, hunting for my clothes.

"What are you doing?" Luke threw out a sleepy arm to pull me back into the sleeping bag.

"I'll have to talk to the police, give them my statement."

"Stay with me."

"You're clingy today. What's brought this on?"

"You mean aside from you being completely amazing? Oh, probably the fact that even though all this shit is going on and you're in danger, you're trying to get me and my cousin talking. You're always thinking of me, Anna, trying to make me happy. Apart from Dad ..." Luke's fingers stroked my cheek, "...no one's ever done that for me before."

"And that makes you want to fuck me?"

"It makes me want to make you just as happy as I am. And I know a great way of doing that." Luke nibbled on my ear. Sparks of desire flew across my skin.

"And Caleb ... do you forgive him ..."

"I haven't decided." Luke lifted my thermal underwear over my head, his hands skimming over my skin. "I'm not thinking about Caleb right now."

"Luke—"

"Anna," he whispered against my lips, his eyelashes fluttering against my cheek. "I love you."

I love you.

The words froze in my mind, like three enormous icebergs penetrating deep below the surface. Cold crept into my body, driving out the heat of Luke's embrace. My eyes flew open. Luke had stopped kissing me – he stared at me intently, his green eyes ablaze with love.

I didn't see him. Instead of Luke's face, I saw Ben, his earnest features frozen forever in my mind, his face in the morgue, blotched and broken. I loved him and he left me. My ears buzzed. *This can't be happening.*

"No," I choked out.

"No?" Luke's mouth curled down. He looked unsure.

"I can't ... I have to go ..." I grabbed my thermal top and yanked it back over my head. My heart pounded against my chest, and a sharp pain stabbed at my stomach, as though someone were twisting a knife into my guts. *I can't do this ... I can't lose another ... I'm not strong enough ...*

Luke reached out to me, but I kicked out with my leg, hitting him harder than I intended right in the solar plexus. He bounced back against the air mattress. "Ooof, hey, what's wrong?" Luke's face fell completely.

"I have to go." I shoved my feet into my shoes.

"Wait, Anna. Let's talk about this—" He reached for me again.

"Get the fuck away from me!" I screamed, panic rising in my chest. Luke recoiled, as though I'd hit him. The knife in my stomach twisted deeper.

The look on his face tore my heart open. I needed to get out. I grabbed my keys from on top of my bag and raced from the tent. Luke yelled after me, but I didn't look back. I couldn't bear to see him fall apart.

"Hey, Anna. Where are you going?" Ruth called out as I fled across the site towards my Mini. "The police need your statement—"

Ignoring her, I slammed the door shut, and gunned the engine. My Mini bounced away from the site. The panic clawed at my throat. I had to get away from the forest, away from Luke and Ben and my father, the men who would not let me be free.

22

LUKE

"*A*nna!" I yelled after the departing Mini. She didn't look up, didn't stop the car. The Mini's wheels squealed as she nailed the corner at top speed, the tiny car carrying away the only woman I'd ever loved.

My chest ached. My whole body shuddered. I felt as though I'd been run over by a lorry. She left. *She left.* The shock of it juddered through my veins.

"Luke?" Frances's voice pierced through the pain slicing across my skull. I was dimly aware I was standing in the middle of the camp, completely naked. But I couldn't bring myself to care. I wiped my hand across my lip. I could still taste the sweetness of her kiss there.

Anna left me. I told her I loved her and she fucking left.

Anger seized me, a rage that rumbled from my toes right up through my whole body, a bubbling heat that seared me inside and out. Fuck her. Only a few minutes ago she'd been telling Caleb that stuff, and now she'd just left.

My eyes pricked with tears. I blinked them away angrily. I hadn't felt that sensation in a long time, not since I was a kid. I hadn't even cried when Dad died. But watching Anna run away, watching her abandon me just as I was ready to open up to her, almost destroyed me.

If Anna is going to run away, let her run away.

"Luke, what's wrong? What are you doing?" I became aware that Ruth was jogging towards me, her gaze scanning my whole body. I tore myself away, and raced back to my own tent. I yanked on trousers and a jacket. Ruth poked her head in through the flap. "The police are going to need your statement about the caves—"

I shoved my way past her and headed into the trees, not even paying attention to where I was going. All I could see were angry red welts. My fists clenched and unclenched, the tension rippling through my body. With nowhere to go, nothing to direct it at, my rage simmered below my skin, the wolf inside threatening to go completely berserk.

As soon as I was far enough away from the camp, I found a spot on the edge of the limestone seam running along the stream. I leaned against a tree and started undoing my shirt. I'd fold up my clothes and hid them in the branches, and then I could let the wolf loose. I needed to run, to burn off this horrible, sickening feeling.

"A little chilly for skinny dipping?" A voice shattered my private thoughts.

"Fuck off, Caleb." My hands froze on the button. "You are the last person I want to talk to right now."

Caleb stepped out from behind the tree. "Wrong. I am *exactly* the person you need to talk to. Because I'm the only one who can tell you when to pull your head out of your arse."

He still hadn't found any clothing. I was really not in the mood for discussing my feelings with a naked man. I turned away from him. "This is none of your business. Why did you follow me, anyway?"

"Because I saw Anna drive off from the camp, and she was

crying, and I figured you must've done something to upset her. Although, you're a Lowe, so you're probably used to women seeing your cock and cowering in fear—"

"Why do you assume I've done something to her?" I demanded, closing the space between us so I was right up in his face. Caleb didn't blink.

"Because you're an idiot."

"Well, you can shove off, because all I did was tell her I loved her, and she bolted."

"Of course she bolted. Didn't you hear all that stuff she was saying to me before about grief and being scared to love again?"

"She was talking about me."

Caleb slapped his forehead. "You're an idiot. She was talking about herself. And you're sitting here being angry with her for it."

"Wouldn't you?"

Caleb shook his head. "I'd be chasing after her, getting her to talk me what hurt her so bad that she's terrified of loving me back."

Shit. The fight went out of me, the tension in my body turning to shame. Caleb was right. Here I was, acting like a selfish idiot because I'd been vulnerable, and she'd shied away. I should have seen that she did that because of what happened to her last boyfriend. I should have found a way to reassure her, but instead I'd thrown a tantrum and run away. Some mate I was.

I sank against the tree, my head in my hands. "Fuck."

"Don't worry. You can fix it. Just find her, and apologise. Women like that, I'm told."

"How do you know so much about this stuff?"

Caleb grinned. "Hey, just because I don't have a mate, doesn't mean I don't know a thing or two about women, or about grief."

I glanced at him then, noticing a flicker of something pass

over his face. It was the first time since meeting him where Caleb looked anything other than in perfect control. He appeared vulnerable, human. In an instant, it was gone, and Caleb's usual smug expression was back once again.

I got to my feet, dusting off my jeans. "I've got something to do."

He nodded. "Good luck. And if she still hates your guts after you're done, put in a good word for me. That girl is *fine*."

I didn't even bother to answer him. I dove into the trees, heading back towards my truck as fast as my human legs would carry me. *Anna, I'm sorry. I'm coming for you.*

23

ANNA

I love you.

My hands gripped the Mini's steering wheel so hard, my knuckles turned white. The words pounded over and over in my head, the echo of memories mingling with Luke's husky voice. Ben shyly saying those words for the first time over dinner at the *Tir Na Nog* pub, his nervous face watching me from over his shepherd's pie. My dad whispering them in my ear as he tucked me into bed at night. My own lips trembling as I fought back tears to get the words out at their funerals.

The frigid night had left a layer of ice on the windscreen of the Mini. I'd tried to wipe it away with my mittened hand, but it was holding fast. I didn't want to go back to camp for water to thaw it and risk running into Luke, so I wound down my window, and navigated my way slowly along the track, leaning out over the car door like the main character in a bad spy film.

Luke loved me. He *loved* me. My chest ached with the weight of that revelation. After everything he'd been through, that must have been such an incredible thing for him to say.

But I couldn't say it back. Not yet. Those words ... they still retained echoes of Ben, of his essence. He'd said them, and then he'd left me, just like Dad left me. The grief had only just begun to recede into a dull, empty ache. I wasn't ready to open myself up to that kind of love anymore.

Luke loves me.

The tears poured down my face, the cold wind turning them to ice on my face. I kept my eyes glued to the road in front of me. I longed so badly to love him back, to fall into his arms and feel completely safe, but it just wasn't possible. I knew I shouldn't have run away. I should've tried to explain exactly how I did feel, but the words caught in my throat like a bone lodged in my oesophagus. Now it was too late. I'd rejected him. Guys like Luke didn't stick around to get rejected twice.

I needed to get out of the forest. Away from the trees and the earthy scent that reminded me of both of them. Of Ben and Luke. Of my past and what might've been my future. I needed to clear my head and think.

I needed tea. And a pie. And a friendly ear to bend about my current predicament. *I'll go to town. Derek will probably be awake. He'll know what to do.*

I kept checking behind me, but Luke hadn't followed me. *Good.* But it didn't feel good inside. I wished his wolf would come sprinting into view, pink tongue extended, powerful legs churning at the earth as he raced after me, ready to claim me back at any cost. I wished I could bear to hear those words from his lips again. I wished like hell I was brave enough to say them back, for I suspected I would mean them.

No. I couldn't think about it. I wasn't ready. I wasn't strong enough. *I have to get away ... get away ...*

By the time I exited the forest, the heat of the engine had thawed enough of the ice that I could see the road ahead. I wound up the window and texted Derek to see if I could come over. He responded that he wasn't home right then, but he would be in about an hour, and he'd be happy to see me.

The *Bewitching Bites* bakery on the high street was open. They were empty at this time of the morning, so the stunning Asian woman behind the counter made me a cup of tea for free and talked me through their extensive cake selection. She looked vaguely familiar, and I gave a start as I realised she was the same woman who'd been sitting on the back of the motorcycle I'd passed earlier in the week. I sat on a rickety table by the window and devoured the best Cornish pasty I'd ever eaten, thinking about Luke and trying to stop myself from throwing it all back up again.

You ruined everything.

My phone beeped. Derek was home. Good. I needed to talk to someone, to work this thing through in my head and figure out if I could fix it somehow. The woman boxed up half of a Heaven and Hell cake for me, and I drove over to his house. When he opened the door and saw my expression, his face immediately crumpled.

"Anna, what's wrong?" He flung open the door and I slunk inside.

"I'm such an idiot. But I brought sugar," I said, moving a giant coil of rope so I could slump down on his sofa. "Why do you have rope?"

"Oh, Rodney's decided to take up rock climbing." Derek took the cake box from my hands and fetched two plates, forks, and a knife from the kitchen, as well as two cups of tea.

"Sounds ambitious." Derek's flatmate wasn't exactly a small guy.

"I think he has the hots for the captain of the climbing club. Here." Derek passed me a small slice of cake. I pushed it away and grabbed the box, digging my fork into the layers of gooey whisky ganache. I shoved another slice in my mouth, and felt a tiny bit better. I was here with Derek. I had cake. I could sort this out, somehow.

"Okay, I can see this is an emergency." Derek nodded at the box as he picked up his slice. "It's about a guy, isn't it?"

"It sure is." I sniffed, shoving another forkful of cake into my mouth in a vain attempt to prevent a sob from escaping. "I met him on the dig and I ... and he ..."

"I figured," Derek said darkly. "You've been pretty distracted the last few days. You're only like that when you're in love."

I choked on my mouthful. My stomach heaved. I cupped my hands over my mouth as I coughed violently. "Don't say that," I whispered as I recovered. "Luke just told me ... that he loved me."

"That's big. Especially after only a few days."

"Yeah." There was a pause while I scoffed more cake.

Derek asked in a strange, hard voice, "And do you love him?"

"I ... don't know. I think so. Yes. But it doesn't matter. I got scared. I ran away. You should have seen his face, Derek. He was heartbroken. He won't be back for me."

"If he's going to bail on you when you're this emotionally battered, then he's a complete bastard," Derek declared. He moved closer to me and placed his arm around my shoulders. I sank back against him, enjoying the comfort of his shoulder while tears streamed down my cheeks.

"He just lost someone, too." I sniffed. "I think we're both a little too vulnerable for this intense emotional shit."

"I say forget about him," Derek said. "You don't need a guy like that dragging you down. You have other options."

"Oh yeah? Like what? Every guy I love dies. I think I am cursed."

"What about me?"

"You?" I turned up to him, smiling. He was joking, right? We'd already talked about this. But his face looked deadly serious.

"Yeah, sure. Me. Why not?" Derek stroked my shoulder with his hand. "We're perfect for each other. We're both academics. We like the same books and movies. We're always here for each other. We're already close. It wouldn't be much to take the next step."

"Derek ..." I shook my head, my stomach churning. Why did he have to say this now? "We've already been through this. I don't see you like that. I'm sorry. We're friends. Good friends, and I love that. But friends is all we're ever going to be."

His face turned hard. His grip on my shoulder tightened. "That's a mistake, Anna, and you know it. We're meant to be together, I can feel it. It won't be long until you realise I'd make a fine mate."

Mate? There was that word again. But why was Derek saying it? Only shifters talked about their partners as mates. But Derek wasn't ...

Was he?

"Come on, Anna. Don't tell me you hadn't figured it out." Derek stared at me, grinning.

In a flash, the pieces slotted together. Derek going away all the time to work on his project, where he couldn't be reached. He'd been gone at the same time as Luke – over the full moon. Derek had been the one who'd given me that book. No one had broken into my house – it was Derek all along.

I remembered Clara talking about her regulars coming in for their monthly pills. Derek must've been one of her regulars, which was why she couldn't tell us if there were other new wolves in the area, which had led Luke to suspect Caleb. When all along ...

Derek was the black wolf: the powerful shifter who'd destroyed the site and killed Misty Sharpe. I tried to scramble away, but he grabbed my other shoulder, pinning me tight against the sofa.

"But ... " I spluttered. "But you're a Peyton. I saw it on your family tree. Your family hated werewolves."

"Correction, my family hated the *Lowe*. The Peytons are an ancient wolf pack, one of the first to settle in England. They wanted to be the only wolves in Crookshollow. This village is built upon two ley lines, a crossroads – it's a vitally important centre of supernatural species coming and going across England. My family wanted to control that, in the same way my grandfather controlled the church. The Lowe stood in their way."

"So why not just kill them? Why hurt the baby and make the villagers do it?"

"Because they were beloved," Derek growled. "And that could never work. You can't exercise control with kindness. We needed to remake the wolf. It's not enough just to kill a person, Anna. You have to kill the myth of them, too. When that baby was found torn to pieces, werewolves were once again creatures to be feared. And that was exactly what my great-grandfather wanted."

"That's awful," I sobbed.

"That's the circle of life. The strong kill those who stand in their way. And now," he added, his mouth twisting into an ugly grin, "you and your wolf are standing in *my* way."

"But why destory the cave paintings?" I cried out, desperately trying to keep Derek talking. If he was talking, he wasn't tearing me to pieces.

"Because your boyfriend and the other Lowe wolf were going to use them to establish their pack in this area. I couldn't have that. Crookshollow is *mine*. I needed to show them what my grandfather had established a century ago – the Peytons are the dominant force in Crookshollow. And we are to be feared."

"Why did you kill the reporter?"

"That *woman*," he growled. "She wrote ridiculous, libellous things about my family. I couldn't allow those words to stand unopposed. If other wolves read that story and knew she still lived, they would believe the Peytons were weak. But I am not weak. I will not have my family name dragged through the mud in some cheap tabloid."

"Is that what you're doing?" I sobbed, trying to wrench my arm out from his grip. "Is this all to prove you're some kind of macho super wolf?"

"I told you. It's all to kill the myth of the Lowe, so that the Peyton myth can live on. I've destroyed the paintings, now I just need to make sure that no one who knows their true origin still lives. Then I alone will have control over the story of the caves."

"But you haven't," I exclaimed. "The photographs have been in all the papers. The BBC did a detailed story about the find. Experts from around the world are going to be studying those images. They will figure out they're fakes."

"No they won't, because they all want to believe in their own myths about the past. That's what always gets me about you archaeologists," Derek scoffed. "You think you're so *scientific,* so *impartial.* But really, you need the meaning just as much as the rest of the world ... the stories, the narrative, the mythos. You need to believe the paintings are a message from the distant past, and so that is exactly how they will be portrayed. No, I'm not worried about the paintings now. There are only three people who know the truth: the two Lowe wolves..." he grinned, "...and you."

He moved his hand to grip my chin, shifting his weight on my other wrist. I took the opening, and rolled to the side, launching all my bodyweight towards the coffee table. Derek cried out as I bent my arm back, my wrist snapping from his grasp. I slammed against the floor.

I grabbed the coffee table, trying to pull myself to my feet. Derek wrapped his powerful arms around my legs, dragging me back towards him. I grabbed my tea mug from the table and flung it into his face. He howled as the boiling liquid stung his skin, and he let go of me to rub his eyes. I scrambled to my feet and backed towards the door, putting the sofa between us.

"Stay away from me, Derek." A few more feet and I'd be close enough to lunge for it. "I know martial arts."

"No you don't." He grinned, shuffling towards me. The skin on his face was all red from where the hot tea had scalded him. Black bristles sprouted from his cheeks and forearms. I could already see his fingers deforming. He picked up Rodney's rope, and took another step towards me. "I'm your friend, remember? I know you took three classes at the YMCA, but then you quit when it clashed with *Time Team* on the telly."

He lunged for me. I scrambled for the door. My hands closed around the knob, but Derek grabbed my hair, yanking me back. My scalp screamed. Derek shoved me face down on the floor, pinning my hands behind my back.

"Hold still." He growled in my ear. I tried to wriggle away. Derek trapped my legs beneath his. My head throbbed, my chest tight with panic. Derek wrapped the rope around my hands, trapping them behind my back. Then he let me fall. I slammed down hard on my knees, then tried to wriggle across the floor like a snail, but Derek placed a boot on my shoulder, stomping on me and keeping me in place. He held up a roll of tape. "I'm sorry about this," he said. "But I think you'll appreciate this. It's a bit like being an Egyptian mummy."

He rolled the tape around my body, taping my legs together, pinning my hands at my sides, and my legs together. Panic rose in my chest, pounding against the inside of my skull. *This is bad, this is seriously bad.*

Derek picked me up like I was a stack of towels and carried me out to my car. He stuffed me into the back seat, pulled the keys from my pocket, and climbed in the front.

"Sorry I haven't put your seatbelt on," he said. "I know you have a thing about that. But I figure you're going to die soon, anyway, so it probably doesn't matter."

It took Derek three tries to start the engine. I hoped in vain that he wouldn't get the hang of it, but after a lot of swearing, it finally turned over. As my poor Mini bumped along the road, I slid around the seats, eventually ending up on the floor with my legs bent awkwardly in the air. I could see trees flashing by through the window. We were heading back into the forest.

Luke, I thought, my mind reeling. *I know you can't hear me, but if you could, I'm sorry. I'm so sorry.*

24

LUKE

"*H*er car's gone," Caleb said, gesturing to the empty spot where her Mini had been parked.

"Yeah. She sped away pretty quick after my little revelation."

"Any idea where she might have gone?"

I racked my brain. Would Anna have gone deeper into the forest?

No. I remembered what she'd said about her previous boyfriend, how he'd had an accident and died in the forest. If she was upset, she wouldn't stay here, among the trees and memories. She'd head back to town, find someone to talk to, perhaps that guy she visited the other day.

"She's in Crookshollow," I said. "She had a friend there named Derek. I bet she's gone to see him."

"Let's go," Caleb pulled open the door of my truck and climbed in. "Keys?"

"Why are you driving?"

"Because you're too upset to think straight. And you're a shit driver."

"I can just feel that cousinly love," I growled, but there wasn't time to argue. I climbed in the passenger seat and tossed him the keys.

Caleb gunned the engine and we tore down the road. Behind us, Ruth came running towards us, the police officer from the other day hot on her heels. Ruth waved her arms frantically, yelling something I couldn't hear. As we sped past, the car wheel flicked a wad of mud right into her face. I would've burst out laughing if I wasn't so afraid.

We turned the corner, past the rotting oak where I'd first shown Anna what I truly was. We bounced along the road, every second feeling like a lifetime. Trees sped past in a blur. Rain pelted the windshield.

"Who's that?" Caleb jabbed his finger at the road ahead. We were coming up to a T-junction – the left fork leading into town, the right deeper into the forest. In front of us, a car sped across the T-junction, hurtling down the forest track. My stomach lurched. It was Anna's Mini. But a black-haired guy was driving it. I couldn't see anyone else in the car.

Something's not right. Anna loved that car. She'd never let anyone else drive it.

"Follow that car!" I yelled, leaning over and yanking the wheel around. The truck lurched towards the ditch.

"I know, fuck!" Caleb batted me away, grabbing the wheel and steering the truck back on the road. He put his foot to the floor. I grabbed the handle as we hurtled towards the Mini.

We quickly gained on them, but the black-haired driver showed no sign of stopping. I could just make out a large shape slumped across the back seats. Was that Anna? My stomach lurched. The Mini skidded around a corner, fighting for control in the mud. Its right front wheel lost traction on the dirt road, and it pitched into the ditch. The bonnet hit an oak, and buckled around it.

"Anna," I screamed.

"Fuck!" Caleb slammed on the brakes. I threw open the door and leapt from the car before he'd even stopped.

I landed hard on my feet, flailing my arms to keep my balance. The air reeked of the bad wolf. I ploughed towards the Mini. As I reached the back door, I caught another glimpse of that object slumped along the back seat. It definitely looked like a person, tied up with rope. I noticed Anna's boots flailing in the air. I grabbed for the door handle. Something large and black and furry leapt from the front window and slammed into me.

I hit the ground hard, my back cracking on the road. The wolf's claws dug into my shoulders, his sharp teeth snapping just millimetres from my face. Hot saliva dribbled over my cheeks. His black fur gleamed from the rain.

As I fought with him for control, I forced my own change, my limbs cracking and shifting beneath the wolf's iron grip. As my snout grew outward and my teeth sharpened, I snapped back at him. I caught his cheek, tearing a piece of skin. He yelped with surprise, then slashed at my shoulder. I winced as he drew blood, pain flaring through my body.

As suddenly as the wolf was on top of me, he was gone. I heard him yelp as he sailed through the air, his vicious claws flailing for purchase. Another shape hurtled through the air, bearing a distinctive reddish hue.

Caleb.

He slammed the black wolf into the earth, his teeth digging into black fur. The black wolf howled as blood spurted between Caleb's teeth. As quickly as I could, I pulled myself to my feet. My front leg shot with pain as I placed weight on it, but I had to push through the pain. I needed to get to Anna.

Caleb and the wolf tumbled across the road, their teeth bared, their claws locked tight into each other's flesh. Blood smeared across the ground. *Can't worry about them now.* I grabbed the door of the Mini and pulled. It wouldn't budge. *It must be locked.*

My heart sank into my knees as I noticed the huge dent along the side of the car. It had buckled the door so badly, it was now clamped shut.

Anna!

I barked at the limp figure, banging on the window with my paw. The shape on the floor wriggled. I heard a strained grunt.

It was her. Her eyes met mine, wide and full of terror. In a flash I changed back to my human form. "Try to move away from me!" I shouted. She heaved herself up and leaned forward, presenting her back to the window. I could see her hands tied to her sides with tape, her mouth also taped shut. My stomach clenched as I saw blood running down the side of her face.

I slammed my fist into the window. Pain splintered through my arm as the glass shattered into pieces. Anna screamed through her gag as glass fell into the car. I grabbed a rock from beside the track and used it to bash out the rest of the glass.

I leaned inside, barely feeling the jagged glass on the edge of the window as it tore at my chest. "This is going to hurt!" I shouted. Anna screamed as I tugged off the tape securing her mouth.

"Luke," she sobbed. "Get Derek. He was my friend but he's really—"

"I know," I growled. "Hold still."

I transformed back into the wolf, and leapt in through the window. I dug my claws under the tape holding Anna's arms in place, and sliced through it with ease. She flexed her fingers, wincing with pain, while I freed her legs. She leaned forward and unlocked the opposite door, sliding across the seat and outside.

I leapt out after her, just as the black wolf – Derek – skidded across the road, Caleb's jaws clamped around his foot. As the wolves barrelled towards us, Derek's body shifted, and he became a naked man, his enormous muscles straining as he dragged himself across the dirt, blood streaming from his wound. Caleb growled, trying to dig his teeth deeper into Derek's leg, but Derek grabbed the wolf around the neck and, muscles tensed, tossed him aside like a cuddly toy. Fuck, he was strong. Caleb hit a tree on the other side of the road, and crumpled into a heap. He didn't get up.

"Caleb?" Anna croaked out. Her voice sounded strained, weak. What had this bastard done to her?

"We meet at last, Lowe." Derek stood up. He spat out my name, as though it were poison. "I'm pleased both you and your cousin fell for my trap. It will make my work all the easier to complete."

"And what work is that?" I demanded, placing my body between his and Anna's. She wrapped her trembling fingers around my forearm.

"I'm here to finish what my grandfather started," Derek hissed. "To destroy the Lowe clan completely, so that Crookshollow will once again belong to the Peytons – wolves who aren't afraid of their wild nature, wolves who are ready to take their rightful place as rulers of humans—"

While Derek was talking over his plan, as all criminal masterminds did, I could hear Anna scrambling in the car behind me. I didn't dare draw attention to what she was doing by turning around, but I hoped like hell she wasn't being obvious about whatever she was trying to do. I had no idea what until I felt something cold and smooth press against my hand. It was a long sherd of glass. A weapon.

"Why now?" I demanded, trying to keep him talking. "Robert Peyton killed off my family, for all he knew. Why did he not establish his pack here and rule Crookshollow with an iron fist, as he clearly always intended to do?"

"After he destroyed your pack, the church decided he was too *spirited* for this sleepy village," Derek scoffed. "They sent him up to Ireland, to root out the infidels there. He was killed in a barroom brawl, and his brothers were not fit to fill his shoes as alpha. They disgraced our name with their drinking and gambling, and our family heMargaretge was reduced to a shadow."

Behind Derek, Caleb was dragging himself to his feet. He started to change, his limbs slowly contorting and clicking into place. His injuries were slowing down his shift ... or was this intentional? Blood oozed from a cut along his leg, but how bad was it really? I still couldn't shift my nagging feeling that Caleb and Derek were working together ... that Caleb wasn't a Lowe at all, but a relative of Derek's. That all their fighting was just a ruse to force me to trust Caleb.

If it's a ruse, it's a bloody committed one. He looks seriously beaten up.

Derek was still talking. "... his son – my father – became a schoolteacher and tried to live among humans. He taught me nothing but shame for my heMargaretge. When I started digging into our history, I knew I had to come back here, to wait for the best time to reclaim our lands. And then Anna found the paintings, and I smelled you on her. I knew a Lowe had returned, and that now was the perfect time."

"It certainly is," I said, my fingers tightening around the glass shard. I leapt at Derek.

He darted to the side, clearly anticipating my move. I tried to pivot towards him, but he slammed his fist into the side of my skull. My head rang. My vision blurred. I hit the ground hard, the shock of it paralysing me.

In a flash Derek had grabbed Anna, holding her around the neck, pressing her body against his. With his other hand, he dug around in the back of the Mini, and pulled out my crowbar, which he held aloft.

"You hadn't even noticed this was missing from your truck. If you come any closer, I'll stave her head in."

Fear coursed through me, mingling with the white hot rage that flooded my veins. *He wouldn't do this to her.* I still had the glass in my hand. I'd been gripping it so tight, my own blood flowed between my fingers.

"Just do as he says, Luke," Anna cried. "He'll let us all go if you just give him the caves."

Luke. Caleb mouthed, waving his arms. *Over here.*

He was in the perfect position. I could toss him the shard as I attacked Derek. If I could grab the crowbar, Caleb could slice his throat before he even knew what's happening. But that nagging doubt wouldn't leave me. Why hadn't Derek checked to see if Caleb was really out of it? If I threw Caleb the glass, and he was really part of Derek's scheme, I'd be handing him the means to kill Anna.

Trust no one. My father's words burned in my mind. My father had lived by that motto, and he'd kept us safe together, alone in the forests my whole life. How could I now trust this wolf who said he was my cousin, with the most precious thing in the world to me?

But then I remembered Anna's words. "You have to learn to trust again, to love again. It's the only way you'll be truly free."

"Fuck it," I said, and I threw the glass.

Caleb caught it in his hands, and as one we advanced on Derek. He swung out with the crowbar, aiming for my head, but Anna chose that moment to sink her teeth into the flesh of his arm, and his swing faltered. I grabbed the bar in mid-air, using the momentum to swing his body around, just as Caleb's arm went around his throat, the glass slashing against his skin.

Derek dropped Anna to grab the crowbar with both hands.

"Anna, get out of here!" I screamed. She ducked underneath our raised arms, scrambling for the car. Caleb gripped Derek's face, his hands slick with blood, his face twisted into an ugly scowl as he dragged the glass across Derek's throat.

Derek's grip on the crowbar loosened, and I wrenched it from his hand. His eyes bugged out as I held the tip of the bar against his cheek. "Time to say goodnight," I hissed. "You won't be seeing the full moon again."

"Don't kill him." Anna's voice penetrated my rage. "Please, you're not a killer, Luke."

The wolf within me surged, begging for flesh. Derek's wild eyes bore into mine, begging me to finish him, to give him the dignity of a true wolven death. But behind him stood Anna, her back pressed against the Mini. Her eyes wide with fear, her hand clutched at her heart. The pain in her voice tore at my soul. Her whole life had been death; she couldn't bear any more of it.

I lowered the crowbar. Derek slumped against Caleb, his body too weak to fight any longer. Caleb kept a tight grip on Derek, pulling him down on the earth. I dropped the crowbar on the earth, and crouched down beside him.

I wiped the smear of blood over his eyes. Derek stared up at me with blazed pupils, wild and defiant even as his body trembled with weakness. I leaned in close, and said, "I claim this territory for the Lowe pack. You have challenged my pack, and you have failed. You attacked my mate, and therefore, I will not grant you the boon of an honourable death. You are to return to your family in Ireland, and tell them of your disgrace. You may tell them that the Lowe once again rule here in Crookshollow. And if I ever see your face around here again, I will not be so lenient."

Derek spat in my face. His warm drool rolled down my cheek. I wiped away the insult, and laughed, laughed right in his face. Caleb joined in; it was the ultimate insult, draining Derek of his last burst of defiance. He slumped to the earth, his hands clasped around the wound in his throat. He was badly wounded, and utterly beaten.

Someone crashed into me. "Luke ... oh, Luke." Anna sobbed as she held me, her tiny body rocking against mine. I wrapped my arms around her, relief surging through me. It was over, it was all over.

Anna was safe; the wolf was neutralised; my family honour would be restored. All was right with the world.

25

ANNA

*L*uke let Caleb drive the jeep back to the site, while he crawled in the back with me. He didn't seem to want to let go of me, which suited me just fine. Our lips met in a long, luxurious kiss. I devoured him, the relief of still being alive and of having him alive coursing through my veins. The adrenaline made me dazed, giddy, and his tongue against mine felt like the most incredible thing on earth.

"I meant what I said before," Luke murmured against my lips. His arms squeezed me. "I love you, Anna."

"I know you do. That scared me."

"I understand."

"But not anymore." I wrapped my arms around him, losing myself in his kind green eyes. "Being abducted by Derek ... it showed me something, something I should have learned from Dad and from Ben. Life can end in a moment, and all we have is what we're given. I don't want to waste a single moment of the life I've been given being scared of what might be or what could happen. I want to embrace all of my feelings, all of my dreams, even the scary ones. *Especially* the scary ones."

"What does that mean?" His eyes penetrated mine.

"It means ... I love you too." The words, once released, hung in the air between us. "And that I want to be your mate."

"You do? Even after almost getting killed and your archaeological site being destroyed and everything?"

"We're meant to be together." I brushed my lips against his. My chest swelled with emotion. My voice hitched a little as I said, "I knew it from the first moment we met, but I've been fighting it all this time. Well, no more. I'm not going to argue with fate."

"If anyone could, it would be you." Luke kissed my nose.

Caleb yanked on the brake, and the jeep juddered to a halt on the edge of the campsite. "Get out," he growled, "before your lovey-dovey shit makes me sick to my stomach."

It took a bit of manoeuvring to get out of the car with Luke's arms wrapped around me, but we managed.

Ruth and Frances came running up to us. "What's going on?" Ruth demanded. "The police are still waiting to talk to you. You ran away, he was naked ... it's as if you two were guilty or something."

"Your behaviour has been very uncooperative over this whole excavation," Frances scolded. "Really, Anna. I'm surprised at you. This is no way to conduct yourself if you want a career as an archaeologist—"

"*My* behaviour has been uncooperative?" I fumed. Luke's arms around my chest reassured me. "I'm the only one doing any actual archaeology here. You've been so busy running your own PR campaign, you haven't even really *looked* at the cave paintings. I know, because I've been researching them, and I discovered that they are fakes."

"Oh, be serious," Ruth flared. "You're just saying that because you're jealous—"

"No, I'm saying that because it's a fact." All the built-up frustration poured out of me. "Even if you ignore the two figures wearing crosses around their necks in the second-to-last frieze, the hunting scene is all you need to establish a reliable date. The painting clearly shows a band of wolves hunting a pig. The artist has done a remarkable job rendering the pig, so remarkable you can even figure out the particular breed of pig – an Oxford Sandy and Black pig. That breed of pig that wasn't present in England until three hundred years ago."

"That's … that's impossible!" Ruth spluttered.

Frances paled. She slumped against the trunk of a tree. I could see in her eyes that she believed me. "No," she whispered.

"She's lying," Ruth said. "I checked over the painting myself. There wasn't a single indication they weren't genuine neolithic. She just wants to discredit me at any cost—"

"Anna wouldn't lie about this," Frances said, her voice barely above a whisper. She looked ill. I felt awful for destroying her dreams like that.

"I'm sorry, Frances," I said, and I meant it. "I didn't mean to ruin everything. I wasn't trying to prove you wrong, I just wanted to do my own research."

"This is a disaster," Frances moaned.

"Cheer up," Luke said. "So the paintings weren't real. They were still an interesting part of what makes these caves unique, and that uniqueness is now forever attached to your name. And besides, at least one good thing came out of this whole adventure."

"What's that?" Ruth demanded.

"Anna is going to marry me."

"What?" I whirled around to face him. Was this another one of his jokes?

"How about it?" he asked, his green eyes sparkling. "We've only know each other for a few days, but I've never felt this way about anyone before. I love your kindness, your passion, your geekiness. I may have lost my family, but with you by my side, I know I'll never feel alone."

"Oh, Luke." My heart swelled. I couldn't believe the depth of his feeling, the intensity of his gaze. Between us, the energy that drew us together danced and crackled in the air.

"What do you say?" Luke gave me a tentative smile. "Want to help me fulfil one of my own scary dreams?"

"Sure," I said, not even hesitating. I was done second-guessing love. I wanted to be with Luke, he wanted to be with me, and that was all that mattered.

Luke grinned maniacally, a sight that melted my heart. He gathered me in his arms. Out of the corner of my eye, I caught a glimpse of Ruth, her petulant mouth set in a firm line, her eyes wide with shock and disgust. But then, I was swallowed up in Luke's embrace, his deep scent pulling me under. I sank into his kiss, lost in the depth of our love.

I was alive, and I was the mate of a strong, kind werewolf. It was the most glorious feeling in the world.

26

EPILOGUE: ANNA

SIX MONTHS LATER

*T*he bell inside the store tinkled. Clara glanced up from her magazine, a broad smile falling across her wizened face as Luke and I pushed our way through the beaded curtain and into the shop beyond.

"There are my favourite newlyweds," she gushed, racing out from behind the counter to embrace us both. "Let me have a good look at you. Anna, you have such a beautiful tan, dear."

"I know." I grinned, twirling around to show off my beach body in my new Italian sundress. It seemed too bright and cheery for the drab English day, but I was still riding the buzz from our honeymoon. Being with Luke made me feel bright and happy, every single day.

"Why are you back from Italy so soon? I wasn't expecting you two for another few weeks." Clara jabbed a bony elbow into my ribs. "Is wolf-boy not satisfying you?"

"Hey! She is plenty satisfied." Luke grinned. "We had to cut our honeymoon short because *someone* got accepted to a post-graduate program at Yale University."

I grinned. I still couldn't believe it was true. We'd been

stuffing our faces at a little pizzeria after seeing the ruins of Pompeii when I checked my phone and saw the acceptance email. *Yale University.* I'd be starting in just a few weeks, so we needed to cut our honeymoon short so I could come home and pack.

Clara wrapped her arms around me. "Congratulations. I knew you could do it."

"So did I," Luke said. "My wife is pretty amazing."

I was still getting used to the concept of being Luke's mate, and now I was his wife as well. I couldn't believe my life had changed so much in the six months since knowing Luke. I'd been so afraid of my mother's reaction when I introduced him. But instead she'd warmed to him as if he were her own son. Now, the two of them did puzzles together and teased me mercilessly about my love of Star Trek.

My work had exploded after the news of the faked paintings came out. I'd published a paper on dating cave paintings based on animal breeds, inspired by my work on the Crookshollow cave site. With Frances's connections, I managed to get it published in a major academic journal. That paper, coupled with my stellar grades, had earned me a full scholarship to the archaeological program at Yale. For the next two years at least, I didn't have to worry about money – I could just study old stuff and soak up a new adventure with my amazing husband.

And, of course, Luke and I got married. The day was wonderful – we had a small ceremony at Luke's cabin in Sherwood Forest. Clara was our officiant. She read quotes from some of our favourite authors, and I carried a small locket containing pictures of Dad and Ben in my bouquet. We followed the ceremony with photographs in amongst the towering oaks, and a champagne picnic lunch. Both Caleb and Luke looked amazing in their crisp white shirts, grey trousers, and ties engraved with a new Lowe family crest. My mother couldn't stop smiling all day.

Even Frances came along to congratulate us. Ruth transferred to Exeter University, so I didn't even have to invite her to the wedding. All in all, it was the perfect day.

"We've just come in to stock up on a supply of Lycan pills," I said. "Luke is coming with me to Yale, and I don't know how long it will be before we can find a reliable USA supplier."

"When do you leave?" Clara asked, suddenly looking worried.

"In three weeks' time. We need to get settled in our apartment before the semester begins. But if that's a problem—"

"Oh, dear." Clara tsked, taking my hand and rubbing it. "That's going to be very difficult."

"If you can't get the pills in on time, you could just ship them over. That is, if they can get through customs—"

"That's not what I'm talking about, dear."

"Oh, you mean leaving my mother?" I grinned. "It's all worked out. She's selling her flat and moving to America with us. It will be a fresh start for all of us."

"No," Clara grinned. "I mean attending a rigorous academic program while being a mother. That could get very stressful."

"A ... what are you talking about?"

Clara pointed to my stomach. "You're pregnant, dear."

"What ..." I glanced down at my flat stomach. Surely Clara was kidding? "No, I'm not."

"I'm afraid you are."

"But how?"

"I think all that smokin' hot sex in the hotel, or on the beach, or behind the cabana might have had something to do with it," Luke growled in my ear. He wrapped his arms around me.

"Luke!" I swatted him away, my cheeks burning with embarrassment. "I mean, how do you know, Clara? Luke and I haven't even been trying. We're not even ready—"

"Whether you're ready or not." Clara grinned. "That baby is

on the way. Trust me, Anna. I have seen more than enough human mates of shifters come through this shop over the years. I know all the signs to look for."

Luke glared at her. "This is serious? You're not making some kind of cruel joke?"

"This is not my joking face, Lucas Lowe."

Luke threw his arms around me. He pressed his lips to mine, his tongue savouring mine. "We're going to have a baby, Anna." His grin stretched across his entire face. "We're going to have a family. A new generation of the Lowe pack. A new science-fiction geek you can mould in your own perfect image."

I touched my stomach. I couldn't believe that inside was growing a tiny person. Would it be a boy or a girl? Would we have a werewolf like Luke, or would our tiny person be fully human? Either way, he or she would be amazing.

Luke and I were going to be parents. I didn't know how we were going to do it, *and* juggle my master's degree at the same time, but I knew one thing – I couldn't wait to find out.

With my mate by my side, nothing was impossible.

THE END

～

Anna and Luke are having a baby! Find out what else they get up to in a FREE bonus epilogue – to read it, all you have to do is sign up to Steffanie Holmes' VIP club. You'll also get exclusive previews, fun giveaways, and hot teasers -
http://www.subscribepage.com/digging_bonus

～

Want more stories from Crookshollow? Check out Caleb and Rosa's story in the hottest new paranormal romance from Steffanie Holmes, Writing the Wolf.

WRITING THE WOLF

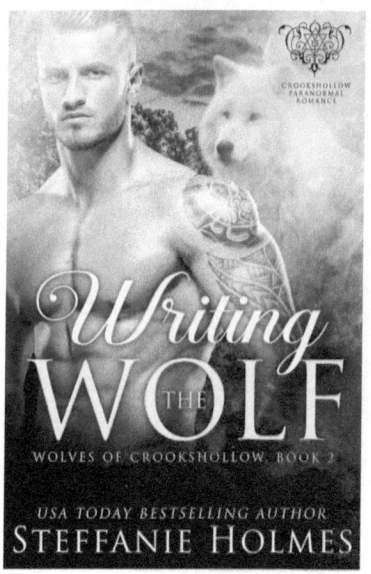

Sink your teeth into the hot new werewolf paranormal romance from USA Today bestselling author, Steffanie Holmes!

Rosa

I need to escape.

After those racist bastards destroyed my home, I can't face the world again.

I've rented a cabin in the heart of the Crookshollow forest. I'm going to lock myself away and work on my book. I'm going to write my story.

And I absolutely, positively WILL NOT think about Caleb, the hunky labourer who's fixing up my cabin.

No way.

I won't think about the way his eyes melt my heart, and his smile melts my panties.

I'm too emotionally raw right now. I can't handle a fling, especially not with a white guy.

Especially not a guy like him. A guy who shags and leaves. I can't handle any more heartache.

Caleb

Rosa Parker – clever writer, black woman, total hottie.

The connection between us sizzles – there's no denying it: this woman is my mate.

When I'm near her, all I want to do is claim her.

If only I wasn't the biggest threat to her life right now.

With a rogue pack after my hide, I can't afford a distraction.

Even a distraction as alluring as her.

I need to keep my wolfish instincts in check.

But I can't help myself.

Rosa Parker has got under my skin.

And I won't stop until I've made her mine.

Writing the Wolf is a standalone novel with an HEA. It's the second book in the hot new paranormal romance series by *USA Today* bestselling author Steffanie Holmes. Read on if you love spunky heroines, pack politics, and a hero so hot he'll have you howling for more.

EXCERPT FROM WRITING THE WOLF

"As you can see," Margaret said, opening the creaking door, "it's a little sparse. But you mentioned you wanted something authentic and rustic, so I thought this was the perfect cabin for you."

Sparse? This wasn't *sparse*. It was the bloody grapes of wrath.

I glanced around the cabin, which didn't take very long, as the room was the size of a postage stamp and contained exactly five items of furniture – a bed, a small desk under the window, a chair for the desk, a long bench along the wall beside the door containing a sink and some shelves, and a faded armchair beside the fireplace. The tiny windows above the desk and beside the door let in a square of grey light, which only made the dark wood walls and low ceiling look even more gloomy.

I want to go home.

The thought hit me like a freight train, dislodging me from the present and sending me back in time, halfway across the country, to where I once had a nice Tudor cottage at the end of a quiet street. I planted window boxes and painted the front door bright red.

Margaret droned on about the plumbing and the handyman

and the sewage and the other quirks of the property. I nodded along, barely listening, lost in the grief steamrolling across my whole body.

It's no use wanting it. You can never go back. You don't have a home anymore.

My therapist, Nancy, said it was normal to grieve for a lost home the same way you would grieve for a person. I hated the grief – it made me feel so weak, so pathetic, pining away for all my *stuff*. I always thought I was pretty grounded, that I didn't place much value on possessions and things, that I could take whatever shit people threw at me and hurl it right back. But while I watched that fire consume everything I owned, I felt as though a piece of myself had burned up along with it.

All my photographs. The diaries I'd diligently kept ever since intermediate school. The furniture I'd collected from estate sales and elegantly restored. The paintings I'd bought at local art fairs. My computer with all my early story drafts. The piles and piles of books. The English Rose crockery Grandmother Mary left me. The gold bangles my mother gave me on my sixteenth birthday, made by craftsman in our ancestral village in Ghana. Who was I without these pieces of a life?

"You need a fresh start, Rosa," Nancy told me, after listening to another of my tirades about the fire. "If you really feel like a shell of a person, then take the fire as an opportunity to remake yourself. Do what you've always wanted to do. Be bold."

Be bold. That was my new mantra. I still wasn't sure it fit, but I was doing my damn best.

As soon as my insurance payout landed in the bank, I handed in my notice at my crappy administration job at the accounting firm in Old Garsmouth; the tiny, backward, completely white village outside of Leeds where I'd lived since university. My boss – the white, leggy Susan, who had done her bit to make my life miserable – at least had the decency to look pissed. "Going back to Africa, then? Going to go steal yourself a jigaboo husband?" she sneered, before informing me she wouldn't be paying me my last paycheque.

"You can keep it." I grinned at her, before walking out of there with my head held high, black curls bouncing over my shoulders. Susan could keep her stupid check. I had 300,000 pounds burning a hole in my pocket. And I knew exactly what I was going to do with it.

I googled "Remote forest cabin England." The first entry that came up was for a collection of cabins on the edge of the Crookshollow Forest. They were owned by an elderly woman named Margaret who rented them out to artists and yogis and any other weirdo who needed a tranquil place to think and create.

It sounded perfect, mostly because it was far, far, far away from Old Garsmouth and the charred remains of my life. I called Margaret immediately and gave her my credit card number for the deposit.

And now I was here, standing in the place I'd call home for the next year. Looking around the drab interior, I couldn't help but think I should have checked out the cabin first. So much for practising being bold.

Maybe bold doesn't work for you, I thought as I dropped my bag beside the battered armchair, sending up a cloud of dust that made me cough and splutter. Stuffing bulged from long gashes in the arms, and I could see more stuffing poking out from beneath the sagging seat. *Maybe you should have just got an apartment—*

No. Stop being so dismissive, Rosa. This is your new life. This is where you're finally going to write your book.

I wandered over to the window, pulled out the chair and looked down at the tiny desk, barely large enough to fit a cup of coffee and my laptop. When I'd come up with the idea of holing up in a cabin in the forest to write, I had visions of those cute

cabins you see on the internet, all comfy beanbags by the fireplace and strings of fairy lights and plush couches covered in
moroccan blankets placed around warm braziers. I pictured
mosquito nets and bright-coloured rugs and a Japanese-style
dining nook and little framed motivational quotes stuck to
the walls.

This cabin barely had room for a beanbag, much less a
Japanese-style dining nook.

Margaret was looking at me expectantly. "Is something
wrong?" She rapped her wooden walking stick against the floor.

I realised I was frowning. Quickly, I plastered a smile across
my face. "It's lovely, really. It's just a little ... bare."

"It's yours for the whole year, dearie. Feel free to decorate it
as you like. JK Rowling used it for the whole summer a few years
back. She put up some lovely cream curtains."

That made me beam. *If it's good enough for JK Rowling, it's good
enough for me.*

"I'll leave you to get settled in." Margaret hobbled down the
front steps. "Don't forget what I said about the plumbing!"

"I won't." I waved, frantically replaying our conversation in
my head to try and figure out if I remembered hearing anything
about plumbing. "Bye, Margaret."

Alone at last with my insanity. I dumped my suitcase beside
the bed, and started pulling out the few possessions I'd brought
with me, mainly stuff I'd bought since the fire. My clothes I had
to leave inside the case until I could buy some drawers. The
torch and ereader and books and drink bottle went beside the
bed. A framed picture of my beloved cat, Lennox (after Lennox
Lewis) took pride of place on the windowsill above the desk.

Poor Lennox. I'm so sorry.

Tears burned the corners of my eyes. *Oh no, you don't.* I was
here, in my cabin, about to start the next phase of my life. This

wasn't the place to get all hysterical again about shit that was in the past.

I slammed my laptop down on the desk harder than I'd intended, placing my new coffee cup, a pad of paper and set of new pencils beside it. This was it. This was where I'd write my novel. This was where I'd pour out all the hurt and pain and anger that had been brewing over the years.

This was where I'd make them all pay.

After I finished unpacking, I went for a walk around the cabin to admire the wonderland that would be my home for the next year.

Margaret owned a small parcel of land at the edge of Crook-shollow Forest, left to her by her first husband after his death. Her house – a beautiful, sprawling eco-lodge built from enormous rough-hewn logs – was up at the opening of the driveway, near the dirt road leading deeper into the forest. Right down the back of her land, some three miles from her house and not even accessible by car, were a collection of six cabins all made from wood felled from the forest by Margaret's second – also late – husband.

Each cabin stood several hundred metres from its neighbour, and the tightly packed trees and uneven ground made them practically invisible, hidden away like witches homes in fairy tales. The whole place had a fairy-tale vibe about it – small paths meandered off in several directions, one leading me down to a swimming hole in the stream, the others leading to lookouts or the day hikes through the forest mentioned on the website. Each cabin had its own letterbox – carved from wood in the shape of animals by Margaret's talented third – also late –

husband. Mine was a wolf. Maybe he would be my spirit animal, to go with my new mantra and my new life.

I headed for the nearest path, and wandered a little way. Branches swayed gently in the breeze, and the cool light of the moon shone between the leaves, creating bubbles of light that danced over the ground. In the distance, I could hear an owl hooting, and the rustle of some critter moving through the undergrowth. I stood silent, taking it all in, wrapping my body in an armour of peace.

Best of all, there was no one else around.

I could see the faint flickers of light through the trees, indicating at least two of the other cabins were occupied. But they'd come here for the same reasons I had, to get away from the world. My only company would be these tall, majestic trees – no one was yelling abuse at me, or telling me to go back to Africa, or threatening to cut me just because I was black.

I sucked in deep breaths of crisp, cool air. It felt *damn* good.

By the time I returned from my walk, I was in much greater spirits. I knew I could make this work. In the moonlight, even the dreary cabin didn't seem so bad. In fact, it had potential. I decided to visit town tomorrow and buy a few things to brighten up the cabin, as well as some groceries. I definitely needed groceries. When I returned from my trip, I could start writing.

As it was, I'd brought a few essential supplies to see me through the night. Dinner was tinned beans on toast, cooked over the little gas stove Margaret had provided. I had a bottle of red wine in my pack, and even one of Sam's old cigars. As I lit up the cigar and took a deep drag, I felt like a real writer.

As the moon rose higher in the sky, casting a cold haze through the trees, I poured myself a third glass of wine, stubbed out the cigar (what a disgusting thing. Why did I like it when Sam smoked them, again?), and picked up my ereader. A few pages into the latest Zadie Smith novel, I realised I desperately needed to go to the bathroom.

The bathroom. Where was the bathroom?

I hadn't given too much thought to it when Margaret had gestured at the rear of the cabin, but now when I went to hunt for the facilities, I couldn't find a doorway inside, which meant only one thing.

Don't tell me. Don't fucking tell me ...

Yup. I had somehow managed to rent a cabin that didn't even have a fucking indoor bathroom.

Cursing at my stupidity, I grabbed my ereader and held it out in front of me, using the screen as a torch as I fumbled my way across the porch and—

"Ow!"

I rubbed my knee. The ereader didn't make a very good torch.

Hobbling around the balustrade, I found my way to the steps at the end of the porch. Sure enough, when I descended them, I found myself facing a tiny wooden shack so small I secretly hoped it was a TARDIS, because if it wasn't bigger on the inside I couldn't see how my booty could possibly fit through the door.

I grabbed the handle and tugged. The door rattled on ancient hinges, but didn't budge. My bladder howled in protest. Squeezing my thighs together, I shoved the ereader under my armpit, gripped the handle with both hands, and yanked it back as hard as I could.

The door flung open, sending me sailing backward. My foot caught on a loose tree root, and I toppled over backward, my palms and ass stinging as they caught the brunt of my fall. My ereader clattered against a stone, and the light flickered out.

Great. This was turning out to be a real disaster. Tears pressed at the corners of my eyes, but I wiped them away with a stinging palm. I wasn't going to let the stupid toilet get to me. That wasn't *being bold.*

Look on the bright side, Rosa, I reminded myself. *At least the door's open now.*

I rolled over and got to my feet, brushing the dirt off my ass. I grabbed the door and walked into the dark closet, pulling it shut behind me, leaving a gap just big enough that the moonlight could give me some visibility. I sat down, did my business, and tried not to think about how many creepy crawlies were lurking in the shadows. I stood up, and grabbed the thin cord hanging from the ceiling to flush the toilet.

The toilet didn't flush.

You can't be serious. I am not doing this. I'm not living in a fucking cabin with a toilet that doesn't work.

I yanked the cord again, harder this time.

The loo made a gurgling sound, but nothing else happened.

"You've got to be kidding." I said aloud, my voice sounding hollow in the darkness. *Great. This is just perfect.* I should have listened more carefully to Margaret's warnings about the plumbing. What had she said, while I was busy thinking about the fire again?

Even when I was hundreds of miles away, Old Garsmouth still managed to fuck up my life.

Well fine, I wasn't going to deal with this problem in the dark. I'd call a plumber in the morning. I slammed down the lid, and turned on the tap to wash my hand. A tiny trickle came out, followed by nothing except a loud, thumping noise from the pipes.

"Aargh!" I pounded my fist against the wall. Something scuttled across my knuckles.

"Aargh!" I yanked my hand away and stumbled out the door, straight into a tall stranger who was standing on the path.

"Do you need some help?" A deep voice boomed in my ear,

with the familiar heavy vowels of a Scottish accent. Huge arms wrapped around my body.

"Aargh!" I flailed my arms about, tearing myself away from his grip. Who the hell was that? Why was some guy walking around my cabin at night?

And why did my body suddenly feel so strange? It was as though I'd stuck my finger in a light socket. All the hair on my body stood to attention. I could only imagine what the frizz on top of my head must look like. My heart thundered in my chest, but this wasn't fear – it was something else. It almost felt like ... excitement.

I fought against the overwhelming urge to throw myself back into the arms of the stranger. *What is that about?*

I backed against the side of the loo, and studied the stranger. Even in the moonlight, it was obvious he was the world's most attractive man. Well, maybe not the most ... Idris Elba was still alive, of course, and Sam Heughan. But this guy would certainly make top five. And he had the significant advantage in that he was in my immediate vicinity, although I still had yet to ascertain if that was a good thing or not.

He had long, floppy red hair that tumbled around his face in tousled waves. A line of dark stubble crossed his strong, square jaw, and the corners of his mouth lifted up into a cheeky half-grin. Eyes of blue ice looked me up and down with predator-like focus. Even with a thick leather jacket on, I could see the dark shapes of a tattoo poking out from the side of his collar. He carried a metal box in his hand. A gold ring dangled from the top of his right ear. God, I'd love to grab that with my tongue and—

What are you even thinking? This is nuts. That's a white guy, standing in the dark. Hot or not, he can't be there for any good reason.

I backed away further, trying to ignore the desire surging through my body. *Stay alert, Rosa. Ignore your body for the moment. It's probably having some kind of seizure. If he makes a move, turn and run for the path at the other side of the cabin—*

"Are you having some plumbing issues?" the stranger asked, taking a step forward.

I held up a hand. "What the hell do you think you're doing?" I demanded, in a voice that oozed the confidence I did not feel. "You're sneaking around my cabin in the middle of the night wearing all black, you scare me half to death, and the first thing you have to say to me is about the *plumbing?*"

He shrugged, a full-on wicked grin spreading across his face, the kind of grin that might move him from top five hottest guys on Earth into the top three. "Why not? I help lots of women with their plumbing."

"Don't be disgusting. Are you here to attack me? I warn you, I'm dangerous when provoked." I tried to make my feet move back, but they were frozen in place.

"Oh, I bet you are." There was that grin again. Cocky, self-assured. Sexy as hell. Damn this guy. "In all seriousness, though. I just came to see if you were all right. I've brought my tools."

He jiggled the box in his hand, which upon closer inspection did indeed look like a toolbox. Certainly not big enough to carry a body around in. That was some positive news.

I still wasn't buying it. "Do you just randomly walk around the forest in the dark, looking for plumbing disasters? You still haven't told me your name."

The guy set down the box, and held up both hands in a gesture of supplication. "My name's Caleb. Caleb Lowe. Margaret hired me to do some carpentry work around the place. I'm staying in the cabin just over there." He jerked his thumb at the trees behind us. "She asked me to come out and check on you, offer my services for whatever you need." Caleb grinned again. "Looks like I got here just in time."

My shoulders relaxed a little. Margaret had mentioned

something about a handyman. But that gorgeous, white face and the thrumming energy surging through my body still left me feeling off-guard. "How do I know you're not just some crazy dude *pretending* to be the handyman? I've seen a lot of horror films that started with conversations just like this, and they always end up with the heroine slashed across the throat and being dragged into some kind of dungeon torture chamber."

"You watch horror films that regularly begin with the protagonist and the serial killer discussing plumbing?" He raised an eyebrow. "Where are you getting your film recommendations, the National Plumbing Association Film Festival?"

"So you admit you're a serial killer."

Caleb grinned again, then leaned into the closet and tapped the pipe on the wall. "Let me guess, you don't have any water, right? But the pipe's making a gurgling noise?"

"Yeah, that's about the size of it."

"Too easy," he grinned.

A flush crept across my cheeks. Thankfully he wouldn't be able to see it in the dark. "Yeah, well, it's been a long day. If I'd known I'd be swapping *double entendres* with an itinerant fix-it serial killer, I would have taken the time to bone up a bit."

I wondered if he got that that one was deliberate, but he burst out laughing, and I found m\y unease melting away. It didn't help that the strange energy was still flowing through my veins, and my hands were itching to run through his hair.

"Funny as well as gorgeous, you might be my new favourite neighbour." Caleb held up his toolbox like a peace offering. "I know what's wrong because the exact same thing happened to me the first day I moved in. I can fix this in a few seconds for you, if you like."

I was still a bit apprehensive, but the energy in my body screamed at me to accept his offer. Besides, I needed to have running water, and all I knew about toolboxes was that they provided a great surface for stacking books. I waved an arm dismissively at the toilet, as if the whole thing really wasn't that big a deal. "Yeah, sure. Knock yourself out."

Caleb set down his toolbox, and took out a couple of strange-shaped tools. He bent down beside the toilet, giving me an excellent view of his tight, muscular ass swinging in the air. A few moments later, his head popped back up again. He leaned in and turned the tap on. Water gushed freely into the sink.

I flinched a bit, sorry I'd been so suspicious. "Thanks so much."

That grin again. Damn, it made my knees weak. "Don't mention it. It was worth it for the excuse to come over here and meet you. It's been fun."

It's been fun. Oh, screw Idris, Caleb was the most attractive man I'd ever seen. Clearly, my body screamed for him. It had been so long since Sam Seymour, and there hadn't been anyone else since. I desperately wanted to be touched, and a guy like Caleb would know his way around a woman's body, of that I had no doubt.

I toyed with the idea of asking Caleb in to finish off the wine. As I opened my mouth, a hard thought stopped me.

Caleb was *white.*

I couldn't overlook that key fact. I wasn't normally attracted to white men. It probably had something to do with the fact that white men had been a source of much of the misery that had invaded my life, especially in recent years. The police never caught the arsonists who burned down my house, but I *knew* they were white. It was pretty obvious when you thought about it.

Sam Seymour, the biggest mistake of my life, had been white, too. After him, I'd sworn I'd never go there again.

And yet here was the most beautiful man I'd seen, and

instead of staring at me with disgust, or calling out some kind of slur, he was friendly, and dare I hope … even a little flirtatious?

I was all alone here in the middle of the woods, in a forest known for strange occurrences. Only six months ago, Crook-shollow had hit the national news after a reporter was found dead, torn apart by some kind of wild animal. There were some mysterious goings-on at an archaeological site, too, and before that, a dead rockstar showing up in perfect health, and some kind of altercation at an art gallery … Clearly, this place attracted weirdos and freaks of the first order.

Maybe it would be good to have someone looking out for me.

I couldn't have a lover, much as I might want one, but maybe … maybe, it would be good to have a friend. Especially a friend who knew his way around a toolbox.

Just friends, that's all. It's okay to be friends with a white guy, if you don't get involved. What's the harm, right?

Right?

I plastered a smile on my face. "While you're here, would you like to come in for a cup of tea?"

Oh girl, my brain berated me as I walked up the steps ahead of Caleb, trying not to let my hips sashay too much. *You are in for a world of hurt.*

TO BE CONTINUED

~

Get your hands on Writing the Wolf right now at
www.steffanieholmes.com

ALSO FROM THE WORLD OF CROOKSHOLLOW …

CROOKSHOLLOW GOTHIC ROMANCE, BOOK 4

Love so fierce it transcends even death.

When Elinor Baxter arrives at the dilapidated Marshell House to settle the estate of her law firm's oldest client, she can't help but feel a little spooked. The creaking gothic mansion is a far cry from her life as an adventurous party girl back in London.

Then she meets Eric Marshell, a man dressed entirely in black with a wicked smile and the ability to float through walls. Eric was the violinist in popular rock band Ghost Symphony until a hit-and-run accident claimed his life. Now he's trapped inside his mother's house for all eternity, and the only one who can see or hear him is Elinor.

Eric and Elinor fight their attraction for each other as they dig into the mystery of Eric's death. But when they uncover a dark and sinister plot that threatens Elinor's life, their bond draws them into a world neither of them understands. Can their love transcend the boundary between life and death?

THE MAN IN BLACK is a steamy gothic romance by USA Today bestselling author Steffanie Holmes, Set in the English village of Crookshollow, it's a standalone novel of love, redemption, and second chances. If you love clever BBW heroines, crumbling gothic mansions, and brooding rockstars who know what they want, then this book will have you shivering all over.

SUPPORT ME ON PATREON!

You can support Steffanie's writing via her Patreon page – it's like an ongoing crowdfunding campaign where you get free books, deleted scenes, random fun stuff, and the chance to name characters and decide plots.

Check out Steffanie's patron page at: www.patreon.com/steffmetal.

ABOUT THE AUTHOR

Steffanie Holmes is the author of steamy historical and paranormal romance. Her books feature clever, witty heroines, wild shifters, cunning witches and alpha males who *always* get what they want.

Before becoming a writer, Steffanie worked as an archaeologist and museum curator. She loves to explore historical settings and ancient conceptions of love and possession. From Dark Age Europe to crumbling gothic estates, Steffanie is fascinated with how love can blossom between the most unlikely characters. She also writes dark fantasy / science fiction under S. C. Green.

Steffanie lives in New Zealand with her husband and a horde of cantankerous cats.

Get your FREE BONUS EPILOGUE

Anna and Luke are having a baby! Find out what else they get up to in a FREE bonus epilogue – to read it, all you have to do is sign up to Steffanie Holmes' VIP club. You'll also get exclusive previews, fun giveaways, and hot teasers. www.subscribepage.com/digging_bonus

Come hang with Steffanie
www.steffanieholmes.com
hello@steffanieholmes.com

OTHER BOOKS BY STEFFANIE HOLMES

This list is in recommended reading order, although each couple's story can be enjoyed as a standalone. Find them all on www.steffanieholmes.com.

Crookshollow Gothic Romance series

Art of Cunning (Alex & Ryan) - READ NOW FOR FREE

Art of the Hunt (Alex & Ryan)

Art of Temptation (Alex & Ryan)

The Man in Black (Elinor & Eric)

Watcher (Belinda & Cole)

Reaper (Belinda & Cole)

Wolves of Crookshollow series

Digging the Wolf (Anna & Luke)

Writing the Wolf (Rosa & Caleb)

Inking the Wolf (Bianca & Robbie)

Wedding the Wolf (Willow & Irvine)

Fallen Sorcery Fae (shared world)

Hollow

Witches of the Woods

Witch Hunter

Coven

The Curse (coming in 2018)

www.ingramcontent.com/pod-product-compliance
Lightning Source LLC
Chambersburg PA
CBHW050716180626
46814CB00002B/468

* 9 7 8 0 4 7 3 4 0 0 4 7 7 *